CALL TO ARMS

MICHAEL G. THOMAS

First published in the United Kingdom in 2014 by Swordworks Books.

ISBN 978-1-911092-39-1

Typeset by Swordworks Books
Printed and bound in the UK & US
A catalogue record of this book is available
from the British Library

Cover design by Swordworks Books
www.swordworks.co.uk

CALL TO ARMS

MICHAEL G. THOMAS

CHAPTER ONE

Private space travel increased in popularity wherever money was there to be made. The new colonies of the Alliance were filled with haulers, mining ships, and traders, but the old worlds of Sol were another matter. Cut off by long journeys and slow communications, the old colonies of Sol developed at a different rate. Even when the Rift brought them into the great Alliance family, their small populations, poor living conditions, and a general distrust of outsiders put them at a great disadvantage. Private enterprise had stagnated and suffered over the decades so much that it fell to a state controlled monopoly to create a workable transport network between Earth, Mars, and the moons of Sol.

Origins of Private Space Travel

Eos was a miserable place, a relatively barren rock with little strategic value to the Alliance. As Wictred stretched his left leg, he thought back to his time on Hyperion and realized he actually missed the place. Where Eos was barren with just a smattering of industrial bases on its surface, Hyperion was a lush forest world filled with the surviving Biomech monsters that his kin so loved to hunt. Hyperion was in many ways a more dangerous place, yet he would rather be there with blades and firearms than on this dust bowl.

I can't even remember the smell of Hyperion.

Wictred checked the radiation markers on his overlay display. The centigray scale had dropped right down to the average for the moon, and even he had been surprised at how quickly it had died down. In the first hours after the bombardment, the sensors had peaked at levels that would kill a man outright. He was just thankful they'd been able to shelter deep enough underground as the radioactive clouds spread. Even though it showed the area was safe, he still checked it again before activating the visor mount on the armored helmet. It was actually all part of the same unit, and it hissed open to let the cool air enter his system. Even as the air mingled with the stagnant air that had been in his armor, he still checked, ever paranoid of the threat of radiation.

Still at safe levels, good.

The visor made a grinding sound where dust had built up around the moving parts until it was completely open. Wictred closed his eyes and took in a long, slow breath. The ventilation unit built into all of their armor versions still took in air from the outside and ran it through a number of rigorous scrubbers. Nonetheless, there was little right now that was better than the feeling of fresh air on his face. He lifted up his left arm and pulled on the levers to open up access to his arm so that he could wipe the sweat from his face.

"Corporal Wictred, I've got the Alliance broadcast. It's different his time. I think it's the General."

Wictred found a mixture of blood and sweat that had stuck to his bruised hand, and he flicked his hand before reactivating the armor that protected his limb. The radiation levels might be safe, but there was still the chance of coming upon contaminated material. He had no intention of dying to radiation exposure. He would die as he'd always intended, with his hands around an enemy's throat, and he really didn't care which enemy, right now.

"Turn it up."

The marine had positioned the deep-space receiver on the ground and tapped the keyboard to alter the settings. It took a few seconds for the system to catch up with the data. At first it was garbled, but after just a few more seconds, the decryption software had done its work, and the noise turned into familiar voices.

"Gun," said Wictred happily.

"...priority is to stay hidden and await help from the NHA. They have been notified of your positions."

"The NHA?" said one of the marines further inside

the cave.

"Are you frigging kidding me?"

The marine began to break out in a laugh that quickly turned to something bordering on the hysterical.

"Come on, they are no army. You heard the reports from Fort Macquarie. When the Biomech landers came in, they just bugged out. We can't count on 'em."

From his position at the edge of the cave, Wictred had a good view of the ground around them. Although he was desperate to hear something useful from the receiver, he had already resigned himself to a bloodbath on Eos. He scanned with his eyes back and forth as he listened, ever watchful for signs of the enemy, or the even less likely help from the NHA. The news from the fleet wasn't particularly positive.

"Alliance is mobilizing...Helios is preparing for a massive assault...War has come to the..."

All of the words coming from Gun told him one simple truth; the Alliance had left them there. If they were going to get out alive, it would be up to them and them alone. If the fleet had left, it could only be for one of two reasons; either they'd been forced to leave because they were needed elsewhere, or they had been chased away by superior numbers. Wictred doubted it was the latter. Gun wouldn't leave them behind.

"It has to be Eos," he said, more to himself than the others.

"What do you mean?" asked the youngest of the marines.

Lance Corporal James laughed and then answered the other marine.

"What the Corporal means is that the fleet had to leave Eos. You heard the message. The enemy is here, and they are heading for Helios. If they can take the planet, they'll control the Nexus and access to all the primary Spacebridges."

He pointed to outside of the cave.

"This is just a moon, one of many under Helion control. They can afford to lose the place, and so can we. We're marines, and every one of us is expendable."

Wictred couldn't argue with that.

"They haven't abandoned us. They will be back."

He looked back at the armored figures of his comrades.

"This is a war, and we've all trained for this. The fleet has to go where it can do the greatest good. We smashed this assault, and we can survive the Biomechs that remain here."

He tapped his head.

"If we use our heads."

It was a calming message but seemed to do the job. Wictred was no officer, but his cool attitude, coupled with his great size, did its job for now.

"Corporal Wictred. Why can't we contact them for help?"

As if in reply, the black shape of a Helion fighter screamed past overhead. A trail of black smoke ran from its left wing. Right behind it moved a Helion fighter, its guns blasting away. The two craft vanished as quickly as they had arrived. Wictred pointed at the sky.

"That's why. We might have wiped out their ground assault and made this moon safe from invasion, but out here away from the towns, they are still here."

The marines looked at him but none spoke.

"You saw what happened to Theta platoon when they called for assistance. We cannot take the chance until we have numbers and weapons on our side."

None of them wanted to speak of that, but it was also a memory none of them would be able to shake off. The depleted unit of less than twenty marines had climbed atop one of the highest peaks and called for help on an open frequency. Wictred had heard it but forced those that would listen to stay down. Less than three minutes later, a hunter killer team of three fighters and a small lander swept down and obliterated them.

He indicated for them to approach and bent down to scrape a diagram on the floor.

"You need to remember that the NHA forces here are spread thin. The intel coming in shows they are dealing with the Biomechs, but it's taking time."

"Why?" asked one of the marines.

Wictred sighed.

"Eos has a small population and an even smaller military. Most of them are still trying to deal with the Animosh insurgency. We cannot deal with the Biomechs ourselves until significant reinforcements arrive. In the meantime, the reports from the major settlements are that they are digging in until relieved."

"Yeah, man, the Helions control the towns," said another.

"And the canners have the desert," answered the female marine from back in the shadows.

"It's true," Wictred agreed. "Until we have air cover and transports, the enemy has the advantage out here."

Their discussion had given him some ideas, however. He brought up the digital map and the last details for their combat operations. He had the flight plans for the rescued Hammerheads that had never landed, as well as the link up routes they were supposed to take with the NHA. The one thing he'd given no attention to since the attack was the Animosh, the personal security force of the previous regime that was now fighting a guerrilla war against the populist government.

"Wait, I have an idea," he said.

At first nobody spoke until Lance Corporal James moved closer.

"What is it?"

Wictred looked out to the main ground car route out in the open. There were seven military vehicles, all of them burned out and abandoned. Four had been hit where they waited, but the rest had spread out to avoid further explosions before being knocked out in turn. It was a painful reminder of how badly things had gone for the Alliance, and more specifically, for Wictred.

I hate this place.

He looked back at his comrades and did his best to look confident.

"Our vehicles weren't destroyed by the Biomechs."

"No man, that was the rebels."

"Exactly," Wictred replied.

The Lance Corporal seemed even more confused.

"What are you getting at?"

Wictred grinned.

"The Animosh are not our friends, that is true. But there is somebody, or more specifically, there is something they hate more than this populist uprising or even us."

"The Biomechs," said the Lance Corporal, as though he had just discovered a great secret.

Wictred looked back to the map and checked on the routes used by the insurgents. They certainly knew the area well, and they had been able to strike and escape almost with impunity.

"Very interesting."

He looked at the rest of his unit, and all of his ideas seemed to fade away. The images of a great union of factions, with Animosh, Helions, and marines fighting side by side now seemed more like a children's story than an actual possibility. There were just five of them now, and all were wounded to one degree or another. There was more than that though, they were suffering, and he knew it. They had plenty of food and water, but it was the radiation that was causing the biggest problem, and it was an enemy that Wictred had no idea how to fix. It was what frustrated him the most, the fact that he could not simply stand up and strike the enemy; because this time it was an invisible wind that killed his comrades slowly over a matter of hours and days.

Who will go next? he wondered.

He had never liked Helios much, but since the attack, he'd found a completely new level of bitterness towards the place. Unlike his comrades, he'd been taking part in a training exercise with the New Helion Army outside of the main compound when the attack began.

That was a week ago, and now look at us.

"Corporal, look!" said Private Harvey.

The middle-aged man still wore his PDS Alpha Armour, and from the analysis provided by the suit's computer, he was the only one in his unit that had managed to avoid a fatal dose of radiation immediately after the bombardment. The man had refused to leave his suit for the entire week now, and Wictred wondered quite how he was managing. The man pointed off to the left and Wictred had to strain to see where he had pointed.

"What is it?"

The man continued to point.

"The smoke trails, they stopped just beyond that ridge."

Wictred spotted a double column of black smoke.

"So?"

"Well, both of them must have crashed."

"Yes, you are probably right. I don't see how this is..."

The man pointed again, and this time Wictred spotted the flickering light. He counted the pattern and then shook his head in surprise. He looked back into the tunnel and nodded at the engineer.

"Smyth, up here, fast. Tell me if this is what I think it is."

The man looked carefully through the enhanced optics of his suit.

"Uh, it's light bouncing off something on the horizon. Could be machine, I guess."

Just the mention of the word 'machine' sent a hushed chill though the group.

"What's the plan?" asked the youngest of the marines, interrupting the quiet.

Wictred didn't even know his name, and after the fighting retreat of the last three days, he really didn't want to know. Back then they had numbered more than fifty. Now the Captain was gone, along with the last two officers and NCOs. He was it, and he didn't like it. Like his kin in the Alliance, Wictred wore the latest Jötnar Assault

Suit armor that seemed to bulk up his already substantial form considerably. Even though he was smaller than the average, Wictred was still massive compared to a normal marine.

"According to our maps, there is a Helion town seven klicks from here. We should get there and report in to the NHA," he said, pointing out to the right of where the burned out vehicles sat.

"What about the radiation though, are you sure it's safe to leave this place?" asked the young marine for what must have been the tenth time.

Wictred opened his helmet visor and spat on the ground.

"How many times must I tell you? Alliance nukes are neutron weapons. They kill fast, and the radiation vanishes in a matter of hours. If you survived the bombardment and the fallout, then you have a chance."

"Yeah, he's right," said the gruff engineer with the dented breastplate.

"The half-life on those things is ridiculously small. They're designed to clear areas ready for ground assault."

"How?" asked the young marine.

The engineer shook his head in annoyance.

"Kid, didn't they teach you anything? Neutron bomb the place and wipe out their ground force ready for assault. Three hours after the attacks, the infantry move in and mop up."

Wictred nodded as the man spoke.

"That's right. They stopped using them a long time ago. It must have been a last resort option."

It was of little comfort to the others though, especially the two marines whose armour had been penetrated during the bombardment. Wictred could see the woman, a young private who'd been hit four times in the chest. Incredibly, the armor had saved her life, but it had broken the external seals and let in clouds of radioactive dust that did their damage before the radiation could dissipate. Wictred knew they would be dead in a matter of days.

She'll be dead soon. Better for her to die with a rifle in her hands than like that. It's a cruel way to die.

He looked away from them and in the direction of the promised town. The fact the Alliance fleet had launched such a heavy bombardment as they left told him everything he needed to know; that the battlefield had been lost for now, and anybody still living there was on borrowed time. He felt no guilt at lying. There was little point in telling them the truth. They were hundreds of kilometers from any known town, and the enemy was coming for them.

I will give them a death, one that is worthy of their sacrifices.

He ground his teeth at the enormity of what he planned on doing and then made his plans.

We'll find whatever is left of these Biomechs, and we will reduce them to ash before our time is done.

* * *

The heat from Prometheus warmed the interior of the Mauler as it circled over the landing zone. The surface was primarily thick rock, but in places molten metal ran in rivers from the scores of volcanoes littering its surface. At first glance the world looked impossible to house anything but an incinerator, yet careful scrutiny would reveal a hive of activity in a dozen locations. This planet was the home of one of the largest research bases, engineer outposts, and naval shipyards in the entire Alliance.

"Hold on, we're moving into our landing pattern," said the pilot.

The Mauler altered its thrusting pattern and moved from its slow circling pattern and onto the correct approach vector for the angled blast doors. They were fitted directly into the side of a massive cliff that reached nearly three kilometers up from the surface. Out in the distance, vast plumes of black smoke filled the red sky, and the telltale flashes of yellow and orange marked the burning of the volcanoes. Teresa looked at the screen that showed a frontal view from the craft as they closed in. She wasn't the only person on board, but she was the senior Marine Corps officer. More importantly, she had detailed knowledge of the base. A handful of the officers from the battalion had also joined her for the visit.

Anderson must have been made to expand this place, Teresa thought.

Back in the War, the enemy had carved out a number of secret research bases, right under the nose of the authorities. These had been the backbone of their efforts to strip organs and tissue from human captives to create Biomech monstrosities. It had been just the start of the horrors they would encounter, and she had never forgotten what she'd seen.

"Outer doors activating."

The surface hangar hatch opened up and released a great cloud of dust into the air. These weren't dust particles of dirt though; the surface of the planet burned hot, and the cloud of super-heated dust could have easily torn away the outer plating of any craft unfortunate to be close enough. The cloud obscured most of the multiple defense turrets fitted around the plated doors, but only a fool would try to bypass them without proper authorization.

"Just a few more seconds," said the pilot. "Entering Alliance authorization now."

The codes varied depending on the vessel, and this particular one was for the Alliance Navy. It took nearly thirty seconds for the code to be assessed and compared to the ship status and description. Even as they waited, the turret tracked the craft and aimed at the center of Mauler. It was obvious to all inside that they could be dead in a microsecond if the inhabitants of the base doubted their intentions.

"Prometheus Research Facility access granted."

The Alliance Mauler was one of the most advanced and dependable vessels in the Alliance inventory, yet even a Mauler would be vulnerable to such a blast. It waited for a moment to let the entrance clear and used its reversed engines to maintain height. Pintle mounted lamps lit up the ground below the Mauler and showed nothing but rocks and marker lights. After what must have seemed like an age, the craft lowered itself gingerly toward the wide entrance and then moved inside. The thick doors slid into place behind them, and the craft went down into the vast tunnels that had been burned into the bedrock of the planet. It was one of the smaller access points to the base and one of the most heavily guarded.

Back again, she thought.

Prometheus looked just as Teresa remembered it. The world was hard, impenetrable, and pounded by heat and meteorites on a regular basis. From space it looked like a barren rock, but she knew better than most what lurked inside. The memories of her time on the planet filled her with an odd mixture of dread and nostalgia.

"Welcome to Prometheus," the pilot announced.

Teresa was sure she could pick up the sarcasm in the man's voice. There was little to like about the place, but it was hard to argue about the value of the site. They moved through the tunnel and into a massive landing area that she suspected could easily house a vessel the size of a heavy cruiser. The Mauler lowered itself until finally dropping down inside a ring of blue beacons. Within seconds of making contact, the doors hissed open and thick, warm air blasted inside. Teresa uncoupled herself, moved to the doorway, and looked out.

"Colonel," said a familiar voice.

She moved onto the ramp and stepped down to stop in front of the tall T'Kari.

"T'Kron?"

He smiled at her and replied through his translators.

"I am here at the request of the Chairman of the Joint Chiefs."

General Rivers.

"What are you doing here?" he asked, "I thought you were with reinforcements for T'Karan?"

"That's a good point, T'Kron. We were hit coming through the Spacebridge. Only one ship made it through."

It took a moment for his translators to do their work, but once done, his expression changed from a relaxed smile to a tense look.

"That is bad news. My exiles are spread thin at the moment. We do not have the forces for T'Karan on our own."

Teresa raised an eyebrow.

"You think the Biomechs will try and take the colonies in T'Karan?"

T'Kron nodded.

"Yes. Even with the Jötnar barracks on Luthien, it will be difficult. The Prophecy speaks of a great devourer that will swallow Helios and then every world. Helios has already put out the call, and all available ships are heading for its defense."

Teresa had seen the reports, as well as the lists of ships from the many races that had been sent to bolster the world's defenses. At first she had given little thought to the general strategy of the enemy, but as she listened to T'Kron, her mind began to explore other alternatives. He continued to speak before finally stopping and watching at her. She noticed him and apologized, looking at him sheepishly.

"I'm sorry. Where were you?"

T'Kron was unfazed by her lack of attention.

"You were thinking of the enemy? You have other ideas for them?"

Teresa was used to their speed of thought and well-trained and logical minds. Even so, she was still surprised to see that her thinking process was so transparent to them.

"Yes. I have concerns."

T'Kron indicated for her to walk with him a little further along the vast hangar space.

"Tell me, please."

Teresa looked at the ship being built and recalled the

awful creatures and carnage that had occurred on this uncomfortably hot planet.

"The Biomechs. We know they are a hybrid race of biomechanical creatures that were treated almost as gods on their worlds."

"Yes, that is true. Before they made contact with us, the Helions and the others, they ruled over many domains. Their experiments in biomechanics repulsed all of us though. Before our terrible war, we learned that all of them were hundreds, and some even thousands of years old."

"So what is their end game?" asked Teresa.

T'Kron didn't quite understand the terminology and had to check his own records before answering.

"We have never worried too much about this. Mere survival against the Machine Gods was enough."

Teresa shook her head.

"No, we know they attempted to dominate your race, along with the others. There's no reason to think they do not want to finish this. The question is, how?"

"I might have a few ideas about that."

Teresa recognized the voice and turned about to see the gruff old figure of General Cornwallis, the Chief of Defense for the Alliance Marine Corps. She only met him briefly before, but his voice and upper class accent were hard to forget.

"General, what are you doing here?"

A number of other senior officers gathered around them while others continued on along the designated pathways to the central hub of the base. He spoke with a junior officer and sent him off on an errand before continuing to speak with her.

"General Rivers' strategy is to split our forces, with half defending our key territories here and in T'Karan while and the remainder are heading to Helios. I'm here to assist Admiral Anderson in implementing this new plan."

"Teresa Morato?" asked a brusque voice.

It could easily have been that of a large man, but when she twisted her head, she spotted the oversized shapes of a large group of Jötnar lurking about near a shuttle. One of them had broken away and was heading toward her.

"Olik?" she asked with surprise.

The older looking Jötnar approached close enough to reveal a hideous face with multiple cuts along one side of it. She was sure a number of the marks were new. The last time she'd seen him, he had been fully armored; he looked much smaller without all the metal attached to his body.

"What are you doing here?" she asked.

Olik moved to the side of the General and nodded rather than saluted, much to his annoyance.

"Colonel Morato, may I present your Jötnar platoon."

He turned and bowed in as grand a manner as he could manage. A number of the Jötnar nearby saw him and struck their chests in mock salute.

"Are you sure you want them in your unit?" asked the General.

Teresa extended her hand to Olik, but as he reached for it, she slipped past and struck him in the cheek with a strong punch. The impact shook his head, and he spat out a tooth to the ground while she nursed her throbbing fist. General Cornwallis stepped back and lowered his hands, trying to calm things down.

"Colonel, what the hell are you doing?"

Olik began to laugh. As his voice became louder, so did that of the other Jötnar. Four more of them moved to greet her, but this time it was just the gabbing of arms or pulling each other in tightly. The General looked to T'Kron who gave him the most curious of smiles.

"They are an unusual race, are they not?"

The General shook his head and then walked away, only turning to say one last thing as he left.

"Colonel, we have an urgent meeting with the Admiral in fifteen minutes. I will see you there."

With that, he wandered off, still shaking his head. T'Kron moved closer to the Jötnar and tilted his head slightly before introducing himself. Olik extended his hand but did no more than shake the Jötnar's fist.

"T'Kron, I have heard much about you from my brothers. We have bled for each other on the battlefield. It is good to meet you."

"And you, Olik, your kin are famed among my people.

Your mercenaries have never failed a mission."

The group moved on while Olik and Teresa discussed news of Hyperion. Their short walk took them far away from the landing platform and to the side of the massive space dock. Teresa couldn't help but be impressed at the sight of the ship in the background that was being worked on. Finally, the entire group stopped to gaze at the gleaming metal. As far as she could tell, it was close to completion. T'Kron noticed her looking and nodded with interest.

"You like the ship?"

"It looks different to normal," said Olik.

T'Kron pointed to the prow of the ship where a battery of tubes were fitted. Teresa looked at its outline but couldn't place it. Most of it looked similar to a civilian liner, yet more storage segments were being fitted out with weapon mounts and additional sensor suites.

"Anderson told us about the Tamarisk, a civilian ship that was equipped with armor and hidden weapons."

Teresa nodded. She was of course far more than a little acquainted with the idea. She had been part of the rescue mission led by Anderson, back when Spartan and General Rivers had been imprisoned on board the planet.

"Tamarisk, that was a good ship."

Olik looked at the shape with fascination.

"I've seen this ship before. Isn't it one of the ancient T'Kari transports?"

T'Kron seemed pleased.

"Yes. We have worked alongside Alliance engineers and technicians to create a new type of ship for use in the Alliance. These are medium size, high-speed transports that are quick and cheap to replicate."

"With what purpose in mind?" Teresa inquired.

T'Kron looked at her and then pointed at the weapon mounts.

"Admiral Anderson proposed the specification over a year ago. They are a...well...a creative solution to a problem."

Teresa knew immediately what the Admiral was doing, and also to what problem T'Kron was referring. The President had little interest in raising taxes to build more ships or expanding the fleet. The cost of running the existing Heavy Strike Groups was already proving more than most colonies wanted to support, and if he pushed any harder, he would simply be forced out of office and replaced by whomever offered to lower public spending.

This is his solution.

T'Kron pointed back at the waiting vessels.

"These ships are designed to provide a civilian, as well as a military capability. By combining technology from your ships and ours, we've come up with something that is more than capable of defending themselves. They have a similar transport capacity to your old smaller troop transports and can carry over two hundred soldiers or equivalent cargo."

Teresa seemed impressed at what he had to say so far. She started to speak but then put her hand over her mouth, as though stopping herself.

"What is it?" asked T'Kron.

"Well, do we need more transports? The Crusader class is already working just fine. I can see private industry wanting to hire these ships; I assume at a price that will benefit the Alliance?"

"Of course. These ships are very cheap. We will recoup our return in less than three years operation of each vessel."

Teresa didn't seem quite so impressed now that she knew more.

"They are not warships though, so what is the point?"

T'Kron walked off to the right of the ship so as to get a better view of the rear of the vessel. He indicated toward the large, yet sleek engine nacelles that were attached just a few meters from the hull itself.

"These ships cannot carry fighters, but they can transport two Avenger drones, with one in each of the flank nacelles. They are as fast and as heavily armed as a T'Kari cruiser, with a mixture of railguns and missiles that can be installed by dropping out the three cargo modules and replacing them with combat modules. This will free up warships and provide additional numbers in times of war."

He lifted his secpad, one that was Alliance issue she noticed, and slid his hand across it.

"If you would check your workspace?"

Teresa looked at him and then remembered her own device. She pulled it out and examined the schematics that T'Kron had just sent her. The main image showed a top down view of the ship with a ladder type chassis fitted around three large square spaces.

"Those are the module spaces. It takes under three hours to change one of them. So far, we have cargo, troop, railgun, and missile modules. Each one is self-contained and quickly replaced here or at any configured Alliance base."

Teresa tried to hide a smile, but Olik spotted it. To her surprise, he said nothing.

This was a smart move by Anderson. He plans to increase the size of the fleet through the back door. It is probably too little, too late though.

"When will it be ready?" she asked.

T'Kron looked confused.

"What do you mean?"

"I mean, when will the first of these ships be ready?"

T'Kron understood and did his best to hide the look of pride from his face.

"The Prometheus shipyards have been very busy, Colonel. This ship is number fifty-two, and one is coming off the assembly line every four days."

Teresa did the math in her head and was shocked at the number.

"That's ninety ships a year."

"What are you calling them?" asked Olik.

T'Kron pointed to three large compartments being moved off to the other side of the massive hangar where a line of machines waited to work on them. It was a production line that made the warship lines look modest in comparison.

"They are called Liberty ships, and each one takes the name of a town or city in the Alliance."

CHAPTER TWO

The Centauri Alliance experienced a seismic shift in both power and size following its adventures into the Nexus. The new colonies at Epsilon Eridani, Gliese 876, Procyon, and T'Karan increased resources at an exponential rate. Though the worlds of the Seven Star Systems were the least advanced of the known races, they were already becoming some of the most important. Colonists and private enterprise continued what the Alliance exploration fleets had started.

Rise and Fall of Interstellar Empires

The sterile surface of Earth looked nothing like Spartan had expected. Throughout his life he'd come across images, paintings, and stories about the lush surface rich oceans and mighty cities that marked the birthplace of humanity. It saddened him a little to think of what it must have been like before it was plundered and exploited. He didn't have the numbers to hand, but he was certain the population had at one point exceeded ten billion. Now the population of Earth and Mars combined was less than sixty million.

What a waste of time.

The view from the triple-layered windows was out across a low valley. It had probably in the past been green, and fields with grasslands and forests. Now the surface was ashen, with dust, weed, and scrawny looking plants that somehow managed to survive in the mildly toxic environment. He looked down to where Khan and Lieutenant Jenkins waited.

"What was this place?"

Khan shrugged while Lieutenant Jenkins spoke with the other three Earthsec guards. Khan didn't seem to like the look of any of the group of men, not even the Lieutenant.

"We're on one of the last military bases in what was Europe. We still use it as a transit point for the high orbit platforms."

"Europe?" asked Khan.

Spartan smiled and looked back out through the windows.

"Yeah, Europe. I've heard of the place. Way back, well before we sent the first ships to Alpha Centauri, this world was filled with countries. I think Europe was one of the oldest."

"You're close," said a stern voice.

Spartan looked down to see a captain in the same uniform as the other men. He looked at Spartan with unflinching eyes and no glimmer of a smile. Spartan had met so many men and women like him, and they always left him feeling a little cold. Of all officers, these were the type to send you on those missions with little chance of coming home. It was his words that surprised him most. There was something familiar about them, but he couldn't put a finger on it. Was it a region he had visited or was it somebody he knew?

Marcus, yeah, it has to be.

The accent was definitely similar to that of his old friend Marcus. The tall warrior had trained alongside him and been a good friend when he'd been a lowly grunt in the Corps. It was a long time since he'd given any thought to Marcus, and it took a moment for him to even remember what he looked like. As the image darted behind his eyes, he felt a pang of guilt at having forgotten him for so long. It made him wonder who else he'd pushed away over the years. Luckily, the officer continued to speak in that cold, dispassionate tone.

He's a hard one.

"This is indeed part of Europe, but you are on one large island, what used to be called the United Kingdom. This is one of the few remaining military bases that survived the exodus. Originally, it was all above ground; now ninety-five percent of the base is below the surface."

Spartan let out a slow breath but said nothing. He'd come across similar places on other worlds before. It was common to build habitation facilities deep underground on worlds that were prone to orbital bombardment. It was the structures on the surface that made the place stand out, and he couldn't quite put a finger on it. The officer saw his confusion and mistook it for his knowledge of the planet itself.

"In the nineteenth century, back when military might was based around wooden sailing ships and gunpowder weapons, this island was at its peak. Yes, there were other empires, but the United Kingdom ruled the largest empire ever seen on Earth. Its ships traveled the oceans, and its language and technology traveled with it. The language we now speak comes directly from them."

"English?" asked Spartan, now even more confused.

The man bared his teeth a little, and Spartan could only assume he was trying to smile. It reminded him of when Gun had tried to do the same soon after they'd met. Back then, his command of language had been worse than a child's.

"English, yes, the name of the people that inhabited the largest part of this United Kingdom.

"What happened to them?"

The man lifted his eyebrows and shrugged.

"Nothing much different to the rest of this planet.

When Earth became almost sterile, so did its people. The population fell, and those that could, left with everything they owned. All that remains now are the underground cities and military sites. There are no countries anymore, and the surface is littered with the remains of civilization spanning thousands of years."

Spartan started to move, but the man shook his head and nodded in the direction of the glass to one side of the dome.

"That is south. You'll see the debris in the indentation ahead, which was an old road system from ground cars. What can you see beyond that?"

Spartan didn't like playing these games, but a twinge in his leg encouraged him to stay in the dome section for a little longer. The road was difficult to identify, being as it was the same featureless color and covered in a thick layer of tough weeds and plants.

How the hell does anything grow anymore?

"Can you see it yet?"

Spartan shrugged. There was nothing of note outside of the military base. He scanned the horizon but saw nothing other than a slight indulation. There was something between the road and the horizon though; an odd shape and it forced him to squint before stopping.

"Wait, there is something out there. It looks like a rock wall?"

The man nodded as if pleased by his find. Spartan was

not amused though and moved down from the observation dome that extended from underground to provide a few of the dead surface. As he did so, he wondered quite why anybody living on Earth would ever want to see the surface again. He'd seen prettier places on the fiery world of Prometheus, after all.

And now these fools think they can manage out here, and on their own.

Khan and Lieutenant Jenkins waited patiently for him as he reached the lowest rung of the ladder. It took him longer than it should have, but that was understandable due to his missing limb and painful muscles. He landed next to the officer and winced as a burst of pain rushed up his leg.

"So, what about that place?"

The man looked back into the tunnel and then to Spartan.

"It is the remains of an ancient city wall, one that was built in the fifth century."

Spartan knew he should have been impressed, but he wasn't. A broken wall, and thousands of years old on a sterile world, meant little to him.

Perhaps for archaeologists or historians, but not for me.

All he'd seen was a modest structure to position several heavy weapons or a foundation for a fortification of some kind. He looked at the man and wondered what would have persuaded such a man to join Earthsec. It wasn't an organization he'd known a huge amount of, although his company had dealings with them prior to his disappearance. His gut instinct told him they were ultra-conservative and jealously guarded access to their own domain. Technically, they were Alliance, but none of them seemed to believe it.

"Your voice, it sounds like somebody I knew. He was from a colony of Earth settlers."

"We are all of Earth, my friends."

Spartan exhaled slowly, particularly unimpressed at this comment.

"Really? I didn't know that."

Khan chuckled in amusement, the sound rumbling in the underground room.

The man looked away from Spartan but kept one eye on him as though assessing him.

"You're from where exactly, Spartan?"

Spartan smiled and pointed up.

"From up there."

The man didn't seem amused at that, something that greatly amused Spartan.

"Your file is interesting, but it lacks a certain detail prior to an incident on Prometheus. Everything before that has been redacted, why?"

Spartan looked at him, took in a short breath, and then changed the subject.

"Your voice. Tell me about it."

"You mean accent?" answered the officer.

Spartan just nodded, but he could feel an anger building inside him. This man felt his was superior in every way, yet he lived on a derelict wasteland. Earth was death and disease, a planet that had been abandoned for good reason. The man seemed unaffected by Spartan's manners.

"In the past, my people were from Northern Germany, part of Europe."

He pointed to the dome at the top of the ladder.

"Like this place, it is no longer a country, just another wasteland with a few isolated underground settlements."

One of the men walked away and disappeared into one of the many passages that seemed to spring up in every direction underneath the military base. The lighting was far more sedate than expected, and it was beginning to hurt Spartan's head as he strained his eyes. That combined with the aching in his body made him feel ancient.

Man, you're not in good shape, are you?

Khan seemed to be thinking the same as he raised one of his large eyebrows and laughed. Lieutenant Jenkins was unsure as to what was going on. The banter between the two was something that was inaccessible to anybody else, even though he had spent time sweating and possibly bleeding alongside Spartan back in the War.

"Spartan, you're looking old."

He dropped down next to the massive warrior and punched him right in the stomach. There was little visible effect on the warrior, but it did stop the laughter.

"Maybe. I can still kick your ass though."

Khan looked to him and wondered if that were true. It was a thought that seemed to consume him and push out all other thoughts. More importantly, the idea of a fight with Spartan seemed to brighten his usually dour expression.

"What are you so pleased about?" Spartan asked.

Khan smirked.

"Just daydreaming."

The officer tapped his temple and spoke quietly, looking at Spartan.

"The Governor will see you now."

He bowed just a little and indicated to his left, into a darker one of the many passageways.

"About damned time," grumbled Khan.

Spartan moved on, and Khan followed right behind. The route took only a brief moment, but he counted six more guards before they reached the surprisingly small door. Spartan approached but found his way blocked by the final two guards. One turned to face him, purposely putting himself in the way.

"Where do you think you're going?" he said sarcastically.

Spartan had done his best to hide his impatience and irritation at these so-called officers. He didn't bother to stop and simply smashed his knee into the man's stomach. The impact was short and savage and sent the man to the ground. Spartan pulled on the handle and walked inside.

The second guard tried to make a show of stopping him, but Khan was next. The massive figure of the warrior instantly encouraged the man to stand aside, which he sensibly did.

"Smart choice," Khan said.

Once inside, the door slid shut and cut them off from the corridor. The room was spacious. Spartan was confused but only for a moment. The room was easily the size of a training hall yet contained nothing but a large stainless steel desk. The walls were filled with cavernous windows that looked out onto the wasteland of Earth.

"Spartan, and Khan I presume?" asked the man seated behind the desk.

Spartan nodded, but Khan did nothing.

"Thank you for coming down to meet me. I am Governor Trelleck."

He indicated for them to sit down in the chairs provided, but it was immediately clear that Khan was much too big to use them.

"I don't think so," he muttered at the suggestion.

"Ah, yes…one of the fabled Jötnar. We have never had one of your kind here before."

He moved out from behind his desk and approached Khan. He was tall, gaunt, and almost skeletal in his build. His face was pale, as were all of the inhabitants of Earth that the two had seen so far. His eyes were pale blue and his hair short and gray. Spartan looked at the windows again. They were like those used on armored ships to present video feeds from other places.

We're underground, you fool; all of this is just a projection.

The Governor ignored Spartan and looked directly at Khan's face.

"Your people were created on Prometheus, a fire world. That's where you met Spartan, isn't it? I wonder how that meeting went?"

Spartan cleared his throat.

"The Jötnar were the final creation of the Echidna Union in the War. A spy on Prometheus interrupted their programming and removed the fail-safes."

"Indeed. I read the report. You Spartan, were there as well?"

Spartan nodded.

"Interesting."

The Governor moved around Khan, examining him as he might a new piece of equipment or technology, and Spartan could see his friend getting annoyed.

"What are you looking for?" he growled.

"Oh, nothing, I am merely curious. In Sol, all forms of artificial life are treated with suspicion, and your people are famed for your assault on Terra Nova at the end of the War."

Khan spat on the floor.

"My people fought under the command of General Rivers and Admiral Jarvis to liberate your capital."

The mention of the word 'capital' seemed to raise the heckles of the Governor. Spartan could immediately spot the innate hostility toward the primacy of the Alliance capital, and it amused him greatly.

"Yes, we took back Terra Nova from the Union troops and their commanders."

The Governor shook his head as if he'd just heard some tall tale. He looked at the two and smiled a thin, almost cruel smile that looked as genuine as Spartan's respect for the man.

"Yes, a rather convoluted tale, as I recall. The Union was under the control of some Artificial Intelligence, buried deep underground on Terra Nova. They were using clones, synthetic warriors, and ship based technology to wage a war of revenge."

Spartan said no more and simply nodded in agreement.

"This is one of the reasons that I have retained as much central control in Sol. Exposure to these unsavory elements had led to all manner of calamities. I suspect this war that ended with Terra Nova was just an attempt by these creatures, the ones you call Biomechs to destabilize our worlds ready for an outright invasion."

Again Spartan said nothing and instead spent the time listening. After a long time dealing with situations with just his fists, he was finally starting to understand the idea of using his ears.

"I plan on keeping Sol out of this, just as we did in the

past."

"What has this got to do with us?" Khan asked.

Governor Trelleck rubbed his chin and then moved back to his desk to examine data on his computer system. There was no way to see what was showing on the screen, and when Spartan tried to move to the side, he shuffled a little to block his route.

"I have a problem, and I need your help."

Khan raised his eyebrows at this.

"Well, problems are our specialty."

The Governor pressed a button, and all the windows in the room changed to show a very different surface; this time it a red and rocky, with a grayish black sky.

"Where is this?" Khan asked.

Spartan answered before the Governor could respond.

"It's Mars."

He then turned to the Governor.

"What about it?"

"Reports came to me in the last hour to say a series of objects has been found on the surface. My people are sending in a team to investigate, but there is something about the description of what they've found that sounds… well…very familiar."

Spartan looked to Khan and then again at the man.

"Familiar?"

Governor Trelleck turned his display around to face them both. It was a still image that showed a shattered structure with some kind of metal leg partially obscuring the field of view.

"This is the last image sent to us by the orbiting relay station. Shortly after sending this, it was shut down."

Spartan swallowed slowly as he looked at the imagery.

"Yeah, I've seen this before. That's a Biomech soldier."

The Governor looked positively shocked at this.

"Soldier? How many more can we expect?"

"Oh, not many. In our experience they are very rare. You'll never find more than three of them on board a single major warship or station."

Governor Trelleck calmed down a little at this piece of information.

"Ah, and these soldiers, what might they want?"

Now it was Spartan's turn to smile.

"I thought you already knew their plans? In the past, they have captured and secured areas prior to establishing forward bases. They've landed at a heavily occupied habitation site with minimal defenses, right?"

Governor Trelleck nodded, and Khan sighed. He walked to the screen and examined it closely.

"They will harvest your people, Governor Trelleck. When they are ready, they will turn them on the rest of Mars, then the Moon, and finally here, on Earth."

He looked truly staggered at this.

"But why? We have no quarrel with these machines."

Spartan shook his head.

"They want you out of the picture while they finish the job elsewhere. If you ask me, the Biomechs are on the move and heading to their endgame."

Governor Trelleck looked back at the screen and said nothing for several minutes. Spartan and Khan just waited there until the man looked up at them.

"I see. Well, in that case it would be useful to have you around. We will be back in contact with the ground station in thirteen hours. I've arranged for you both to have guest quarters. I will send for you when I have information."

Neither made a move to leave the room.

"Is there something else?" he asked.

"Yeah," Khan muttered, "What about the Spacebridge back to Terra Nova?"

He left his computer and walked to one of the nearest fake windows. He pointed up to the sky.

"That is where it used to be, a busy transit point between different parts of our great Alliance."

The sarcasm in his voice was bitter and obvious.

"The last reports from the barge around Mars said that an unknown vessel tried to take control of it the station. We've put a lot of time and money into building up the defenses on Mars. My teams deactivated the station and shut down the Rift immediately. In the subsequent battle, the ship was destroyed and the barge heavily damaged, but not before the vessel released several large objects that dropped to the surface of Mars itself."

He looked to his right and pointed to more open space on the surface of the Red Planet.

"That is where one of them came down. Less than an hour later, all communication with the mining base ceased, as well as contact with the dozens of civilian ships docked on the planet."

He looked at Spartan and tried to smile at him.

"I know you have fought these things before, and I suspect I will need your help very soon."

He pressed a button, and in walked the guard Spartan had put on the ground. His face tightened at seeing Spartan.

"Governor Trelleck."

Trelleck looked first to Khan and then to Spartan.

"I suggest you get some rest, perhaps visit one of our biomedical stations and see to that arm."

Spartan started to speak, but the man continued.

"I will not give the order to reopen the Rift until I am satisfied that Mars and the rest of Sol are clear of any contamination. As soon as we make contact with the planetary bases, I will be in touch. In the meantime, you have unrestricted access to this facility, as our guests."

Spartan moved to the door and stepped through before stopping and turning back.

"Governor Trelleck. If Biomechs have landed on Mars, you will need to evacuate the entire colony. They will leave no one alive."

The Governor lowered his head in acknowledgement and then indicated for the guard to escort them from his room. The door shut behind them, and the man attempted to block their path once more.

"Really?" Spartan asked.

"Yeah, are you that stupid?"

The man looked at them both, closed his eyes, and pointed in the direction he wanted them to leave.

"No," said Spartan.

"Take me to this biomedical station the Governor was talking about."

The guard clearly didn't want to assist, but the hard lines on Spartan's face and the bulk of Khan, as well as the pain in his stomach, encouraged him to do otherwise. He let out a sigh from his chest and reluctantly nodded to his left.

"This way, to the plaza."

* * *

The lights flickered inside the Governor's personal quarters as a priority video message woke him up. He hadn't meant to sleep and was still dressed in his smart Earthsec uniform, albeit it in a creased form.

"Governor Trelleck, we have the signal. The full report is coming in now…"

That was the news he'd been waiting for. Just a quick

toggle of a switch, and the feed switched instantly onto his system. The imagery of the surface of Mars was nothing unusual, but the new craters and damaged buildings near one of the shuttle landing stations shocked him.

"What happened?"

The view shifted, and the camera panned quickly to the right to show a large refinery structure. A number of towers rose up hundreds of meters into the sky, and one had collapsed down and crushed three large structures. A rail track was torn and damaged on one side, as well as several dozen cars strewn about.

"No," he said, unable or unwilling to accept the fact that something terrible might have happened at the colony.

Finally, a woman in an Earthsec uniform appeared. Her face was cut, and she had lost her cap at some point. It was only then clear that she was inside because her face was partially reflected on the glass behind her.

"This is technician Evans. We are in trouble…"

She looked back at the glass window, watching as another of the towers crumbled and then collapsed. A massive cloud of dust obscured all but the peaks of the towers and partially blocked the view from wherever the woman had been stationed. She looked back at the camera.

"The things smashed through the hangars. All of the security detail are dead, and the survivors, they've been given evacuation orders to head for the water towers."

More explosions rocked the background, and cracks

appeared on the glass.

"Their commander broadcast a message before landing and demanding our surrender. Captain Peterson led a patrol out to their landing site."

She sobbed, and more blasts shook the buildings.

"We've not heard from them since."

The sound changed to a banging noise and then gunfire. The woman looked out of shot and then ducked down for something. A sickening screeching sound followed. She reappeared with a long metal tendril thrust through her body. She slumped out of view along with the limb.

"What the hell is going on?" asked the Governor.

He had already pulled on his boots and rummaged about for his utility belt and firearm. He knew he needed to speak to somebody else, but there was something akin to a sickening fascination in watching the young woman die such a painful and bloody death. There was nothing showing now but the ruined control room and the cracked glass. He made to leave his room but stopped when a figure moved into shot. He watched, completely amazed at the sight of the thing.

* * *

Spartan sat on the bed and looked at the device the technician proposed fitting to his severed arm. There were plenty of marines in the Alliance that had been fitted with donor limbs and even organs if the need arose. It was very rare, however, for the fitting of augmented limbs or body parts, especially since the war against the Echidna Union. More than enough people still distrusted the Jötnar, even after their sacrifices to end the War. The fitting of technology directly to the body would allow the creation of more powerful and potentially more dangerous people. He looked back at the device and couldn't help but smile.

Maybe it isn't so bad.

"Very pretty," Khan said, trying to be helpful.

Spartan had imagined the team on Earth would be able to fit some kind of exotic device, but instead it was something more akin to a small claw attached to an engineering machine. It was jointed and could pivot shut but not with any great level of precision. It was slightly bigger than his hand had been and was based around two fingers and a thumb fitted around a central cylinder section; all built from a lightweight unpainted alloy. The fingertips had a thin rubber material to help with grip, and the back of the hand was open and exposed to show the wiring and motors.

"Well, what do you think?" asked the technician.

"Uh…do you not have something a little, well, more lifelike?"

The man looked offended at the question.

"This is the best we have. With a simple neural linkup, you will have full motor control of the lower limb and hand within a few days. I can make a few tweaks, and then we'll fit this over the top."

The man opened a cabinet and pulled out an odd pale jelly material. He placed it on the desk and it flattened out under its own weight.

"It takes less than an hour to mould it to create a reversed match for your other hand."

Spartan reached out and touched the lukewarm material. It was clearly supposed to replicate flesh but instead left him feeling a little queasy. He looked to Khan who just grinned back.

"Hey, maybe we could fit some weapons on that thing. You know, man it up a bit?"

His friend was trying to be helpful, but at that particular moment, it sounded more like a cruel joke. The material did seem odd, but the hand was more of a small robotic pincer than anything he'd seen before.

"Would you want one of these?"

Khan nodded excitedly.

"Of course. It looks better than the one they took from you, and it could be handy in a fight."

Spartan thought about it for a moment.

"Okay, let's fit this on."

The man pointed at the base of the unit.

"You have two choices when it comes to fitment. Either we can use a strap system to attach it to your elbow. Or we can go for the more direct route."

He pointed at Spartan's elbow.

"What do you mean?"

The technician brought up a set of schematics on his screen and enlarged a metal structure that looked very similar to bone.

"We can mount a support unit directly onto your elbow. It is small and would fuse directly to the joint. At the base would be this triple pinned socket, and you could just clip the arm on whenever you wanted to use it."

Spartan actually quite liked the idea of having the unit as more a part of him, but it was the expression on the man's face that put him off.

I don't know him, so why would I let him root around inside my arm?

"No, the straps will do fine for now. You can still connect it up via the neural link?"

"Of course."

Spartan watched him carefully, noticing how his body language had shifted slightly, as if he had been disappointed by the decision taken by Spartan.

Who cares? It's my arm, and I don't trust any of you down here.

The video communication panel flashed, and the technician immediately turned from his patient and toward the unit. With a hand gesture, it changed to show a serious looking Governor Trelleck.

"Is Spartan there?"

The man nodded.

"Yes, Governor, I have Spartan and the Biomech here."

Spartan winced at the man's use of the word. It wasn't because he was worried for Khan. On the contrary, he was far more concerned about what he would do. As expected, his friend reached out and tapped the man on the shoulder. He twisted about and glared at him.

"I'm busy, can't you..."

Khan's fist finished the man's question when it connected directly with his nose. The man was knocked to the ground, stunned, and knocked out cold by the blow. Blood streamed out around him from the wound. Spartan pushed the man aside and approached the screen. He could see the worry on the man's face, and it wasn't because of what they had just done. Spartan had seen the expressions on people's faces before that matched what he was seeing right now.

"Governor, we're here. What's wrong?"

The man's muscles in his face tightened just a little.

"It's Mars."

Spartan looked at Khan, but his friend was already next to him.

"You don't say," said the Jötnar.

"What about it?"

The Governor took in a long, slow breath before answering.

"A Biomech machine has taken control of the main mining facility. The soldiers are dead, and the rest of the colonists have vanished."

Khan shook his head in frustration.

"Governor, we told you this would happen."

Spartan nodded in agreement.

"That's true. Now the machines have control of the colony and its resources. They will start harvesting as soon as possible, and then you can say goodbye to the rest of this star system."

"Harvesting?"

Spartan gave the Governor a grim smile in reply.

"Of course. The machines will use your citizens as fodder for their Biomech factories. Once their equipment is ready, it will take just a few weeks, and then they will be ready."

"Ready for what?"

Khan knew exactly what was coming, and even he didn't relish the prospect.

"They will consume every facility and compound on Mars. When it is theirs, they will then do the same for every planet and moon in Sol."

Spartan looked even less impressed.

"Governor, by closing the Rift you blocked our ability to contact Terra Nova or to ask for help. Mars isn't ready for a war against these things."

He looked at the mechanical hand and forearm on the desk in front of him and picked it up to examine it. Even he was well aware of the irony involved in fitting a machine augmentation to his body.

"And when Sol has fallen, they will reopen the Rift and send their reinforcements in to open a second front against the Alliance."

The Governor paused and wiped his brow.

"Can you stop them?"

Spartan smiled at this.

"Removing Biomechs is our specialty."

The Governor closed his eyes, his face deep with concentration. Spartan was not impressed by what he had seen so far but had little doubt the man was genuinely concerned about his territory, even if his distrust of the rest of the Alliance was excessive.

"Very well, I will call for you shortly. In the meantime, I suggest you get some sleep."

CHAPTER THREE

The universal warship design, one formed alongside the creation of the Alliance itself, is an undoubted success and has proven sturdy and reliable against all manner of foes. Over the years the design has been improved, but the basic principle of a ship with interchangeable mission modules is now standard practice in the Alliance Navy. The Conqueror Class Battlecruiser is the latest in the line of universal ships, and it is expected that frontline operations will be taken over by these larger and more capable craft over the next two decades. The Crusader class will be reconfigured as required to better support their larger and even more advanced cousins.

Naval Cadet's Handbook

Spartan threw back the glass and swallowed another long mouthful of the yellow liquid. It wasn't a drink he was familiar with but found he quite liked it. Instead of the usual drinks, this one was a local delicacy. At least that was what the woman at the bar had said. As he swallowed another mouthful, he recalled how the woman had explained it was made from apples, a fruit that grew on the trees in their underground orchards.

Not bad, not bad at all.

The bar had a strange name with an excessive number of consonants that Spartan still thought they'd made up. The resulting name was nigh on impossible to pronounce, at least for him and Khan. He'd traveled far and wide and had never come across such a long and confusing name. The passageway leading to this social part of the underground base contained multiple businesses, including places to buy food, exercise, clothing stores, and even a place selling trinkets and memorabilia supposedly of Earth's past. He gulped the last few drops and dropped the empty glass down on the table. He could have done with more sleep, but right now he was enjoying a chance to relax before getting the call from the Governor. Khan spotted him finish the glass and took it from him before signaling for the woman to approach.

"Two more," he said a little louder than he intended.

The bar was much like any other Spartan had been to, with just one exception, the amount of weaponry on display. The walls and ceiling were covered in a bizarre collection of edged weapons and pieces of armor. Spartan had been fascinated by the number of helmets of many shapes and sizes but especially the one shaped like the head of an ox. A line of brackets held up nearly thirty very long weapons, including glaives, spears, partisans, and big swords. The ceiling was almost five meters above their heads, yet even more equipment hung down above those beneath enjoying a quiet drink.

It looked like a popular place, with nearly a dozen people relaxing prior to Spartan's arrival. It had taken the two of them less than an hour to get themselves into trouble, and all because Khan had made a comment about two women in one of the Earthsec bars. Two officials were now propped up on the bar while a third wiped blood from their faces. Khan and Spartan, on the other hand, looked revitalized, both pumped up on a mixture of alcohol and adrenalin.

"I like this place," Khan said.

He walked toward the bar trying to find his drink, but instead the three guards raised their hands to protect themselves. Khan stopped and growled at them, and then burst out laughing so violently that drool ran down from the corner of his mouth. When one of the guards recoiled even further, it merely encouraged him to lean in.

"Khan, come on, they've had enough," said Spartan.

Khan looked at each of them in turn and then stumbled back while grumbling something about Spartan. He staggered and then made an odd noise upon finding his drink, threw it back with one gulp, and then smashed the glass on the bar. He walked back to Spartan and dropped himself onto a long sofa that groaned painfully under his weight. Spartan sat directly opposite, took a swig from his own glass, and then placed it carefully on a small round table.

"What do you think is happening out there?"

Khan shrugged. Spartan could only smile at his discomfort. Khan looked to the door and back to Spartan. He had a helpful look on his face.

"Go and have a look."

Spartan laughed at his friend's dulled senses and complete lack of understanding.

"No, Khan, I mean I wonder what Jack and Teresa are doing now? The last reports they have here confirm something about an attack on Helios, Biomech ships being spotted at Rifts, and a full-scale mobilization of our entire military."

"What about APS?"

Spartan looked at him for a second before remembering that his company had a small regional recruitment office at one of the Alliance buildings on Earth. He'd not had much to do with it, as they hadn't even rented an entire floor. It was from memory a shared location with other firms in one of the state business centers. At least that was how he remembered it.

"Good point, I need a working computer terminal...or datapad. Where the hell can we get one?"

Spartan stood up and almost crashed into a tall man wearing a smart suit. The man began to speak, but at seeing their faces, decided discretion was the better part of valor and headed for the door.

"Smart," Khan said.

The man vanished to be replaced by another figure. He stepped inside and stopped. He was an overweight man in an Earthsec uniform, and carrying the same utility belt and weapons as his comrades. He looked about at those sitting or drinking before stopping at he sight of the three Earthsec operatives. He sighed and walked over to them.

"Spartan," Khan said quietly. He looked in the direction of the newcomer and nodded at him.

"We've got a suit heading our way."

They were partially obscured by the smoke of cigarettes from their position in the far corner. Even so, the size of Khan was almost impossible to hide, and after speaking for a few seconds, he touched one of them on the arm and indicated for a pair of guards to come in and help them leave. Khan clenched his fist at seeing them, but Spartan shook his head ever so slightly.

"No, not yet."

At the same time, he checked the motorized hand he'd been equipped with was also working. It was almost silent, but he was still finding the neural connection cumbersome to use. The last thing he wanted was to end up in a fight with a hand that ended up causing him problems. The man looked at him and then walked from the bar through the smoke toward them. By the time he appeared underneath the low-level lighting, they could see his face, and Spartan instantly relaxed.

"I see you've been making friends," said the man.

Spartan laughed.

"Lieutenant John Jenkins. What are you doing in our private hell?"

He moved up to Spartan and lowered himself down. Shapes near the doorway betrayed additional guards, but Spartan chose to ignore that, for now. He suspected they were keeping an eye on them, but so far had made no overt moves. He looked to Spartan's left arm.

"You want to see it?"

The man grinned sheepishly.

"Do you mind? I heard you went for something… well…something that is a…"

Spartan moved his hand up from where he'd rested it under the table.

"I've been checking our records prior to the closure of the Rift."

He handed him an old datapad, one that must have been at least forty years old. It took him right back to their shared time in the Corps.

"And?"

Lieutenant Jenkins pointed to the top right of the device.

"Your wife, she isn't with your company anymore. In fact, the entire private security industry is gone."

"What?" Khan snapped.

"There was some trouble while you were away. It seems the Alliance bought up some of your services and assets before shutting down the business, leaving it a corporate shell or something."

"What about my wife?" asked Spartan, his tone lowering and sounding less friendly.

"That's what I thought you'd like to hear. She's been reinstated to the Marine Corps. She made Lieutenant Colonel."

Khan raised both of his eyebrows at that.

"Colonel?"

Spartan wasn't sure whether he should have been happy or saddened at the news. Teresa had loved the Corps, but neither of them had been able to progress much further, and after the War the opportunities for people like them had shrunk every year.

"Not much of a surprise though, is it? She would be a good Colonel."

He looked to the Lieutenant.

"Anything on the rest of my family?"

Lieutenant Jenkins took the data and moved to a second page of data before handing it back. It showed a list of personnel on a number of warships, with three names all highlighted in red.

"Not much other than this."

Spartan looked at them carefully and then handed back to the device.

"So, my family is knee deep in all of this."

He turned to Khan who was now looking around for another drink. Spartan grabbed his chin and tugged him back to face him.

"Khan," he said forcefully.

"Yeah, I'm listening."

"Jack is with a task force at Helios led by Gun. He's got three marks on his record here."

"Just like his father," he muttered in reply before the name of his kin registered.

"Gun got the command, huh? I wonder who he killed for that!"

Spartan wiped his brow and nearly poked himself in the eye. He shook his head, trying to force the alcohol from his body and regain a little more composure.

"Thanks, Khan."

His friend looked at him and swayed before righting himself.

"What about Matius and Ingo?"

Spartan's face tightened like a single angry muscle at the mention of their names. They were not his children. They were from Teresa's past, and he got on even worse with them than he had with Jack in his early years.

I don't like kids, he thought.

Khan continued to look at him though, and he felt obliged to answer.

"They are heading out with the fleet, to join the rest at Helios, I think."

Khan leapt up and almost crashed into the wall. Only by resting a foot on the sofa was he able to remain upright.

"Then we need to get going. If there's going to be a fight, they'll need us."

Lieutenant Jenkins reached out to help stabilize Khan and found it harder than expected. When both of them were ready, he leaned in and spoke quietly.

"That's why I'm here. The Governor has authorized a special operation, and he wants your advice."

Spartan rose to his feet and did his best to ignore the pain racking up through his body. He dreaded to think how many bones he'd broken or damaged since vanishing with the T'Kari ship so long ago. The medics had explained to him over and over that he needed a long period of rest and recuperation, and to a man he'd explained to them all that he would, but only when he knew his wife and son were safe, not a moment earlier.

* * *

The room was dark, lit only by the antiquated looking two-dimensional projector device. The unit cast a highly detailed video image directly onto the specially coated wall to give a wide view of the awful scene being depicted.

"Ladies and Gentlemen, this has just reached us after the last survivors of the refinery security detail on Mars were killed. The last two made it off planet and used a relay satellite before being cut off."

His tone altered to something far more somber.

"We suspect both were killed in action."

The video continued, but so far nothing particularly interesting had appeared. The imagery was shaky because it came directly from the helmet mount of a security operative. To those in the room unused to combat, it must have come as quite a shock to see the terror and confusion of those being looked at. Spartan scanned quickly around the conference room, noting it looked more like a business boardroom than somewhere suitable for a military briefing, if that's what it was.

"Here," said the Governor, "this is where the main attack began."

Spartan watched as the figure moved to a window and looked out at a number of tumbling shapes surrounded by smoke. The camera jarred about and focused on the left of a small barrack room. Two men lay dead on the ground, and a third screamed out as his left arm hung down, shattered by some impact. They wore Earthsec uniforms, but unlike those on Earth, they were all wearing full tactical armor. It was nothing like the gear the Marine Corps used, and Spartan could see it was cheap, privately manufactured equipment designed more for internal security work. Their torsos and limbs were protected by plates of layered metal and plastic held on to their bodies with Velcro straps. The limbs were bulked up with additional plates on the knees and elbows, yet large gaps remained unprotected on the inside of the limbs and the ribs.

"They won't stand a chance," said Khan.

A pair of men in black suits at the back of the room whispered to each other whenever Khan said something and once again, when he finished, he looked at them to see them busily chatting away. Khan narrowed his eyes slightly and watched them until the taller man spotted him. He nodded politely and turned back to his comrade.

Yeah, you do that, Khan thought.

"Get the hell back!" cried out the figure they were observing.

Unlike the shouting and crying from others off camera, they were calm and remarkably restrained.

"This is Special Agent Aaron Smith. I am making this a category alpha attack. Unidentified forces are landing around the refinery site. Evacuate all Earthsec installations and head for the escape shuttles. Seal the tunnels!"

Another voice screamed, and a metallic shape ripped its way through the wall. Two long pointed arms pushed through and skewered the man like a kebab spike. The razor sharp tip punched through his front and out of his spine. A man near the front twisted about and vomited on the floor. Another nearby recoiled from the involuntary action and then stepped away.

The Governor sighed and indicated with his hand for two security guards to enter. A third person came in with cloths to clear up the mess. More sounds of violence turned the attention of the audience back to the screen. The machine had completely torn its way into the room, and the special agent had taken aim with a thermal shotgun of the type often used by internal security and police units.

"Get back!" he shouted.

The machine stabbed again at the first of the men who had already stopped moving. There was no reaction from him, just the foul sound of sharp metal punching into flesh. The shotgun safety clicked, and a pair of loud booms interrupted the sound. Everything else lowered in volume as the electronics tried to compensate for the spike in sound levels.

"He's a brave man."

"Brave, but foolish, Spartan," Khan agreed.

The thermal shotgun sent chunks of molten metal projectiles in a tight pattern against the machine. Incredibly, the man succeeded in blowing a number of fist-sized holes in the thing, yet it refused to stop. A scream off to the left made him turn about, and another machine filled the view. This time the machine was busily smashing a number of computer system and displays.

"Special Agent Smith. Abandon the refinery, now!"

He turned from the machine and began to build up speed. The door to the room quickly approached their view, and then he was through and into a wide passageway. Screams continued from all about, but he was of a single-minded purpose and ran the few hundred meters while ducking and jumping past smashed computer systems and broken walls.

"What the hell is going on here?" he asked himself as he ran.

He rounded a corner and slid to a stop. The ceiling had collapsed in on itself, and the level above had broken down to his level. Movement caught his eye, and he lifted the shotgun, but the face was that of a female civilian.

"Up here," she said.

A hand came down and helped lift him up. The camera struggled in the blackness, and finally adjusted by pumping up the volume. The resulting mess was much harder to make out.

"Who are you?"

"Anna Fitzgerald, technician for Amcord Mining. What the hell is happening?"

The camera panned back and forth.

"No idea. It's some kind of machine attack."

He looked back at the hole in the ground that led back the way he'd come from.

"There are machines back, and they're killing

everybody."

The woman wiped her face with the back of her forearm.

"Where are you going?"

"The evacuation shuttles, we can get to one of the habitation compounds beyond the mountains."

The young technician laughed; a hint of hysteria welling up in her voice. She started to speak, but no words came out. Special Agent Smith pulled her close and tried to comfort her.

"It's going to be okay. The rest of the colony will have received our communications. Earthsec will send in help soon."

There was a short but uncomfortable moment where he held her, and she lost control. The two of them just waited there for what felt like an eternity in a stunned moment of fear and compassion. It couldn't last though, and finally Special Agent Smith pulled her away and looked into her face. She looked back, and it was only then he saw the blood trickling down her left cheek.

"No, they don't know anything about this," she said, desperately trying to stay composed.

There was a delay before he spoke.

"How do you know?"

She looked behind her and pointed.

"I was monitoring a high-bandwidth stream to our head office when we lost power to most of our system.

My manager said something had destroyed the main and backup power generators for the refinery complex. By the time we got the communication system onto the reserve supply, the transmitter station had gone. We've been trying to reach other bases and installation on Mars. So far nothing."

Again there was a short delay.

"We have to find a way to get a signal to Earthsec command."

Anna shook her head.

"No chance. With the transmitter array gone, we just don't have the power to get a signal to Earth. Only one of the Lagrange stations is still functioning, and that will not come into range for another...two hours."

A volley of gunfire shook the floor from a dangerously close position. It was followed by shouting, more gunfire, and then screams. A powerful explosion shook the ground, and both were knocked to their knees by the power of the attack. Agent Smith lifted himself up, helped Anna do the same, and then leaned in close.

"We don't have much time. Let's get to the shuttles. We can use their communication gear to reach the Lagrange Station One when we're in orbit."

The image paused, and the light increased in brightness for a few seconds until those in the room could see each other clearly. The Governor moved to the front and stood directly in the path of the agent.

"The transmission continues for another eleven minutes. Copies have been sent to all of your accounts. These two made it to the shuttles, but shortly after sending in their report, we lost contact with them and any other craft that had escaped."

He let that sink in and found to his surprise that not one of them had a thing to say. He panned across until finding the annoyed looking expressions on the faces of his two newest arrivals.

"You have something to add?"

Spartan looked to Khan who saw the question as an open invitation.

"You're kidding, right? We told you what these machines would do, and now they have. Right now, they have this refinery and will be sending out their forces to secure the rest of the colony."

"Khan's right. How many people were there on Mars?"

Governor Trelleck looked at them both for a few seconds and then turned his head to nod in the direction of a short, dark skinned man. He stood up and faced them but didn't introduce himself.

"Mars Colony has just over three hundred thousand personnel, mainly workers for the refineries and their families. There are two main refinery complexes, a small engineering base, and a number of large habitation complexes. On top of that, there is City One where over half the population live, but it's nearly four hundred kilometers from the refinery site."

Spartan looked confused.

"I thought Mars was a major colony? That is not much more than a decent sized space station."

The man looked disappointed with this question but sat back down and left it to he Governor to continue.

"No, Spartan, we do not have the personnel or resources that the rest of the Alliance has in abundance. Mars...continues."

"Well, not for much longer," stated Spartan.

He lifted himself up and walked toward the Governor, ignoring standard protocol. This simple movement sent consternation through the small throng of people. A number of guards moved from the two main doorways, but on a signal from the governor they backed off.

"Well?"

Spartan pointed at the display.

"How many people are there at this refinery? The one where the Biomechs attacked?"

The Governor didn't even need to consult his system to answer.

"Three hundred and twelve plus a small security details. The site has underground tunnel access via light rail to the secondary refinery, as well as a major tunnel system leading directly to City One."

Spartan shook his head again.

"Those three hundred plus people will get them started.

In just a few days they will strike out to the rest of Mars, assuming they haven't already. I can promise you that City One will fall and will become a Biomech forward base in a matter of weeks. You need to open up the Rift and contact Terra Nova for help. They can have a rescue team at Mars in less than a day."

Some of the civilian staff in the room murmured in agreement, but the look on the Governor's face turned from that of calm and patience to anger. The lines of his face tightened, and his jaw twitted. The dark skinned man approached and stepped alongside Spartan to face him.

"Governor, I don't completely agree with our guests, but my officers think a rapid search and rescue operation on Mars should be conducted as a matter of urgency. We can move in, contain this threat, and put things back the way they were."

He then leaned in so that only the Governor could hear him. They spoke for a few more seconds before standing back. The tightness of his face softened just a little, and he then moved back to Spartan.

"No, we will not risk opening the Rift."

Khan burst out laughing from further back inside the room.

"Then Mars is gone, and you will be next. Three hundred thousand foot soldiers, all modified, butchered, and one hundred percent loyal to them. Earth won't stand a chance."

This time the Governor did give the nod to his guards, and a group of four closed in, each trying to look calm and relaxed as they approached the two visitors. Spartan faced off against one side while Khan looked to the other two, without even moving his body.

"You really don't want to do this," Spartan said.

The nearest man stopped in front of Spartan and then saluted; to Spartan's surprise it was his old comrade Lieutenant Jenkins.

"You keep showing up, old timer."

The man remained impassive and waited for the Governor to speak first.

"As Governor, I have already put plans in motion for a full-scale operation to retake Mars. I would very much appreciate it if both of you would travel along with the team, in an advisory capacity."

Khan looked at Spartan and grinned.

"They want us along, to advise?"

Spartan was less than amused at the suggestion though.

"Governor, you've just shown us a feed of your refinery operation. I promise you, these machines are just the lowest of their war machines. There will be at least one machine in overall command, perhaps more."

"Yeah," Khan added, "and those machines are something else."

Governor Trelleck indicated for them to move to his side so that he could see the rest of his people. Khan dutifully did as asked, but Spartan wouldn't easily do so. It took an additional request from Lieutenant Jenkins for him to agree.

"As you can see, our friends from the Alliance are experienced in fighting these machines. As experts in this field, I think we would all value their contribution to our rescue party."

Three men and a woman stood up and began clapping in appreciation. More followed, and it was very quickly clear it had been planned right from the beginning. It wasn't a particularly sophisticated plan, but it had put Spartan into a rather difficult position. He looked to the Governor, who gave no indication other than a courteous nod.

"Thank you, Spartan. Your skills will be very much appreciated by our combat team."

Lieutenant Jenkins extended out his hand for Spartan to shake, and he felt obliged to return the favor. In that one moment, he knew he had just sealed his and Khan's fates. It didn't make him feel bad though. As he looked back at the group of people, many of whom wore their Earthsec uniforms, he realized he had absolutely nothing in common with them. They were isolated, and it seemed they liked it. He looked to Khan who'd tilted his head a little, as if to question him.

We'll help them, all right. And when the colony is secure, I'm getting that Rift open, if I have to use my bare hands.

Khan couldn't hear his thoughts, but as Spartan looked at his bruised friend, he was convinced he knew exactly what Spartan had planned.

Yes, the quicker we get this Rift open, the quicker we can get to Terra Nova and see what mess our great leaders have moved us toward.

* * *

The underground hangar was much less impressive than Spartan had expected. Like everything else on Earth, it was old, antiquated, and poorly maintained. In days gone by, it might have been the home to a dozen medium sized shuttles, but now over half was taken up with very thick metal poles holding up the stone roof. There were four large shuttles lined up along one side, although only one had its doors open and seemed ready for action. Lieutenant Jenkins moved to the hatch nearest the front of the craft and then looked back.

"Spartan, Khan, it's this way."

It didn't need to be said, but the two of them had already stopped to look about the place.

"Before we go, Jenkins, I need to know something."

The officer waited patiently. His face was relaxed, but Spartan could see there was something he wasn't telling him. As far as he was concerned, this entire operation had been activated on a whim. He even wondered if it had been concocted just to get Khan and him off Earth, and where they could cause the least trouble.

"Is this on the level?"

The Lieutenant looked confused at the question.

"What, the mission?"

Khan nodded, evidently wondering the same thing.

"Of course. I met with the Governor and his senior advisors less than an hour ago. He showed me the rest of the footage which..."

"We still haven't seen completely," Khan interrupted.

Lieutenant Jenkins nodded in agreement.

"Yes, that is true. I have it on file, and we can watch it as many times as you want on the way to the Lunar base. As for the operation though, it is necessary and above board. Mars is not just one of our most important settlements; it is the primary refinery and transport hub for Sol."

Spartan now looked even less convinced.

"It's also the point in Sol that controls access to Rift that can send ships over four light years to the rest of the Alliance. It will take months for engineers on the other side to construct a new system to reopen the Rift somewhere else, assuming they are not already under attack."

Lieutenant Jenkins didn't seem to know what to say to that. He waited for a few seconds before indicating for them to join him inside.

"Look. There is no Rift, no communications, and no help coming until Mars is secured."

He leaned in close to Spartan.

"This isn't public knowledge yet, but eleven minutes into the attack, we lost control of the Rift control system."

Spartan recoiled almost a full meter when he heard this.

"You idiots. You've lost the Rift?"

A number of technicians heard him shouting and looked up to try and understand what they were talking about. Jenkins tried pulling him to the door, but Spartan blocked his arms and gave him a hard stare. Based on the interest shown by the technicians, the secret of the Rift was now well in the open. Spartan looked to Khan who laughed at his friend's discomfort. He looked back at the Lieutenant and indicated for him to move aside.

"Okay, we're coming."

He moved past the man and into the cramped interior of the craft. He sat down, noting the technicians had modified part of the stowage area into somewhere Khan could sit. He shook his head and pointed to where Khan was to go.

"I'm getting sick of this place," his friend grumbled.

There were four other Earthsec operatives on board, but none made a move to look at them or even to engage in conversation. Instead, the three new arrivals strapped themselves in and waited for the start-up sequence. As they waited, Lieutenant Jenkins twisted about to face the two of them.

"Look, we have a ship and escorts waiting assembling at

the Lunar military base. The Governor has even arranged for a squadron of armed shuttles for escort. It's not exactly a major Alliance operation, but it's the biggest thing I've ever seen Earthsec organize."

Spartan tried to look outside, but the windows were small and badly burned, presumably from multiple landings through the planet's atmosphere. It didn't exactly inspire much confidence.

"I've not seen a plan, information on the site, or any idea of the kind of resources you're putting into this. I still doubt your people have any real idea what they are getting into here."

The Lieutenant tried to smile, but it came out a little crooked.

"Maybe, but the three of us know what's down there. That's why I recommended all three of us should be attached to this little operation."

Spartan looked at him carefully. He had a few vague recollections of the man back from over twenty years ago. There were others like Marcus, and even the kid that he could visualize, but nothing much with this man.

"Why?"

The man looked even a little whimsical at this question.

"Really? Well, we have a specialist Earthsec security force with the best gear around. Until these machines attacked Mars though, this was the first we'd ever seen of an extra-terrestrial threat. To be honest, most people out here see this enemy as being a political ploy, nothing more."

Spartan scratched at his eyelid with his good hand.

"Political? Have they not seen the vids?"

Khan was less interested in politics and growled at the two of them.

"You said they were good. How good?"

Lieutenant Jenkins looked to Khan and shrugged.

"Not Confed Marines Corps good, but they are fit, well trained, and capable. With the right leadership and direction, they can get the job done."

He leaned back in his seat as the engines powered up.

"You might as well rest for now. It's going to take us nearly a day to reach your new home."

"The Moon," said Khan miserably.

The lump of space rock was known throughout the Alliance as being the very first human colony. For that it had a special place in history and for most, a visit to the satellite was almost a pilgrimage. To Khan it was just another lifeless rock, in a star system he found he liked even less than he expected.

"No," said Lieutenant Jenkins with a grin.

"We aren't going to the surface."

The two looked at him suspiciously, waiting for an explanation.

"We're meeting up with the ES Dauntless."

He looked at the two, expecting some kind of reaction.

Khan did nothing, so he turned his attention to Spartan who seemed equally unimpressed.

"Dauntless, you know, the oldest commissioned ship."

Spartan shook his head slowly. Lieutenant Jenkins looked disappointed.

"She's a museum ship in orbit around the Moon. Earthsec has commandeered her, and she is being refitted by an emergency crew for immediate departure."

"Wait, a museum ship?" Khan asked.

"Well, yes," answered Jenkins. "Dauntless is over four hundred years old. She's one of the old Commando Carriers. Twelve crew, and space for four assault shuttles and two platoons of commandos."

He sounded excited at the prospect, but Khan just rolled his eyes at the description.

"Sounds like a piece of junk to me."

Spartan said no more and instead reached for one of the wired datapads, of a vintage that seemed older than even the ones back in his short-lived quarters on Earth. The small craft shuddered, and then he felt the familiar kick as its engines blasted them off and away.

Now, let's see what this ship is all about.

CHAPTER FOUR

The descendents of the Jötnar Battalion would find their services being called upon during the great call to arms of 361CC. As scattered Biomech raiding parties made their way from around the galaxy to reach Helios, the Alliance sent out the call to all military units. The response was rapid and substantial, and in a matter of weeks, entire units of reserve troops and mothballed ships were hastily brought back into service. Even the deathly world of Hyperion, now home of the Jötnar, made a contribution, one of many thousands of Jötnar warriors. Their contribution would mean more than an entire division of Alliance Marines.

The 1st Jötnar Battalion

Teresa and her entourage of three captains, T'Kron, and a handful of Jötnar had just finished a short tour of the dismantled Biomech assembly equipment, and she wasn't particularly enjoying it. Most of the facility had been removed or destroyed a long time ago toward the end of the War, yet small sections had been retained, partially for posterity but also for research. The problem she had was too much of it brought back memories of that time, and there was little good about it. The fighting on Prometheus had been more than just a violent rescue. It was her first experience of the massive Biomechs that would later become the loyal Jötnar like Khan and Gun. They had moved away from the equipment and machinery and toward the central hub where the command staff lived and worked.

"Are you okay, Colonel?" asked Captain Nathaniel Rivers.

They had sat down in the large, open central plaza that was decorated with a bizarre mixture of sculptures, each of them constructed from the rusted remnants of machinery. It was the very heart of the underground complex, and Teresa could see with her experienced eye that large parts of the plaza had been modified since her last visit.

"I'm fine, Captain. I just need a moment before we meet the Admiral."

She pulled out her secpad and checked her schedule, breathing out slowly with impatience at seeing she had only a few more minutes of respite before they had to leave the place. He was sitting opposite her on a metal bench that looked like it might lift itself up and walk away at some point.

"My father told me about this place, about the torture and brutality by the Union soldiers."

Teresa looked down the floor. It was strange seeing the metallic surface that always seemed to ooze warmth. She looked back up and tried to smile.

"That wasn't the worst part."

She looked to the rooms they had recently left.

"Those chambers were used to harvest bone, flesh, tissue, and organs to build war machines for them. This entire place was an abomination that took thousands of lives."

She rubbed her chin and shook her head as though surprised.

"The strange thing about this place though, well, until prisoners were brought here, we had no idea of the research bases, underground factories, or the shipyards. They had been constructed here in secret."

"Why is that strange?" asked the Captain.

Teresa looked at him with raised eyebrows.

"That kind of construction takes time, a long time. The engineers here said most of the oldest parts of the place dated back to near the early colonization of Terra Nova."

Now the Captain looked confused.

"I thought Prometheus wasn't fully explored until much later."

"Quite."

The Captain nodded and looked back at the small group of Jötnar strutting about like a group of trolls. Every now and then, they would stop directly in front of a statue and start shouting or arguing. Olik in particular kept returning to one of the larger sculptures and touching the metal. Teresa found it curious how much more interesting this place was to him, far more than it would ever would be for her.

"Why are they so interested in them?" asked the Captain.

Captain John Tycho, the second of her three captains, lifted himself with a groan and nodded in the direction of Olik.

"Being here might be filled with horrors for us, but to him and his kin this is where it all began. Don't forget, the Union used it to research and manufacture the first synthetic warriors."

He looked to Teresa.

"Isn't it true that the first of these larger Biomechs had human parts inside them?"

Teresa closed her eyes and slowed her breathing. When she opened them, all three of the captains were looking at her. Ever since what happened on Prometheus, she had encountered bitterness and distrust towards Gun, Khan, and their people. Although she could understand part of it, the basic criticism always came down to the first of their kind, those built with the butchered body parts of the living.

"Yes, a small number of the first Biomechs were made from organs taken from the dead. I think the brains and nervous systems were used from a number of prisoners, and the final production models were replicated from these."

She looked back to Olik who was still some distance away. The only other time she had seen Khan or even Gun show as much interest in something was when they were examining a new weapon or piece of armor. Prometheus meant so much more to them, more than even she would probably be able to understand.

"This place is like nothing we, as humans, will ever have. It is their birthplace, and no matter how many years go past, they will always be reminded of it. Unlike us, they were manufactured, at least the generation during the War. Don't forget that with the help of people like Anderson, we've been able to support the Jötnar to procreate naturally, instead of in factories.

"Yeah, so their numbers go up. Is that good?" asked Captain Rivers.

Teresa looked confused.

"You should know the loyalty of the Jötnar better than most. Why should they not enjoy the same as us?"

Captain Thomas Thompson, who had until now remained seated, quietly lifted himself to his feet. He was a tall man and had said nothing so far. Unlike the others, his interest in the Jötnar was out of courtesy only. Teresa suspected this was due to his considerable amount of time spent training alongside them. Of the three captains, he was the only one who had spent anything more than a few hours with the Jötnar.

She and Spartan had been on a Biomech hunt on Hyperion with the Jötnar, and it was an experience that left you both bonded and scarred. It was a time she would never want to forget, not least because that was the first vacation the two of them had spent following their marriage. She looked back to the young Captain again.

They are probably nothing more than other marines to him.

She noticed him looking at his secpad, and he began to speak but stopped. Something on the screen almost made him choke.

"Colonel, there's a priority message going out to all officers."

Her secpad began to vibrate and make a gentle humming sound.

"It's from the Admiral, here on this base."

"I don't understand," she said.

She pulled out the device and examined the data carefully. By the time she was past the third line, her body was shaking. She looked up. All of her officers, as well as T'Kron and Olik, were there.

"You've heard then?"

Only Olik shook his head.

"What is it?"

Teresa wiped her brow.

"You recall the Biomech ship that Gun and I boarded?"

He nodded.

"Well, we captured its commander, and it was taken to the Naval Base on T'Karan."

"So?"

She took in another long breath.

"It's not there anymore. Anderson has sent out an urgent message to all commanders on this station. He arrived three hours ago and has brought it with him."

Captain Thompson shook his head in surprise.

"What?"

Teresa tried to answer, but the imagery of the Biomech commander was pushed to the forefront of her memory. The fight to stop it had been one of the bloodiest single engagements she'd ever seen on board a warship. Her own marines had suffered badly, but in the end they had captured the ship and disabled the great machine. Its great black metal chassis had been twice the size of Gun or Khan and had killed dozens of fighters before it had been disabled.

"I don't understand the thinking behind this, Colonel. The enemy commander is a major intelligence asset. Why bring him back here?"

Teresa looked at more information coming in, read it,

and then lifted the device so that her officers could see the imagery. It showed the blackened shape of the great machine, and to their surprise, it was moving.

None of this makes sense.

She looked at her officers and the bemused look on Captain Thompson's face seemed to answer her questions there and then.

If this is so secret, why are messages being sent to so many officers?

It was a simple ruse, but she had to admire its boldness. It was a great risk, of course, but then she wondered if the story about the machine was even true. Was it actually being shipped there, or was it another lie on top of many more?

"What the hell is he doing?" asked Olik.

Teresa read further and shook her head at the news.

"According to the flash report from Admiral Anderson, the Biomech managed to break out of its holding facility and accessed Alliance communication systems for almost seven minutes before being stopped. It's being brought here for safety."

Teresa knew full well how powerful the Biomech machine was, and that if it had escaped for that much time, there would have been heavy casualties on the base. That was of course if the story was even true, and now she was beginning to have doubts about almost everything she'd heard. She looked at Olik and nodded.

"I don't like it."

He twisted his head about sharply, and it looked like he might even reach for a weapon. Instead, he settled for adopting a solid stance with his hands kept low. Teresa knew this position, and it was the classic defensive posture taught in the Corps for uncertain situations.

Non-threatening, but ready. What is it?

"Colonel!" he said, answering her unspoken question.

The entire group looked in the direction he had indicated. A group of black clad marines entered the space and was heading directly toward them. Teresa counted eight in total, and all were fully armored in PDS Alpha armor. None wore any form of identification, and they moved in unison, unlike any marines she was used to. The group finally stopped and from behind them came a man in a dark suit and long gray coat. He moved to the front and looked at each of them before stopping at Teresa.

"Johnson?"

"Intelligence Director Johnson, Colonel Morato," he answered politely.

Teresa ignored those around her, walked right up to him, stopping barely a meter from the man. They looked at each other before Teresa finally moved in closer and grabbed him. They held each other for a short moment while the others watched on uncomfortably. She finally stepped back and looked at him.

"You've grown...more serious."

He tried to smile, but his expression was more of a

grimace.

"The schedule has changed, and I need your officers with me in the lower landing dock."

"Anderson?" she asked.

Johnson merely nodded in agreement.

"I take it you received the flash communication? We have to keep this quiet as long as possible. Are you ready?"

Teresa indicated with her right hand for the others to come with her. Johnson looked at them and finally smiled.

"No matter what rank you reach, you are always surrounded by the oddest of people."

She looked in the same direction as him but saw nothing more than a small group of Alliance officers and a large number of Jötnar. She looked back at him.

"They are coming too?"

"Just the officers."

Teresa began to speak with Olik, but he was already explaining to his own people before joining the party. They moved away and left that part of the vast underground base and exited via a pair of guarded glass doors. As soon as they were through, the doors were clamped shut, and more guards took up opposition around them.

"So, Intelligence Director. Do you intend telling me what's going on?"

They didn't stop moving as he answered.

"Teresa, we intercepted and deciphered part of the Biomech's transmission. It wasn't an escape attempt.

It was an intentional lapse of security. We gave it the opportunity."

She grabbed his arm as they continued on.

"I saw a casualty list of nearly a hundred personnel."

Her friend closed his eyes briefly and took in more air.

"I know. It was a high price."

He stopped for just a few seconds, and the others carried on.

"You know the position we're in. The Alliance is spread out, the Helions are fighting themselves, and the Biomechs, well, wait till you see what we've found."

* * *

Teresa had expected to find people and machinery at their destination, but the smaller of the landing docks contained just a single transport. She suspected it wasn't a ship that was being worked on, as it looked older and smaller than anything similar on the base. As she moved closer, she found her eyes were drawn more to what was missing than what was present. The cargo sections were of a normal size, yet she could see where ribs and plates had been fused to close them shut. It was as if the ship itself had been closed up in numerous places to create the equivalent of a space-worthy security safe.

This is weird.

Her gut instincts were rarely wrong, and each extra

second she spent staring at the thing merely added to her suspicions. Her quick estimation was that it could hold something about the size of the Tamarisk, the deadly Q ship that she had arrived at Prometheus on so long ago. Just that thought alone made her think it might be a ship designed for a similar purpose. Teresa spotted Director Johnson looking at her, and for some reason that made her uncomfortable, but only for a moment.

"So, this is it? An old space freighter?"

Johnson said nothing and looked away before turning his attention back to her. His expression looked as if he was questioning her observational skills. He looked at her face and saw right through her and smiled. He then looked back to the ship and pointed at the narrow ramp leading inside.

"You'll find answers to your questions inside. Follow me."

Teresa and her officers moved in single file to the ramp while watching several dozen engineers fitting additional ribbing on the large blast door that marked the entrance to the dock.

"Looks like they intend on staying," suggested Olik.

Teresa looked at the exterior but didn't recognize the design. As far as she could tell, it was a generic transport, one of a thousand designs that plied the trading lanes of the Alliance. The only giveaway that it was even an Alliance vessel was revealed as she moved nearer. The outer hull plates were actually a multi-layered mesh that extended out several meters ahead of the outer skin.

Layered armor to catch and explode mines and low-tech ordnance; she's a blockade runner, not a transport.

That was even more interesting to her. Admiral Anderson wasn't just the commander of the Admiral Jarvis Naval Station. He was also commander of the outer territories and regional governor, yet he had ventured away from his territory to bring back this deadly machine while using a heavily modified civilian transport.

What is he playing at? Why not use a conventional Alliance ship?

The hull itself was heavily scored, and she could see dozens of markings that could have been caused by anything from high-velocity dust, to weapons fire, or landing in dust storms.

"I don't get this, Colonel. Why is the Admiral not preparing the outer territories for the war?" asked Captain Rivers.

It was a simple question, but one she was beginning to worry about, too. By traveling back to this part of the Alliance, the Admiral had left a large swath of territory without a commander.

"Captain, I really do not know."

Teresa looked at the ship and thought back to what she knew of the colonies and bases on the border. The bulk of Alliance controlled systems was based around Alpha

Centauri and the stars within a four light year radius. Anderson had full control over the Alliance operations at Prometheus that operated as the gateway to the Orion Nebula. It was there the massive Rift control station and apparatus had been assembled in a project that had taken years. He was the senior Alliance officer on the other side of the Spacebridge, effectively a military governor of the entire T'Karan system, and of operations beyond the borders of the Alliance.

"Follow me," said Director Johnson from the top of the ramp.

He disappeared inside, but not before giving Teresa the oddest of looks. The others followed him into the dark and cavernous interior. It took nearly four minutes to navigate their way to the centre of the ship. Rather than many small compartments, this vessel was equipped with a single circular storage section of a size large enough to contain a full company of men. They moved to the wide gantries a third the way up the compartment and spread out to face the Director. The globe of shinning metal looked more like a sculpture than a cell, and in front of it waited a group of officials. Teresa moved closer and stopped upon seeing another familiar face.

"Admiral Churchill?"

The aged former commander of the 7th Fleet nodded and gave her a gentle smile.

"None other. I'm retired, of course."

He twisted about and pointed at the sphere.

"Not quite what you were expecting, I suspect?"

Teresa nodded in agreement.

"I thought you had moved into politics?"

"Yes, well, politics is not for everyone, and Admiral Anderson needed somebody with a military background to assist in the interrogation of this specimen. You'll recall the incident with my ships back in the War?"

Teresa could do much more than just remember what ships he had commanded.

"Admiral, it was surviving ships like the Valiant and the Ark Royal that allowed us to turn the fight to the enemy in the War. The 7th will never be forgotten."

Teresa could see the thanks in the old man's eyes. He and Anderson had both done their part in the War, but she couldn't imagine the damage the losses of so many at the start of the War must have had on the Admiral. From memory, she was certain he'd left the military not long after she had. Like many other officers, the War held bitter memories, and there were more than enough citizens waiting to point the finger of blame on the soldiers of both sides. She could see how time had taken its toll on him, yet also how this new project of Anderson's had revitalized him.

"Admiral, you look more alive than I've seen you in a long time."

"You'll see why in a moment."

He indicated for the almost two-dozen officers to look at the sphere.

"Admiral Anderson has sent me back to Prometheus for one reason, and one reason only. We have to keep this machine as far from the frontline as possible. We cannot risk the enemy finding it, and with war coming to our borders, it needed a new home."

"Why here, on Prometheus?" asked one of the engineering captains from the station.

Admiral Churchill licked the side of his mouth before replying.

"We've obtained substantial information from this... thing...to suggest the enemy want to locate it. It is not just a soldier of theirs; it is one of their leadership, the master race if you will."

"And us?"

Teresa extended her hands to encompass her captains. The old Admiral shook off a twitch in his cheek and cleared his throat.

"Teresa, your task force's mission was kept a secret, even from your commander. We have intelligence from this thing that a rescue party was coming from somewhere near the Terra Nova Rift."

Director Johnson indicated for the two to come nearer to the side of where the metallic sphere took up so much space.

"Teresa, your ships were bait. We copied the

communication coding from the machine and directed it at your force."

He saw the look of anguish on her face but kept on, wanting to give her as much information as he was allowed. He tried to speak, but Teresa grabbed his hand.

"Wait. You pretended this Biomech was in our fleet? You know what happened, don't you? We lost the entire force with the exception of Dreadnought."

Johnson lowered his head. Teresa could see he was hurting, but it wasn't enough. A vast number of naval personnel had been lost, for just one machine. Teresa shook her head bitterly.

"I was brought into this project to manage the research of this thing, and to protect everything we know and might learn from it in the future. Things are getting a little wild out on the border, and Anderson recommended a move to Prometheus. It is the gateway to Orion, and if the Biomechs want him, they will have to get past Anderson and his forces first."

He turned and faced the sphere and then spoke quietly to Intelligence Director Johnson. They seemed to disagree about something, and their conversation dragged on for almost a minute before the Admiral look back. Teresa found herself unable to speak, the weight of the news that so many had died for this still stunned her.

"You are the first to see this outside of the AJ Station."

All it took was for both him and Director Johnson to

place the palms of their hands onto a console in front of the sphere. Almost instantly, a pattern of sparks and flashes rippled around the sphere. With a groaning sound, like that of a heavy stone object being dragged across sand, it moved open. When the sound finally stopped, a bank of floodlights flickered on all around the prisoner. Everybody, including Teresa, had to cover their eyes for a moment while they adjusted to the conditions.

"I give you the Biomech regional commander of T'Karan, known as Krani to his people. He is one of less than a thousand of his race still alive."

Teresa stood completely still as she looked across at the dormant Biomech commander. The last time she'd faced the thing had been during its capture and defeat, yet even in this motionless state it appeared just as deadly. Even now she could visualize its destructive power and capability, and it sent periodic shivers through her body. There were differences now though. Its limbs were encased in multiple rings of metal, and arcs of electricity flashed about it as a series of powerful nodes kept it effectively asleep. Johnson looked to Teresa and gave her a grim smile.

"The enemy knew we had him captured, and thanks in no part to the brave sacrifice of our marines, we have brought it here undetected. The temporary collapse of the Terra Nova-Prometheus Rift destroyed a number of our own ships, but it also eliminated the entire Biomech rescue party."

Admiral Churchill took over.

"This Biomech commander has given us privileged information, and it is imperative that we retain control of it. That is why you were sent here, and not to be sent to the Helion meat grinder. No, your job is to help fortify this entire sector. Prometheus is a tough nut to crack, and if it were ever to fall, we would lose our link to the Orion Nebula as well as our new allies. The 1st Heavy Strike Group is already here, and we have reinforcements from Hyperion coming."

That sent a murmur of surprise through the small cadre of officers.

"That's right," said the Admiral, "We have an entire battalion of Jötnar en route. Prometheus will be our bastion, the buffer between Orion and us. I want this sector of the Alliance to become a rock, the strongest defensive location ever built."

He was greeted with a deafening silence.

"What about T'Karan? Surely we should spend our efforts building up our defenses there?" asked Teresa.

Admiral Churchill nodded in agreement.

"That is a good point. Admiral Anderson is commanding the border and all territories outside of our own area of control. The Orion Nebula is his domain now. It falls to us to protect our heritage, these core worlds of Alpha and Proxima Centauri, and our other colonies just a few light years apart."

He looked directly at Teresa.

"Colonel. You will take temporary command of the ground forces on this fortress. This comes directly from General Rivers."

She nodded in agreement but found herself unable to speak. Olik pushed forward and pointed at the Biomech.

"So, you've brought it here and you've been studying it. What do you know?"

Director Johnson smiled.

"Captain," he started, for a second unsure as to the correct position of Olik in the military structure. He looked at his secpad and checked the security access for those assembled in front of him.

"You are the senior officers responsible for the defense of this fortress. Access to this Biomech and any intelligence learned from it are expressly for command level officers only."

Olik in particular seemed unimpressed at this.

"Then why show us?"

Johnson was surprised at the speed and authority in his voice.

"A good point. We have shown you to ensure you understand the significance of this place. Prometheus is not just a foundry and research site. It is now the single most important location outside of the Orion nebula. While we hold this leader, we have a bargaining chip worth more than an entire planet to the Biomechs. That is all for now."

The more junior officers were politely escorted from the ship, with just Teresa, Admiral Churchill, and Director Johnson remaining. They waited until everybody else was off the vessel before Johnson spoke.

"Information from this enemy operative is limited. We want the enemy to know their commander is here, but nothing more."

Teresa looked at him, carefully examining his face and the lines running down to his mouth. She'd known him a long time, but this almost callous attitude to people and resources had taken her very much by surprise.

"You just explained this to a group of officers, many of which are my own. And you expect this information to be leaked somehow?"

The Admiral tried his best to look conciliatory.

"Teresa, with the best will in the world, when information is shared so freely, it will work its way into the open. It might take a day, maybe a week, but I can guarantee that in less than a month the enemy will come knocking. And we will be waiting for them."

Johnson pointed to the machine.

"What we've learnt in the last few months would shock you to your very soul, Teresa."

She looked at him with a whimsical expression on her face. She looked up at the machine and shook her head with amusement.

"Really Johnson? You think you can shock me?"

Johnson's expression remained the same.

"Frankly, yes I do."

"Well, come on then, what is it?"

He paused, and for a moment it looked like he might say nothing. He looked past Teresa and checked once more that the others had gone. Then he winked with a single eye.

"They have no idea we have their commander on this planet. Anderson is laying a trap for them at the AJ Naval Station. He's got the place rigged with charges and over a hundred ships hidden in orbit."

Teresa was confused.

"I don't understand. In the briefing, you said we were converting Prometheus into a fortress. Is that not true?"

Johnson leaned in closely and spoke even quieter.

"We will be, just not yet."

He squeezed her arm for some unknown reason and then stepped back.

"We've lost dozens of ships in a matter of weeks, and it's getting worse. We cannot support the Helions and defend our own territory with these kinds of losses."

The Admiral looked at Johnson and nodded in agreement.

"It's true. Over the next two weeks, we're pulling back from Orion and fortifying at the AJ Naval Station. It's going to be a few weeks, but we are already assembling assets to ensure the Prometheus-T'Karan Rift is secure on both sides. Helios is a lost cause; they will have to defend it themselves if the fight with the enemy fails."

Teresa looked up to the machine and tried to fight back the fear she could feel in her bones. Jack was in the Helios system, and no matter what these men said; she knew he was in serious danger. Deep down she knew they were lying. It was a show to misinform the machine, or at the very least designed to instill a sense of urgency to the situation. Their story had a ring of truth to it though, and that was what concerned her most. She'd always heard that the best lies were those based upon truths. Teresa closed her eyes for a moment and then looked up to where the sunken black helm of the machines head was.

"And what about him? Shouldn't he be brought back to Terra Nova, for safekeeping?"

Johnson looked up at the machine and then to Teresa.

"Why do you think we brought him to the best research and manufacturing stations in the Alliance?"

Teresa thought about it for a few seconds. She knew everything the two men were saying was being put on as a show; she just didn't know whom the intended audience was. A slight crackle of light around the head of the Biomech machine caught her eye's attention, and then she saw it, the glimmer of movement in its frame.

The Biomech, they're feeding it false information.

"We need troops and we need war machines. Can you

think of a better way to rebuild our ranks?"

Teresa looked at him and again to the machine. The truly frightening part though wasn't that he was making things up. The one thing that scared her more than anything else was that he might actually be telling the truth.

No, he can't be serious. He's suggesting we build Biomech warriors to fight for us.

CHAPTER FIVE

The AI Core was perhaps the most advanced and most elusive piece of intelligent computing in the history of humanity. For the first time, a piece of technology had been found that could absorb the intellect, memories, and intelligence of a human and use it to perform critical analysis of data. The destruction of the AI Core on Terra Nova in 338CC was one of the great achievements and losses in science. Ever since that destruction, the greatest minds of the Alliance have tried and failed to meld the mind of a man with a machine. It would appear the only solution would be a technological exchange with the Biomechs themselves.

Computer Science 101, 7ᵗʰ Edition

Teresa had spent the last hour modifying and expanding the defensive plan of Prometheus that had been in use now for several years. Her new home was the station

Marine headquarters, positioned directly alongside the newly constructed barracks. Unlike other facilities, everything about Prometheus was cut directly into warm rock. No matter where a person went in the facility, there was always the sound of mining and cutting equipment, as workers and machines alike continued to burrow their way inside the resource rich planet. Her four captains, now including Olik, stood alongside her and around the wide table in the centre of the room. Above it was a projected three-dimensional model that sat just a few centimeters from the surface.

"The defensive systems on the surface are solid enough," said Captain Rivers.

"True," answered Olik, "but who is going to start an assault from the surface? Have you seen outside?"

Captain Tycho shifted on his artificial legs and groaned, though quiet enough only to be heard by Olik.

"The Biomechs are able to land mechanized troops on the surface. They can take the heat, and their machine warriors can operate in a vacuum. Hell, our own marines could manage it for a while."

Teresa nodded in agreement.

"That's all true. Even so, the surface defenses are strong. The surface is well protected where it counts, and all entrances are protected by layer gun systems."

Captain Thompson pointed to the orbiting red shapes.

"Don't forget the orbital defense station either. They

are small but can fire into space as well as down on the surface. If they rush things, we can use the satellite to rain fire down upon their heads."

Teresa felt a little happier with that thought. Then she recalled the footage she had watched of the assault against Fort Macquarie. The base of operations on Eos had held two full battalions as well as multiple Marine aviation units and large NHA contingents.

They were well prepared as well, a strong garrison with an entire Heavy Assault Group in orbit. They had the best we have to offer, and yet what happened? A scouting party of Biomechs overran the place, and we evacuated at the very last minute.

She then looked to her captains and again at the map.

"Prometheus is different to any other battlefield. We could afford to lose control of an entire planet but not this one. Without Prometheus, the Alliance will be split in two."

Olik looked confused.

"Wait, I thought we were pulling back from the new conquests through the Rift?"

"That's true," added Captain Rivers, "If we pull back, Prometheus will just be a border fortress, and we can pull the plug on the Rift whenever we want."

Yes, and even if that fails, we have the T'Kari weapon for collapsing Rifts.

Teresa wanted to tell them what she knew, that the Alliance had no interest in giving up its Orion territories, and that the feigned withdrawal was all a plan to draw out the Biomechs and destroy the rot from within. But Teresa knew the fragility of secret keeping. If she couldn't keep the secret, how could she expect her captains to?

* * *

Teresa pulled on her jacket and checked herself in the mirror one more time. She'd tried hard, but her face still looked tired. It wasn't just the physical demands of her new role in the Marine Corps. It was the strain of not knowing what was happening with her family. She was just thankful her new posting had full access to encrypted internal communications once again. There were two messages, both containing video communication, and they had finally decoded and were ready to view. Alone in her quarters, and with the lights on low dim, she reached for her secpad and activated the stream. An image of Jack in his Marine Corps uniform appeared on her main computer screen, and she felt immediately at rest.

"Mother," he started.

She took one step back and then dropped to her bunk. The bed was stiff and far from comfortable. Her eyes were glued to her son's face as she listened to his general account of his trip toward Helios. The words interested her much less than his gaunt face. His voice sounded firm, but she could tell something was wrong. He'd lost weight for sure, but his eyes.

What happened to him?

Parts had been redacted, and she found it a little confusing when the feed seemed to jump past sections. The video was almost twelve minutes long, but by the time she'd reached the end, she found herself in tears. Jack had been involved in some of the heaviest fighting on Eos, and the reports from that battle showed massive casualties and losses. She knew Jack had been in the middle of it, and also what the fighting on Helios had done to him. Teresa placed her hand across her mouth as the video ended.

He's suffering with PTSD, and there's nothing I can do about it, not yet.

Teresa closed her eyes and waited for her pulse to slow down before starting the next stream from her other two children, Matius and Ingo. As with Jack, they had taken her name, not least because Spartan still refused to give her any indication as to what his name might have been in the past.

Spartan, he does like to keep things to himself.

The twins began speaking and unlike Jack, they were buoyant and excited. They were junior officers in the Navy, and as far as she was aware, they had managed to avoid getting involved in any combat so far. The first words from Ingo felt like a stabbing knife to her chest.

"We've got our orders. We're going to the front!"

The specific details were blocked even from her, but

she needed nothing more. There was only one front in this war, and it was always facing the Biomechs and their puppets. She had seen the fleet dispositions throughout Alliance space, and over half were either near Helios, or being sent in to support that operation via T'Karan. She made it halfway through before the feed paused on its own and changed to show a priority signal from the Admiral.

"Colonel, I need to see you, right away."

"What is it, Admiral?"

The man looked to his right and then repeated himself.

Teresa noticed a few pale green displays in the background but nothing gave away quite what he wanted to say. Teresa had her suspicions. She just hoped it was related to Prometheus alone. The last thing she wanted right now was more news concerning her family because no matter what the message was, it always seemed to be bad news.

"Understood, I'm on the way."

Teresa had expected to be called to see the Admiral at some point, but not this soon. With him taking over the security of the Biomech, he had been given great authority and responsibility on the base. It took almost eleven minutes for her to reach his office without breaking into a run. The guards motioned her inside, not giving her time to pause outside. As she stepped through the doors, they quietly slid shut behind her.

Strange!

There were many things she had expected to see in this place, but four Jötnar waiting at the back of the room was not one of them. The room was rectangular in shape and with a completely transparent wall that looked down onto the station's central hub. Teresa recalled the design of the facility, and it did little to rest her mind.

"Colonel, thank you for coming here so quickly."

He indicated for her to approach the wide transparent wall that they might look out. She moved toward him and looked down, even though her mind was on the Jötnar. The ground below them was wide and open, with small narrow gauge transports following tracks that moved about the base.

"It's not so different to when Spartan and General Rivers were here."

Admiral Churchill looked in the same direction but waited before speaking.

"I've seen your revised defensive plans for the station. They are interesting to say the least. You think stationing the reserves so close to the entry points is wise?"

Teresa looked back at him and then pointed her forefinger toward those marching back and forth in the base. At first glance, the facility appeared impregnable. There were no walls on Prometheus, as every single room, passageway, and shaft was cut from the rock itself.

"This underground base can be breached in multiple ways. I know; I've done it before. Once you're inside, it is easy to hold ground. The enemy is expert at all manner of assaults, but their greatest strength is the ability to conduct operations long past our ability to fight them. Once they have a foothold on this planet, they will spend hours, days, or years clearing each room until they get what they are looking for. They really are a machine enemy."

The Admiral seemed to understand her assessment but didn't seem convinced.

"Hence your plan?"

"Yes. My strategy is a simple one. We keep them from ever getting enough troops inside to make a difference. So we keep the most experienced units in small mobile reserve and maintain a strong layered presence on the perimeter."

He handed her a secpad with a list of combat units. She examined them, but there was nothing of any real surprise to her. It took nothing more than a cursory look before she turned her attention back to him.

"Yes, I've already assigned them their posts and schedules. My captains are taking their own units to join them at key points under the command of my second, Major Terson. It is a strong garrison. The enemy would need a major assault to even consider breaking into this place."

The Admiral looked at her carefully as if he could understand something more by just looking directly into her face. He finally stopped and motioned for her to sit down. Teresa did so but not before giving the four silent sentries a good look at too. They were not too different to any other Jötnar she had met, but the heavily modified PDS Alpha armor was a surprise to her. She had never expected such a precise and expensive piece of equipment would ever be granted to them. They were usually kept as assault troops and wore armor more appropriate to their task. This made them look more like regular marines.

Apart from being nearly twice the size!

Their faces were hidden behind their blackened raised visors on their armored helm, yet she was sure one of them had turned its head slightly to look at her.

Do I know this one?

"Teresa, I know this is a difficult position for you. I'm sure you understand that the briefing on board the ship wasn't just for our benefit?"

Teresa nodded but said nothing. That was what he wanted to hear.

"Good. Because that machine has given us critical information, information that Anderson wanted me to share with only three other people."

Teresa's first thought wasn't what the information might be, but who the three people were?

"Teresa, I know you've been helping as much as you can, in no small part to help our understanding of the Rift networks, and to find out where Spartan had gone."

She nodded.

"Yes, as part of the agreement for me returning to the Corps, I was promised resources would be put into place to do just that. With APS, well, I'm sure you know what happened. My resources are somewhat depleted."

"Indeed," replied the Admiral before she could continue. "Admiral Anderson and General Rivers have both pushed for considerable time and resources to be put into use to locate your husband. Even so, it would seem you've been liquidating your assets on Epsilon Eridani and other places to fund your own private investigation?"

Teresa looked surprised, but he lifted his hand to stop her speaking. He then placed the back of his hand on his mouth, took a breath, and carried on.

"Teresa, this might be a little hard for you, but we've had information on him for some months now."

He saw the muscles change in her body and decided to continue rather than wait to hear what she might say.

"It was all speculation with a mixture of material taken from out interrogation of Krani. Until he arrived in Sol, all we had to go on was that Biomech forces were mobilizing in Alliance territory, prior to being given a signal."

The two were silent for a short time while Teresa digested what she had just heard.

"Wait, what signal?"

The Admiral changed the imagery on his screen to that of Helios and Comet C34A.

"The comet?" she asked.

Admiral Churchill took in a long, almost pained breath.

"After what happened in the War, our intelligence division has spent significant time in developing technology and procedures for intercepting and bouncing back alien communications. One day, we might even work out how to modify it. When the comet arrived, the first thing to happen was the transmissions. One came right to the T'Karan-Helios Rift where the Biomech Krani tried to respond."

Teresa didn't quite see the connection. She looked at the imagery, moved the image where her right hand was, and brought it back to Sol.

"What does this have to do with Spartan?"

Now Admiral Churchill seemed to brighten up.

"That is exactly the point. The signal arrived at almost the same time as Spartan's escape from the Biomechs. His report says he was imprisoned on their ship where he learned a number of things; all of which match up exactly with our interrogation of Krani."

Teresa rose to her feet.

"Admiral, he is hurting, and he needs my help. What the hell am I even doing here? He needs me."

Admiral Churchill shook his head apologetically and motioned for her to sit down.

"Spartan is important to all of us, believe me. But, and this is a big but; he has a part to play that we are only just beginning to understand, and it concerns both us and the enemy."

He looked at her and tried his best to appear sympathetic.

"We've had broken reports from a number of scouts over the last month concerning his whereabouts. It was only his arrival in Sol that confirmed them though. The last transmissions sent from our agents on Earth confirmed that Spartan has made contact with the enemy, and that they are still in pursuit of him."

He smiled.

"Your husband would appear to have something of a reputation with the Biomechs now. I suspect he has caused them more strife than any single man...or woman. They are interested him in a way I still don't understand."

He changed the image again to an overview of Helios and then moved the model to show a region of space far out on the rim of the sector.

"The Black Rift?" said Teresa through clenched teeth.

"Yes, and according to our information from both Krani and from Spartan's own testimony, it would appear this entire offensive is being conducted to gain secure access to this Rift."

Teresa looked nonplussed.

"So? What does Spartan have to do with that?"

Admiral Churchill leaned back in his chair.

"That's what concerns us. All traffic from the comet and from Krani confirms Spartan is involved in some way, and we don't know what that might be."

The image changed to the same video communication Teresa had received from her husband prior to the signal stream being cut off. Her heart felt as though it might stop when she saw him again, and in obvious discomfort.

"Apart from losing his hand and part of his forearm, we have a list of injuries that can mean only one thing. He has been tortured and presumably interrogated. What has he given up and have they been able to interfere with him in any way?"

Teresa twisted her head just a little, and he could see the anger in her eyes.

"We are not holding this against Spartan, but we have to safeguard the Alliance. We have no way of knowing what happened to him or what his intentions might be."

Teresa was already on her feet and marched the short distance to the display and grabbed it with both hands, ripping it from its mount. In one swift action, she hurled the unit at the wide clear wall that looked down into the base. It crashed into the glass with a crackle of blue sparks and then flashed. Chunks of glass flew out of the unit and dropped out of sight. Admiral Churchill glanced at his four Jötnar, but only one even looked at Teresa, and for a second it looked like he was smiling.

" Colonel!"

Teresa turned her attention to the old man, and even though he'd known her for many years, there was still hesitation in his movement, even a little doubt as to what

119

she might do next.

"That is what worries us, Colonel Morato. We know Spartan's loyalties, but we also know how far he will go when his blood is up."

Teresa 's blood was pumping fast through her veins, but even she could see what the man was trying to tell her. She leaned over the desk and placed her palms out on the warm surface and tried to calm herself down. He'd always been a little hot-headed, but being married to Spartan had taught her new and more interesting ways for her to lose control.

"You think they will try and use his...passion to help them? How?"

It was an interesting choice of words, but Admiral Churchill couldn't disagree.

"Look, we know where he is right now, and when he arrived we lost contact with our Rift station. More than that, we've lost contact with Mars, Earth, and the entire Sol system."

He rose from his chair and walked to the side of his desk and to the cracked and damaged transparent wall. The hardened glass material was strong, but nowhere near as tough as he'd expected. He ran his forefinger and thumb down his nose.

"Spartan is in just the right place right now. Luckily, we have a few agents and Alliance funded operatives still there. Johnson sent out a priority message just before the

Rift closed."

Teresa now looked at him with interest.

"We want the Rift reopened, but not until the taint of the enemy is removed from Sol. If Spartan is being controlled in some way, then the next time that Rift opens, we can expect a Biomech assault. If he's loyal, as you and I both believe, when it opens, I would expect nothing less than total Alliance control and a pissed off Spartan waiting to come through."

Teresa wasn't quite sure she liked the sound of what she was hearing, but she did appreciate the vote of support for Spartan. Admiral Churchill knew her reasonably well, but nothing like Johnson or Anderson did. He looked at her expression and tried to gauge her feelings, but found he really had no idea.

"There's more. Our information suggests there are another seven Biomechs in Alliance space. We've obtained this information from the dig sites, the T'Kari, and even the prisoner himself. It's fragmented, but we know for certain that one is in Sol, and the others are apparently somewhere near here, in hiding and using hidden Rift gateways. The thing is, we know they have been hiding for a long, long time. They will only come out for one of a few reasons, and it has to be damned important to them."

He looked up at the ceiling even though there was nothing of note there.

"The call has been sent to all Biomechs to return to

Helios. We monitored the traffic from the prisoner, and the signal was simple. All Biomechs are to assemble at Helios, ready for the apocalypse."

Teresa wasn't religious even though she had been given the traditional conservative religious upbringing on Carthago. The word 'apocalypse' had spread via many of the small cults throughout the Alliance. Even worse had been the stories and rumors from the new territories at Helios and beyond. These helped spread the very idea of an end to all things, nothing but mass hysteria.

"Why attack Mars? It makes no sense."

The Admiral scratched his forehead and then slid over his secpad.

"This is between you, me, and Director Johnson. Understood?"

Teresa nodded and then looked down, almost excited. She read the first few lines, but it was the imagery that fascinated her the most. The image showed a vast crater with machinery, cables, and elevators moving down deep into the heart of Mars.

"I don't understand."

He pressed the unit, and the image shifted to a lower level where a massed bank of flood lamps lit the base of the shaft.

"This is nearly three kilometers under the surface. We've had Earthsec working down there for over a year. This is all based on information we found on Hyperion.

The data is fragmented, but it did contain hundreds of locations, some of which are in our own territory."

He leaned in close.

"You see; we have information that there's something down there. Last time we found something similar was in the Outer Rim. Our mining teams made it down to the last layer, but as soon as news got back to Terra Nova, the entire facility was vaporized in a nuclear meltdown. Luckily, the site was fully automated, and the monitoring crews were aboard a resupply ship. We can only assume the Biomechs have been looking for these sites as well."

Teresa looked at him a little confused.

"They don't know where these sites are?"

He shook his head.

"Not quite. Director Johnson suspects the list of potential sites is massive. That would explain why so many of these Biomech sightings have been of scouting parties."

Teresa tried to assimilate the information as best as she could but found it far from easy. The Biomechs were hard enough to understand in open warfare, and their clandestine machinations were unlike anything she'd ever encountered.

"Wait a minute. The Biomechs showed up, as well as Spartan, just as you reached these ships at the bottom of the shaft. What did you find and how did they find out?"

The third image stunned her.

"It can't be," she muttered.

"It's true, Teresa. Look at it."

She did, but the sight of a long-buried Ravager class Biomech warship sent a shudder through her body. The vessel was one of the symbols of the struggles they had all faced. Even though the color and markings were different to those they had found before, it was clearly one of the dreaded ships.

"We've located signs of three more already."

But Teresa's attention had already shifted to the symbols running along the faded colors of the ships. They were emblems made up of six pairs of metallic arms that almost looked like the rays coming off a star.

"What is that?"

Now the Admiral smiled.

"That, Colonel, is the mark of the Twelve."

The next ten minutes seemed to merge into one great mess as he showed her as much as he was able of Mars and the large number of tunnels that had been dug. The more she saw, the more it reminded her of what she'd seen on planets like Hyperion and the moon of Hades. Finally, the conversation returned to the defense of Prometheus itself, though Teresa found it hard to take her attention from the distant planet and back to her current predicament.

"Colonel?" he asked.

Teresa shook her head and tried to banish the memory of the Red Planet, at least for now.

"I...uh. Well, these Biomechs? The ones you believe will

be attacking here, where could they be? Under the rock, too?"

He shook his head.

"No, though trust me, we've dug deep to check that. I suspect in the middle of the storm regions, and they will be coming here."

"Why?"

Admiral Churchill grinned at the question.

"For starters, there have been sightings of their ships in this area over the last four days. Their patterns have been recorded, but we've taken no immediate action."

Teresa looked annoyed.

"But why keep it quiet? We could strike now, when it suits us."

"No, Teresa, we have to get them all. The only way is by doing this. We need to give them a real chance of succeeding. I might be old, but I have just as much experience of these machines as you. They are cunning, and they are hard to goad. They like to stay close to their prey though, and with Krani here, they will have to act. Now, if it were me, well, I would stay as close as possible, just far enough into the storms to avoid our sensors."

"Why bring the machine here then?"

"Anderson has T'Karan bottled up tight. The first batch of Liberty ships has boosted the defenses at the AJ Naval Station, and more ships are arriving every day. We've put out enough false intelligence over the last ten days to guarantee the machines will know what we have here, and that our forces here on Prometheus are thin."

Teresa's attention shifted upon seeing more Jötnar marching in a column down in the open space of the base. Many were wearing a localized version of the PDS armor used by the Marine Corps while just a handful the more bulky JAS armor designed for direct assault. It wasn't the numbers that surprised her; it was the way most of the engineers and personnel reacted around them

They are used to them. They've been here a long time.

"Wait, I thought the Jötnar here had been assisting development programs for new weapons and armor. Are you telling me that you've had Jötnar combat units here as well?"

The Admiral wiped his brow and then looked directly at her.

"Teresa, what do you think?"

He pointed down to those in the open central section of the base, so many meters below the surface.

"Prometheus has been a home to them for two decades now. Is it much of a surprise that many of them wanted to join combat units? All of the Jötnar here are trained in combat on Hyperion, as you might expect. They fulfill both an engineering and a military need here."

Teresa sighed and pulled out her secpad to make a note.

"It might have been handy to know that before I revised the defense plans. I have three companies of marines, a platoon of Jötnar, plus twice that number already stationed here."

She nodded to the four Jötnar who still said nothing.

"How many Jötnar do we have?"

Admiral Churchill smiled at this.

"Just under two thousand Jötnar work here, and every single one of them is part of the newly activated Red Watch."

Teresa hadn't even noticed it, but a quick glance at the nearest of the Jötnar showed a Marine Corps patch on his chest with a burning shield emblazoned upon it.

"The Red Watch?"

"Yes, it is the name of the newly assembled 24th Marine Corps Regiment that has been raised here, all under the watchful eye of their new commander. The name is apparently because they watch the border, and they wear maroon colored armor."

Teresa raised an eyebrow at the last part.

"Maroon? Are they insane?"

The Admiral laughed at her question.

"They are Jötnar, don't forget. It's not like they are particularly proficient at hiding. As for this red, well, it is very dark, as you can see."

Teresa looked at the four Jötnar carefully. She'd assumed it was the lighting in the room as their dark PDS Alpha armor looked like it was reflecting a red colored lamp. He was right. It was a dark maroon, more a brownish-red color. She looked back at him and sighed.

"It was General Rivers' idea," he answered, almost apologetically, "After the Jötnar were given full access to the Corps, they were very keen to create their own identity within the Corps itself. The unit was only officially activated in the last three months, and in secret, of course."

He licked his lip before moving to the next part, and it was clearly something he wanted to avoid.

"I can't beat about this anymore, Teresa. Your deployment to the AJ Naval Station was a ruse. It was always our intention to bring you and your people here to provide the backbone for this new battalion. Ever since your injuries on Helios, you've been earmarked for this role."

He expected Teresa to be please, but she seemed angry.

"You dragged me out here on yet another false promise. What will you want next? For me to lead an assault on the Black Rift?"

That question seemed to stun the Admiral more than any other. Teresa even gave the idea some serious consideration before lowering her head and placing her hands at her temples.

"Admiral, I'm sorry. I'd just like some kind of stability. One minute I'm fighting on Helios, then I'm on Terran Nova, then I'm assisting with the 39th instead of rejoining my unit, only for this to happen."

The Admiral nodded in agreement.

"I know, it is a lot to take in. Your efforts in the 17th have not been forgotten. It will take weeks to get you back though, and they have their own problems right now. Your talents and experience in working with the Jötnar are second only to Spartan. Nobody else can pull this off."

He tried to point to his display, but it had gone, along with part of his usual window.

"Look, Prometheus is more than a base to us now. It is a trap to finally give us the chance to put our house in order before tackling the big problem of our time."

"The Biomechs," she said quietly.

"Exactly. We want, no, we need the Biomechs to reveal themselves so we can shut them down, permanently. Once this remaining Biomech is destroyed, we will turn our attention to the Terra-Nova-Sol Rift and whatever Spartan has stirred up. That is why the rest of the fleet, including Dreadnought, have been sent through the Rift to T'Karan, to draw them out."

The mention of the cradle of humanity put just a single thought in her mind.

"Spartan."

She didn't mean to speak out, but she'd been thinking of his whereabouts for so long, she couldn't help herself. The fact he'd just told her that Prometheus was effectually undefended seemed to go unnoticed.

"He's there, as is Khan and a few other Alliance contacts. We know the other Biomech is there. That is why Johnson's agents deactivated the Spacebridge. It is trapped, and there's nobody better to deal with it than…"

"Spartan," she said again, but this time her face had actually brightened.

Anybody else might be worried, but not her. Spartan and Khan were born to destroy Biomechs, and as long as Spartan had a focus; she knew he would do whatever he needed to get the job done. She walked around the room, much to the Admiral's surprise before stopping a few meters away and looking back at him.

"The two of us have given the Alliance, and the Confederacy before it, everything we could. My family has suffered, and now my three children are all on the frontline. You want me to sit here and babysit marines while Spartan plays your little game for you in Sol?"

Admiral Churchill was not used to taking this kind of attitude from a mere Colonel in the Corps. Teresa was different though; she was of the same stock as General Rivers and even Spartan. He considered her request for a few seconds.

"I don't think you quite appreciate the gravity of this situation. You see…"

He wiped his head, and for the first time Teresa spotted the sweat on his forehead.

"Spartan was captured in T'Karan space, and that is in the Orion Nebula."

Teresa didn't look as though she quite understood the

point he was making.

"So how did Spartan and Khan get to Earth?"

Teresa considered the question, but the answer was clear.

"The Rift network. They must have used a different entry point and from there moved to Sol."

Admiral Churchill smiled at her answer.

"Over a thousand light years? If there was a Spacebridge of that length, our scouts would have found it."

Teresa shrugged.

"Well, there must be another Nexus out there somewhere, and it is the link between T'Karan and Sol, and who knows where else. That would give them a backdoor into the Alliance and completely bypass Proxima Centauri."

"Perhaps," answered Admiral Churchill, "Luckily, it seems Spartan disabled the Rift station, at least for now."

Teresa smiled as he spoke.

"Disabled is not destroyed, Admiral."

It didn't take her long to realize what Spartan would be thinking.

"This Rift isn't a weakness for us. It's an asset, and it will give Spartan a backdoor directly to T'Karan. Once he gains access to their network, you know exactly what he will do."

Teresa appeared happy, but the Admiral was anything but.

You fools! Spartan will do anything but what you want him to do.

Even though they were light years apart, Teresa actually relaxed at this news. As far as she was concerned, it was the best news she'd heard for days. Teresa rose to her feet and motioned toward the door.

"Admiral, I think Spartan will resolve things just fine on Sol. If you give him a chance, he might end this war without even having to come within a light-year of Alpha Centauri."

The Admiral was so stunned at her words that he said nothing as she left. Only when the door shut, did his lips finally move. The planning with the other senior commander under the watchful eye of General Rivers had covered many eventualities. He couldn't believe that none of them had come up with that possibility. Alliance scientists had postulated the fact that there could be many more Nexus than those around Helios and the Biomech territories. The archeological digs on the T'Kari moon of Hades and on the planet Hyperion had already confirmed the existence of multiple Rift hubs, but the idea that there might be one that could link T'Karan and Sol was not one he ever remembered seeing.

Either they have another Nexus, or they've been using our own Spacebridges without our knowledge.

That very thought sent a cool chill through his body. He looked for his computer display, but Teresa has smashed it beyond use. He shook his head in annoyance and so pulled out his secpad and checked the secure Interstellar Network chart that listed every Rift from the modest planet, to planet locations through to the massive Prometheus-Orion Rift. He looked at it for a moment, especially the location of defunct Rifts that the scouts had already found.

How did you get there?

It only took a few presses on the secpad, and he was through to Director Johnson.

"Admiral? What's wrong with your secure terminal?"

"Ms Morato is the problem."

Johnson seemed to smile at him via the tiny screen.

"I see. What's the problem?"

"Spartan. Are we any further with identifying the route he took to Sol?"

"Not entirely, but with help from the T'Kari, we have been able to access some of the Rifts in their area of space. One of them might be the one he took."

"Interesting. Do we know where it went?"

Johnson pressed a button, and a series if maps popped up on the Admiral's secpad. He found himself squirming as he tried to read the details. Director Johnson continued while the Admiral examined the map.

"It's not much to go on, but the signature left behind shows a short journey of just a few light years."

"That's it?"

Johnson lifted his lip a little and nodded.

"Yeah, there's no station or even remains there. Whatever they used to create the Rift has gone with them. Wait, I need to check on something."

They exchanged pleasantries, and then he was gone, leaving the Admiral on his own and still looking at the starmap.

I don't like this. We have to send a team to Sol before Spartan kicks up trouble, and fast. God help us if the Biomechs could appear in that godforsaken backwater.

He moved through his list of contacts on his device and selected Admiral Anderson. It took only a few seconds to activate the secure channel through the Rift and out to ANS Beagle, the station that managed the Rift on the other side. It would then take minutes for his signal request to Admiral Anderson to reach the AJ Naval Station deep in the heart of T'Karan, the Alliance's foothold into the Orion Nebula. He started to speak to himself, deciding exactly what he wanted to say, but something completely different interrupted him.

What the hell?

The sound wasn't the secpad. It was the internal security alert.

"Emergency alert, hostile warships have broken the outer perimeter. Defense plan Titan is in effect."

Gods, they're here already!

He moved to the door, and his four escorts stayed close with him as he emerged into the well-protected corridor.

The sirens continued to blare and marines, engineers, and crew rushed to their stations about the base.

"Colonel Morato got here just in time," said one of the Jötnar.

The Admiral looked at the massive warrior and tilted his head to the right.

"Your job is to keep this base secure. This Morato, can she do it, Osk?"

The Jötnar activated the helmet, and it slid open to reveal the slightly narrower face of a female Jötnar.

"It's Commander Osk, Admiral."

The Jötnar looked to her comrades before looking back at him.

"And yes, if anybody can fool these machines, it is Teresa Morato."

CHAPTER SIX

The official colonization of Terra Nova took place over three hundred and fifty years ago. On that day, the few remaining colonies of Terra Nova united under a single banner and declared the colonization of the planet to be complete. In the century before, thousands had perished in the failed colonies that littered the surface. It wasn't until the arrival of the third and final wave that brought with them machines, people, supplies, and terraforming equipment that a viable colony was established. Tens of thousands had lost their lives, but their sacrifice guaranteed that mankind's foothold in Alpha Centauri would be a permanent one. From that day forward, migrants to Terra Nova would truly consider it the New Earth.

A Concise Guide to Interstellar Travel

Teresa had been angry, and no matter how much she tried to calm down, the imagery of Spartan kept coming back to haunt her. She'd made a deal with the Alliance and the Corps to offer her service in exchange for all the support they could muster. Now it appeared they had found him months ago, and instead of helping, they had elected to use him as part of some elaborate plan to bring the enemy out into the open and reveal their remaining Rift network.

Bastards!

But even as she sat there, she knew it made sense, and that was the part that really made her angry. There was little the Alliance could do other than protect its interests and continue to send scout ships and probes through every Rift they encountered or opened. The maps created so far were impressive, but none of them had yet explained how the Biomechs had spirited Spartan away through a Rift in T'Karan, only to appear many months later on Earth. It seemed perfectly obvious to her, but she wasn't the scientist.

There has to be another nexus, like the one in the Orion Nebula. That could mean an entirely new area to explore.

Just thinking about it hurt her head, and to try and relax she'd brought out a series of notes assembled for senior command regarding interrogation of prisoners and the captured Biomech commander. There was also collaborating information from the other races, specifically the T'Kari, and a small amount from the Helions. There were two key areas that interested her the most, and the more she read, the more she wondered if

Alliance Intelligence had far more secrets up its sleeve. Moving several pages away on her system, she brought up a series of reports from the T'Kari. It took a while before she reached one of the old historical summaries. The translation was long and ponderous, so she skipped to the summary at the bottom.

It would appear that the T'Kari civilization of the past consisted of at least four star systems, all of which were within a four light-year radius of T'Karan. Most of the colonies were lost in the war with the Biomechs, but a few lingered on after the Rifts were closed, and the Biomechs were banished back to their own domain. These last few colonies lost contact with each other over time, and all efforts to reach them through the old Rifts ended in disaster. The T'Kari sent their last ships to their one remaining colony where they were ambushed and destroyed. After that, the T'Kari went into hiding and left just their scouts to watch for signs of the enemy. This continued for generations until the coming of the Biomech commander and his Guardian ship entered T'Karan and established a base on Hades.

Teresa skipped past the next section as it dealt with events she was quite familiar with. The machines attempted to open up a massive Rift to Hyperion, and the bomb that destroyed the Biomech commander and its base on Hades. Instead, she brought up a report on the war with the Biomechs, a poorly translated text that described how the original races had turned on one of their own, and how this augmented race of Biomechanical creatures had declared a war of eternal vengeance on the rest.

The part that truly interested her, however, was the mention of a dead race, known as simply as The Twelve. Apparently, they were one of the nine races involved in the massive war that ended in the banishment of the Biomechs. From memory, she couldn't quite remember them all and was forced to load up a detailed list summarizing the people met so far in the last decade.

So, we have the Biomechs, obviously. Then come the Helion League, the T'Kari Empire, the Khreenk Federation, and the scattered powers of the Klithi, Byotai, and Anicinàbe.

She moved to the next page and found the two lost empires.

So, The Twelve and the Trusska. I wonder if one of these empires had links from the Orion Nebula and back to Sol?

It was a lot to take in, especially as there was so little known about the last two other than the Trusska had killed themselves in a massive ritualistic suicide pact before sending an automated weapon to destroy access to all their Rifts. The Twelve apparently were named for their twelve stars that were separated by a vast gulf of space. Each star contained a number of inhabited worlds. One of these worlds was nicknamed the highway to the Gods in their own tongue, and another given the name Taxxu. What really caught her attention was that this particular race was famed for its use of long-range exploration. Apparently, they had been the first to come across the T'Kari and the wandering Biomechs way back in the distant past.

Interesting. So the Twelve and the Biomechs were more than neighbors. They lived together.

As Teresa read further, she found that the Twelve had intermixed with the Biomechs over the centuries, based on a mutual desire to see technology improve their lives. The Biomechs had been granted land on Taxxu and made it their home for hundreds of years. The Twelve were the masters of long-distance space travel, and the Biomechs supreme at the melding of machine and flesh. It sounded too perfect until she reached the part about the war. The Twelve had suffered horrendous losses at the start of the war, before viral bombing wiped them out as a species, and their sterilized worlds overrun by the machines of the Biomechs. She almost ignored the last few lines before coming across a section that said a number of moons had fought against Taxxu and its Biomechs before they too were annihilated. According to myth, the last of their kind, a mixture of races, including Biomechs, escaped through their Rifts and were never seen again.

Biomechs fighting Biomechs? Could these refugees have reached Sol in the past?

The more she thought about it, the more Teresa realized it was a tenuous link at best; although it was interesting enough for her to submit an information request for the stellar organization of the old Empire of the Twelve. It had never occurred to her that the Biomech territory encompassed much of what had been known as The

Twelve.

You live and learn.

Teresa walked to the water dispenser and filled her glass with the cool liquid and reflected on her new position. This new post was one she had never expected to be granted, but after reviewing the plans for the defense of the base, she was almost pleased they had chosen her. As so many had tried before, it was almost impossible to contain a Biomech assault once it made headway. The latest reports from Helios confirmed her reasoning, and against complaints from many of the other officers, the Admiral had accepted her proposal. Now the entire plan was based around her idea of a very aggressive defense, with only a modest reserve centered in the middle of the base. She had only just sat down in her room for a moment's respite when the sound started. Her first thought was that it was an attack, but when she looked over at her secpad in its charging stand, she could see it was an urgent alert. Teresa cleared her throat and tapped the device. An image of the Admiral Appeared.

"Colonel. A number of unregistered transports have just arrived. I suspect this is the first of many."

Teresa was confused for a few seconds.

"Transports, Sir?"

The Admiral looked annoyed, as if Teresa's brain had slowed down or she'd lost her wits.

"Yes, unregistered transports of a very old configuration.

Looks like from about twenty years ago to me."

The mention of them being old sent a surge of adrenalin through her body. The date matched the Great Uprising, and that could mean one of very few options.

"You think this is the beginning of an attack?"

The Admiral nodded in agreement.

"I've run through your plan with the commander of the Red Watch. She will be with you shortly, along with the status reports for her units."

He rubbed his chin and then looked hard at the camera.

"Teresa. Use her and any other assets we have to keep Prometheus safe. If Johnson is right, this is the first stage in their operation to reclaim the Biomech."

"They won't make it, Admiral."

He didn't smile, but she did recognize a look of determination on his face.

"Teresa. The modified cargo ship, it contains more than just the Biomech. It is also home to a miniaturized atomic warhead, more than enough to vaporize the machine, ship, and entire hangar space. If we fail, just make sure you're somewhere else."

"Understood, Admiral."

"Good. I will be sending out the general alert in ten minutes. That should be more than enough time for you and your commander to get acquainted. Good luck, Colonel."

The image cut and was almost immediately replaced

by a banging sound at the door. Teresa twisted about, grabbed her cap, and straightened herself.

"It's unlocked," she called out.

The door slid open without a sound and in walked the shape of a maroon armored Jötnar. She recognized the gait and overall size as being one of the four that had been in the Admiral's quarters.

"Colonel Morato," said a familiar voice.

The warrior's visor lifted up and exposed a female Jötnar's face.

"Osk?" replied a startled Teresa.

The only response was a wide grin. Teresa stumbled toward the Jötnar who grasped her arm firmly. The strength in Osk was substantial, but Teresa bit her lip and ignored the pain until she released her.

"What are you doing here?"

"Secrets within secrets, my friend."

Teresa indicated for her to sit, but Osk shook her head.

"I cannot, I am sorry. News has just arrived that several unidentified ships have arrived."

"I know. I just spoke with the Admiral."

Teresa looked a little confused.

"Why did you not introduce yourself to me earlier?"

Osk sighed.

"Yes, it was the Admiral's idea. He wanted to meet you without distraction and to get your ideas on the defense of Prometheus. The last commander of the station fell ill and was taken back to Terra Nova. He is in charge now, but overall command of the defenses has been handed to me. I would value your assistance in any way you can."

Teresa lifted her secpad from its unit and passed it to Osk.

"I thought I was in charge here?" she asked in surprise.

Osk pointed to Teresa's secpad.

"That's the official line. This operation is complex, and your role is to be, well, more flexible than defending this base."

Teresa lifted the unit and examined the first page before lowering it.

"So, I am in charge but on standby, waiting for the word from the Admiral?"

Osk nodded politely.

"Churchill, Johnson, and Anderson apparently came up with this one."

Teresa raised an eyebrow to that and then shook her head.

"Very well. It doesn't really surprise me. Let's look at these defenses then."

She would much rather have found out what was going on but was equally aware that events were already in motion, events that she had played no part in. Just as at every time since she'd first joined the Corps, Teresa Morato was only another cog in the massive machine. She resigned herself to the task she'd been allocated, and only then did she realize she'd missed the bottom of the page from the Admiral. Teresa lifted the unit once more and looked at the wording. It did indeed confirm her role as commander of Prometheus' defenses, but it also mentioned a code. One she recalled from her days back in the last war.

Code Hypos Alpha. That was the code for Alpha Teams to perform an immediate extraction from a combat zone.

It put a smile on her face.

"So, the Admiral is planning on sending me somewhere. I wonder where?"

She looked back to Osk, but it was clear that even she wasn't privy to the entire plan.

Secrets within secrets, indeed.

"Right, you've gone over my layered defense already. What do you think?"

Osk didn't even need to look.

"I think it is simple and leaves command to the junior officers. They are ready to do their duty. I made just one change. I hope you do not mind?"

Teresa lowered her head a little as she looked at Osk.

"Oh?"

"The Alpha arm. It is the oldest of the eight arms and has been heavily expanded and extended to make way for larger Alliance ships to land. It is twice the size of the others and has multiple access points. I have kept a single landed frigate there and stationed a company of marines on board."

"Interesting...and to what end?"

Osk laughed in reply.

"An old trick I learned on Hyperion. When you are unsure what is about to happen, you dig in and wait with every weapon available. The frigate is a heavily armed and armored bastion, and it is positioned directly in the middle of the Alpha arm and in a cavern the size of a Battlecruiser."

"I see. Well, that makes sense to me. I had your forward position already set up to use that location. That is acceptable?"

Osk bowed politely.

"Indeed. From the defenses we have been working on, my marines will stop anything getting inside."

Osk moved to the doorway.

"I must ask your leave, Colonel. Time is against us."

Teresa pulled on the front of her tunic and straightened herself.

"Of course, Commander. Good hunting."

Osk saluted and started but hesitated and looked back to Teresa.

"I heard what happened to Spartan. He is in Sol, is he not?"

Teresa found it hard to breathe and found she could do no more than nod.

"My people have no greater friend than your family, Teresa. When we are done here, we will be duty bound to offer our help."

She paused to emphasize the next part.

"In any way my people can."

With that, she exited her quarters as quickly and as silently as she had arrived, leaving Teresa in her civilian uniform and completely alone. Teresa looked about her quarters and then placed her head in her hands.

What did she mean? Is Osk offering me the help of her Jötnar to find Spartan?

* * *

Dauntless wasn't just an old ship. She was technically the oldest functioning vessel anywhere in the Alliance. Dating back to fifty years before the colonization of Terra Nova, the ship was a throwback to the time when ships were designed for journeys of up to a year through Sol. Back then, she had been a flagship for the United Nations Fleet. That small flotilla of ships had been funded by scores of nations on Earth to protect their fledgling operations on the Moon, Mars, and beyond. Inside the vessel, just a short distance from her aged plasma powerplant was a small reliquary, the room not being much larger than crewmen's quarters.

"Interesting," Spartan said as he examined the brass plaque fitted to the wall. It was heavily corroded, and the corner had been broken off sometime ago. It was the remaining wording that intrigued him the most.

"What about it?" asked Khan, barely concealing his boredom.

"Well, for starters look, the ship is using the old Earth system of dating."

Khan scratched his head in confusion.

"I don't get it. What are the A.D. bits for then?"

Spartan shook his head and sighed before pointing at the numbers.

"These are apparently the number of years since the birth of Jesus of Nazareth."

Khan straightened himself and immediately struck his head on the metal ceiling. Something clattered, and a metal box dislodged and dropped to the ground, only to crack and shatter on the floor. Spartan bent down and opened up the damaged unit. A brass object fell out onto the floor.

"Now that is more interesting," said Khan.

The plaque and the date of the ship faded from memory as Spartan lifted the item and held it in front of them both.

"What is it?" asked Khan.

Spartan examined it carefully and turned it about in front of him. It was made from metal and glass and felt rather heavy. The brass and iron framing was pitted and fitted along a partially curved rail. On one side were a number of thin lenses or mirrors, and on the other what appeared to be a small telescope. Spartan fiddled with it until something snapped off and dropped to the ground. He then handed the device to Khan and reached down to the broken piece.

"This is a museum ship. It must be related to that."

Khan spent even less time than Spartan looking at the device and handed it back. Spartan placed it inside a velvet-lined case sitting on the floor at the side of the room.

"For such a famous ship, I thought there would be more here."

Spartan agreed with him and walked about the room, examining trinkets and small artifacts as he moved about. One cabinet was filled with nearly a dozen small models, each one the size of a man's hand. Spartan opened the door at the bottom and took out one. Khan watched him as he placed the object in his hand.

"Fascinating," said Spartan.

Khan walked over and looked at the object. It was rectangular in shape but with a narrow, slightly lifted front. The rear was raised, and three tall poles jutted out from the top. Thin wires ran down to join with the rest of the structure. It was only then that Spartan spotted the name inscribed on its side.

"HMS Dauntless, 1804," he said quietly.

Khan was intrigued and opened another door and pulled out a similar model. It was painted gray, and much of it had chipped off to expose the metal underneath. This one was much sleeker and lacked the wires and details of the other. There was a small, slightly rounded turret, with what looked like a gun pushing out of it.

"Dauntless, 2010," he said to himself but loud enough that Spartan could hear him.

"I see. These are old Earth warships with the same name. That one is from 2010, and the other one is nearly two hundred years older. This is from a time when warships traveled across water and fought each other."

"Have you ever seen one?" Khan asked.

Spartan looked for somewhere to sit, but there was nothing other than old relics and boxes. He'd already caused enough damage so decided to stay upright instead.

"What, a ship?"

Khan nodded.

"Well, there was a replica of a wooden ship on Terra Nova. I've not seen it, but there are video streams of the thing. It is very similar to that model, the one with the wires."

Satisfied that they had now explored this small part of the ship, Spartan had Khan moved back into the main passageway. They had examined the entirety of Dauntless almost four times now. If either of them had an interest in old ships, they hid it well during the long walks. Even the ship's Captain, a curt, slightly angry looking man called Thomas Cobb, had grown bored of their investigations. He was a sprightly old man with a thin layer of white hair, as well as a neatly trimmed beard and mustache. Spartan had found it best to avoid him when he could.

"Well, what do you think of him then?" Khan asked.

As Spartan moved through the ship, he had been looking at more than just the shape, design, and condition. He'd been using the long days of travel to loosen up his limbs and to assess the rest of those on board. Captain Cobb was something of a mystery to him. He was old enough for senior command, yet had been put in charge of an ancient museum craft. They had just left the Captain to deal with a routine thruster problem with his crew and were busy making their way to the appropriately named mission bay.

"Cobb?"

Spartan tried not to laugh when his friend knocked his head on the low level bulkheads for what must have been the tenth time that day.

Khan nodded.

"Well, for a man in his mid sixties, he is in surprisingly good shape."

It was true; the man had looked after himself, either through personal effort or substantial amounts of money. He was average height, but his arms and torso betrayed a level of fitness that would have impressed even a Marine Corps physical training instructor.

"Well, he's a tight ass for a start. I don't think he was particularly impressed with your little speech about the merits of Jötnar infantry."

Khan smiled, and this time managed to avoid cracking his head on a bulkhead. He ducked down and then pushed on down the narrow passageway. The metallic wall on the left dripped with condensation, and there were marks of corrosion in places, none of which inspired much confidence in the two of them.

"Maybe he could spend some of that energy getting this ship ready for combat. This thing is a disgrace."

They finally reached a wide-open access point that led into the mission bay. This section was more frequently used, and at least part of it had been cleaned up for the mission. Even so, it looked far from what either of them was used to. They both went inside and stopped to see what progress, if any, was being made by the hastily assembled troops.

"Spartan," Captain Cobb called out from across the bay.

Khan bowed his head a little in the direction of the man.

"Looks like the Captain wants to play…again."

Spartan did his best to hide his amusement and walked over to him, carefully avoiding the groups of men who were busy going through their drills. Unlike the Marine Corps, this unit was entirely male, and not one of them had shown even the slightest bit of interest in Spartan or Khan. Once past them, he moved to the space between two of the assault shuttles where a table had been put up and a number of weapons and pieces of equipment laid out. Spartan stopped in front and looked down at the gear.

"Interesting selection."

The Captain waited behind the table and looked singularly unimpressed with his comments.

"Interesting? These weapons are the best equipment Earthsec has to offer."

Khan moved alongside Spartan and scooped up one of the rifles. It looked like any other small arm, but with the magazine inserted behind the trigger and under the stock. It kept the weapon short, but it looked strange to him. He turned to Spartan and held it out to him.

"Why?"

Spartan coughed and did his best to hide the smile on his face.

"It's, uh, a Bullpup, I believe?"

Captain Cobb nodded.

"That's right. Short, compact and ideally suited for close ranged firefights."

Khan wasn't particularly inspired by its diminutive size, placed it back down, and picked up one of the magazines. He was amazed upon seeing the column of projectiles fitted inside, all of them pushed up by a kind of spring, presumably at the base of the magazine.

"What is this?"

Spartan took it and withdrew one of the bullets from the magazine. The shape was odd, nothing more than a rectangular block that felt like a kind of resin or wax in his hand.

"Uh, I have no idea, old friend."

"This, Gentlemen, is one of Earth's most advanced exports, the TEK-40 tactical weapon. The small size hides an electronic firing system with state-of-the-art 6mm caseless ammunition and a rate of fire in excess of fourteen hundred rounds a minute."

Khan lifted just one eyebrow at the figures, but Spartan said nothing.

"The TEK-40 has been exported to the security forces on Mars, Lunar, and a dozen stations throughout Sol."

Spartan lifted the weapon to his shoulder and aimed it at the wall of the mission bay. He intentionally kept the magazine well away from the weapon, and as soon as he spotted an operative moving into his line of sight, he lowered the gun and examined it even more carefully.

"It looks well made, Captain Cobb. I'm not sure it will be enough to deal with the enemy though."

The commander of the Earthsec operatives looked unimpressed at his words.

"Spartan, your account of these machines and their capabilities has been examined in detail, and we are confident our training and equipment will be more than adequate to deal with them."

Khan lifted the weapon once more and then cast it down on the table.

"No, this will not work. Small caliber, conventional weaponry is not the solution."

Spartan noticed a vein on the Captain's neck started to pulse.

Good work, Khan.

"Enough!" grumbled the man. "We will be at Mars in less than forty-eight hours. I suggest you check your own equipment and review the layout for the base."

Spartan looked to Khan and again at the Captain.

"What? You want us to leave? We only just got here."

The room fell silent, and Spartan glanced quickly into the centre of the mission bay. All of the soldiers had stopped whatever they were doing and had turned their attention to the noisy disagreement.

Here it comes.

Spartan knew only too well that the Captain would now have to do something or risk looking impotent in front of his men.

"I don't care what you two did in a previous life. Out here you're just a pair of old men with a knack for getting into trouble. My boys are more than capable of doing this job."

Khan began to move, but Spartan placed his hand on his friend's arm.

"No, not today," he said in a whisper.

The Captain looked back to his men.

"Let's run over the landing and dispersal drill again. On

your markers!"

As the men ran about to the pre-arranged positions, the Captain turned his head sharply toward them.

"I need your experience on the operation, but I don't need you. That's why both of you will be staying in orbit during this mission."

Spartan looked at him and grinned, much to the man's annoyance.

"That's no problem, Captain. When your boys get whipped, just remember to give us a call."

* * *

The barrack structure on Prometheus was one of a dozen similar locations spread throughout the base. Multiple rooms were attached to the central area, with sleeping quarters and weapons lockers fitted at regular intervals. In the center of the main room was a line of PDS Alpha armor suits, each one fitted around a metal frame for quick access. Only a handful remained in the barracks as Teresa moved out through the door and into the wide passageway.

"Watch your feet!" shouted a worker from his position on top of a tracked vehicle.

Teresa stepped to the side as the yellow vehicle trundled past her. It was a similar size to the military Bulldog vehicles but was fitted with hardened rubber tracks and a digger blade to the front. Red lights on the front and back flashed as it moved quickly and then twisted about, making its way along one of the many long passageways. Behind it ran a group of six Jötnar, all of them in their dark red armor. They carried massive rifles the size of the gun fitted to an armored personnel carrier. Teresa checked the status indicators inside her PDS armor and then activated the communication network to the rest of the Alliance forces. The digital network expanded out to nearby combat units and permeated throughout the entire base in less than fifteen seconds.

Good, we're ready.

She passed small squads of marines as they grabbed their gear and then headed for their pre-selected zones, all without any intervention by her. That was the simplicity and what she hoped could be the strength of the defense, its ability to operate fluidly and independently of central command. One thing Teresa had learned over the years was that a rigid chain of command led to inaction, especially in the heat of combat. For this fight, the junior officers would command the battle, not her. Teresa reached the wide-open central plaza at the heart of the underground facility at the same time as Olik. Marines and crew ran to and fro, but she was pleased to see they all moved with a purpose. There was no sense of panic, just of urgency and professionalism. Two squads of marines waited in two rows; all standing to attention and with their carbines at their shoulders.

So it begins.

Captain Rivers appeared from one of the massive doorways to the right that led down into one of the many tendrils extending out to hangars and barrack buildings. Teresa had often likened the place to something reminiscent of an octopus.

"Colonel," he called out as he moved at a fast jog. A single fireteam of marines ran with him, and they and stopped when making it as far as Olik.

"All units are in position, Captain. It's just our reserve that remains here."

Teresa already had her secpad out and was busy examining the spider shaped layout of the base. There were eight long legs that extended out in a star shape and ran deep into the rock of Prometheus. All of them were equipped with multiple entry points and hangar doors leading to the surface.

"They are getting close."

She looked to her officers and stopped upon seeing the Jötnar.

"Olik, your people, are they ready?"

In the distance, she could see the shapes of an entire platoon of heavily armed and armored Jötnar coming toward them. Olik looked in their direction and then to her.

"We are more than ready. We are itching for some

action. I have my platoon here at the center and another squad positioned two hundred meters back from each entrance."

"Good."

The Jötnar wore the same armor as the Red Watch on the rest of the planet, much to Teresa's amusement. It allowed them a full degree of movement, yet still offered their large size a fully protected and sealed environment with modest ballistic protection.

"Very pretty," she said with a smile.

Olik looked at his comrades and then to her.

"We'd rather use our own armor from Hyperion, but this equipment is smaller and better suited for combat in a cramped station. Plus, we have our new guns."

Teresa had wondered what exactly the Jötnar were carrying. Unlike the normal equipment, they all held large firearms, each around the size of a marine and much too big to be carried by anybody other than a Jötnar warrior. The body was short and extended into a ring of five snug barrels. A pair of thick ammunition feeds ran from the gun and around the flanks of each of them to a large backpack unit built into the rear of their armor.

"Okay, Olik, what the hell are those things?"

Olik feigned insult.

"What, these things?" he asked, holding up his weapon.

Teresa grinned.

"Well, the reports from Helios confirmed the use of

these new guns for use in the Jötnar units and heavy marine battalions. Gun himself recommended them in his after action report."

Of course he did.

Teresa was hardly surprised. As she looked at the weapon, she noted the profile matched the primary weapon mount fitted on some of the Bulldog vehicles. From memory, it was an L56 Mark III weapon, one of the newest pieces of equipment being fitted to frontline vehicles. Teresa looked away but then spotted two of the Jötnar were carrying an even more ridiculous looking weapon. This time it was a single barreled device, but much longer and fitted with four pairs of thick power cables that attached somewhere on the back of the armor.

"And that?"

Now Olik did look a little sheepish.

"We're testing these; they're the latest model 60mm railgun from the Bulldogs."

One of the other Jötnar pointed the weapon up in the air.

"Perfect for materiel destruction!""

He was evidently very pleased with his new toy, and Teresa found it almost impossible for her to disguise her amusement, so she looked around at the vast open passageways that were big enough to fly a Mauler through. Cramped was hardly the word she would have used to describe it.

"They're here!" called out a man in a gray pair of overalls. He was off to the right.

Teresa glanced at him and then to her motley group of warriors.

"You know the plan, people. We're the reserve, now let's get to that machine!"

She'd only made it a few meters when Olik blocked her path.

"Excuse me, Sir, but shouldn't we be putting you in a secure location?"

Teresa shook her head and nodded in the direction of their objective.

"No, Olik. You know the Moratos. We're not the kind of people who stay at the rear and direct the battle. The Commander of the battalion will conduct the perimeter defense. You and I will ensure that if any stragglers make it through, they will be stopped."

She pointed off in into the distance.

"This central hub is the key to the station. None can make it through to the ship. Understood?"

An approving chorus of acknowledgements met Teresa.

"Good, then let's do this. I want to see a win for a change!"

CHAPTER SEVEN

The establishment of the Red Watch, the aptly named Heavy Marine Corps Battalion, was the first official Alliance unit to emphasize the strengths and benefits of the Jötnar in combat units. This elite unit combined not only the brute strength and aggression of the Jötnar, but also combined them with the best modern armor and weaponry in the Corps. By modifying existing vehicle mounted weapons, a whole new arsenal of close and long-ranged weapons would be used to equip this new force. In the Great Uprising, the Marine Corps had relied upon men and women with small arms to win wars. Now the Corps would feature the same as well as Vanguards and Jötnar in almost equal numbers.

Equipment of the Alliance Marine Corps

The central hub was as large as a city plaza and based around a series of colonnade structures that were primarily there to function as ceiling supports. The middle was a sunken hexagonal area that could easily have been a pool. Instead, its perimeter had been enhanced with low walls and precut positions for the heavy weapons that were now fitted throughout. When she'd been sitting there earlier, her mind had been elsewhere, but now she knew the exact configuration based on the blueprints shown to her by the Admiral and Commander Osk. The defenses were impressive, made more so but her insistence that as many heavy weapons were installed as could be found.

"No, I will stay with you and the main reserve in this central plaza. This is the key battleground, and the Biomechs will know this. Don't forget, it was through their planning that Prometheus was mined and developed to start with."

He bowed his head slightly, the classic sign of respect amongst the Jötnar.

"Yes, Colonel."

His words reminded her of Gun, and she felt a pang of loss that her old friend wasn't going to be around for this battle.

"We have at least an hour before we can expect any kind of effective ground assault. We will use that time to reinforce our defenses further."

She looked to Captain Rivers.

"Stay here and get at least twice as many heavy weapons in position."

He looked surprised at her request.

"Sir? We already have a heavy weapon for every ten fighters."

"Exactly," Teresa answered.

The Captain said nothing for a moment, and Teresa appeared to become agitated.

"I've seen the weapon inventory here. Prometheus isn't just being used as a shipyard, is it? Even ten years ago it was a factory world for the Alliance. There are crates of weapons in the lower docks."

"But, Colonel, those are all designated for Alliance shipments to the…"

"Really?"

The Captain saluted quickly and sharply.

"Yes, Colonel. It will be done."

The last thing Teresa was concerned with right now was the potential problem she might be causing for Alliance logistics. As far as she was concerned, if Prometheus wasn't held, then the weapons would either be destroyed, or more likely used by the enemy against them.

"Now, the rest of you come with me. I want to see how the defenses at the Biomech hangar are coming on."

Olik recognized the importance of keeping his commander somewhere safe, but the idea of his Colonel staying alongside him and his fighters seemed to make him happy. Even better though was the tour of more of the layered defenses they had rushed into service. The only part that didn't seem to impress him was the fact they would be so far from the frontline.

"Everything is ready then, follow me."

With that, she marched away, and the odd assortment of Jötnar and marines moved with her. It was only a few minutes for them to reach the hangar, and she was pleased to see that a squad had already heaped up two layers of masonry around the large doors to shelter the marines protecting it. Portable defense units had been installed to bolster its strength, and there were four tripod-mounted weapons guarding the open approach.

Not bad, she thought.

She returned the salute of the men and women as they continued their preparations and then passed through the large doorway and into the massive open space. There before her was the ship that the Admiral had arrived on board, and inside it waited the precious cargo the enemy had apparently put so much faith in.

"Where is the Admiral?" asked Captain Rivers.

Teresa didn't stop and continued away from the doorway and toward the circular defensive line that had been built in the last three hours. The shape was basic and included six small bastions, each large enough to accommodate a dozen marines and a few heavy weapons. A wall nearly a meter high joined them together and created a barrier that ran around three quarters of the ship. Over half of the defense line had been erected using the large shipping containers, each one large enough to house an entire

Bulldog vehicle. The unprotected front of the ship pointed directly toward the massive layered blast doors that led out into a wide shaft. That in turn moved up to the surface.

"Are her weapons active?"

A crewman leaned over from the side of the ship and shouted back down.

"Commander Osk had us network the forward gun systems into the defense grid. If anything gets the outer door open, it will have to deal with the entire forward arsenal on this ship."

He twisted about and pointed to the multiple turrets and gunports. In space they would be modest at best, but in the confines of a hangar deep inside an industrial world, they would prove undoubtedly powerful.

"Excellent work, people. I think we might have a chance here."

It was almost as though the universe wanted to punish Teresa the minute she started to calm down. The communication system inside her armor activated, and an image of the Admiral popped up on one side.

"Unidentified vessels have emerged from the storm regions. Prepare yourselves for what is about to come."

"We're ready," she said, looking back at the well-arranged defenses. There was an odd look to her face though, and it was just as well the partially mirrored visor on her helmet blocked her facial expressions to those a short distance away.

"Because when we win this thing, and Prometheus is secured, I'm going to be taking Osk, a battalion of Jötnar, and any of my marines that will follow me to Sol. And if anybody tries to get in my way…"

She clenched her fists inside the armored suit.

"…there will be hell to pay."

* * *

The operations room on board the Dauntless was less than inspiring and reminded Spartan of a throwback to military commands centuries earlier. If he'd given it any real thought, he might have remembered that the ship was much older than that. There must have been a water leak somewhere because damp vapor had managed to affix itself onto so many of the internal surfaces. Spartan could smell the damp in the air, and it reminded him of so many places, where he'd taken shelter in warzones, places like Prime and Hyperion.

Hyperion, he thought happily.

It was an odd thought, and there were probably very few people that would see a place like that violent and dangerous jungle world as anything but a deathtrap. He had more than just wartime memories of it though. Spartan and Teresa had spent many times on that world alongside their friends, including Gun and Khan. The great hunts were unlike anything else in the Alliance and had a knack for bringing people together.

Or getting them mutilated and killed!

He looked back at the small space being used as the operations room and sniffed the air once more. Due to the need for artificial gravity, it had been attached to the mission module. This meant a reduced size, but at least they weren't drifting about the ship.

"How much longer?" Khan asked.

Unlike Spartan, who now wore a pair of military surplus camouflaged pants and an Earthsec black jacket, Khan was dressed in something rather less inspiring. Incredibly, the workers on Earth had managed to supply him with absurdly large black boots they had cut open, extended, and then reinforced with metal plating on the sides. The toes were encased in steel, and although it looked primitive, he felt quite proud of them. More hastily modified clothing that was then covered up by separate thin sections made from riot armor and strapped into place, protected his lower body. Spartan saw him examining the protection around his knees and laughed.

"What?" Khan complained.

"Why are you wearing all of that? I doubt the armor would stop a crossbow bolt."

Khan shrugged.

"Probably true."

He then gave Spartan one of his infamous lopsided grins.

"But it looks nasty, and that works for me."

Khan's arms were bare, but his chest was wrapped in what could only be described as a dark gray vest and padded armor plates tied directly to his torso. It was a mess, and most of it he'd had to bring with him to put on once aboard the ship. Spartan recalled the looks from the other men upon seeing Khan dressed in his improvised garb. Only one had been foolish enough to comment.

What was his name? Spartan thought. *Jenson, I think. Well, he won't make that mistake again!*

The gear Khan had chosen to use actually reminded Spartan of the kinds of equipment chosen by the Jötnar on Hyperion for their annual Biomech hunts. Of course, those were a mixture of ritual and sport, and it was expected that the armor would protect them just a little. After all, what was the point of a blood sport if the other side had no chance of winning? Gun had often complained to him that he expected the animals to have at least as good a chance of winning as his own people. If not, how was it a sport?

He had a point, more a ritual killing, in my opinion.

Spartan shook his head and began to wonder why his mind had shifted from the operation to what Gun thought about hunting on Hyperion. He looked down at his new left arm. It was proving useful, if a little clumsy. More importantly, he was now complete, even if his body ached from the numerous fractures and bone breaks he'd sustained in captivity.

Get a grip and focus!

The seating was designed for human crews of centuries past, and Khan had taken to sitting on a pair of ammunition crates he'd unceremoniously dragged into the room. If any of the senior officers had remained there may have been a complaint, but with just Lieutenant Jenkins staying behind, there was nobody to counter order the two. The man leaned in closer and tapped the icons on the touch screen. Spartan shook his head at the speed and antiquity of the technology on offer.

"Three more minutes. They will come down here, right on the flank of the shuttle landing station."

Spartan felt something and turned his head about to look around. The ship was unlike anything he had served on before. It wasn't the age of the vessel either. It was the way the entire thing had been run. Normally, the ship would be crewed by a captain of some type with a crew of experienced people. The combat team or assault party was almost always a separate element with its own commanders. Earthsec did things very differently, and although there was a small number of crew on board, so far he hadn't seen any kind of commander outside of Captain Cobb, who was in charge of the ground element.

"Hey, who is in charge of this ship, anyway?" he asked, his curiosity getting the better of him.

Lieutenant Jenkins smiled.

"I wondered when you would get to that."

He indicated with his thumb to the rest of the ship.

"The crew is nothing more than technicians. They have their individual stations and report to the command system on the ship. Course changes, corrections, and mission planning are all done on Earth."

"Okay, but who sets the course or docks the ship? Surely you don't leave time-critical tasks like that to your bureaucrats back on Earth?"

Khan looked around, equally confused.

"Yeah, if something goes wrong, who makes a decision?"

Lieutenant Jenkins shook his head as if he'd just heard a private joke.

"No, it doesn't work like that out here. You see; Earthsec is very rigid. All official transport is controlled from back on Earth. There is no captain on this ship because the computers on Dauntless are commanded directly from people on the ground."

"I knew it," Khan muttered, "Didn't I tell you?"

Spartan was forced to lower his head and acknowledge his friend had been right.

"Yeah, okay."

They moved their attention back to the large computer system and watched as Lieutenant Jenkins moved the flat, two-dimensional schematic along to show more of the site. Unlike the richly detailed information Spartan would have expected on an Alliance system, this one was very basic, with the plans already looking only partially up-to-date. As the imagery moved, it stuttered and jerked about while the computer system loaded the data. It moved a few centimeters and then vanished before reappearing with a number of off visual artifacts. Spartan shook his head in amusement as the system attempted to fix and reposition the missing data.

"Man, how old is this tech?" Khan grumbled.

Lieutenant Jenkins lifted his hand in mock apology and continued moving the imagery until it showed the landing area, as well the sections of the refinery complex.

"There, you can see where the damage occurred during the initial attack."

Spartan looked at the imagery and then to Khan who looked equally annoyed.

"This plan sucks. You know that, right?"

Spartan nodded to Khan.

"You've got no argument from me, old friend."

He then pointed at the screen.

"John, you saw our reports, and you know what landings under fire are like. Do you think two shuttles and fifty private security guys are going to be able to pull this off?"

A flash on one of the smaller screens showed the first of the shuttles had come down low and was near the taller structures on the surface. Light glinted from the metal and flickered white on the screen.

"If the Biomechs have secured the refinery, then they will also have established a strong perimeter. They aren't stupid, and they are tough to fight when they're dug in."

"That's why we suggested the discreet approach," Khan said, with a wide grin on his face.

The two of them were hardly known for their subtlety in combat operations, but even Khan could appreciate the benefits of a more considered approach to what could prove a deadly operation. Lieutenant Jenkins sighed and moved along the screen to watch the view from the second shuttle.

"You remember the landing on the Titan Naval Station, don't you?" asked Spartan.

It was a painful memory for the two of them, as it had been their baptism of fire. After months of training and work, the unit had been thrown into a full-scale assault where hundreds had been cut down in the first waves. The survivors had become the veterans for the rest of that long war.

"Don't forget, that was only against Zealots and their rebel friends. The Biomechs are something else. They are able to take on a Jötnar in hand-to-hand and have the firepower to deal with decent armor.

"I know. I read your report, and I saw the video briefing you gave Earthsec command before we left. They have given your tactical assessments of their strength to Cobb and his unit commanders. The plan comes directly from

Cobb though."

"Plan?" Khan laughed out.

The three of them waited and watched as patiently as they could. The lower levels of the refinery complex were a dangerous place at the best of time, and now they had to contend with battle damage. It wasn't just impact damage where the small number of Biomech landing teams had crashed down, it was also the destruction wrought by the fighting that had taken place.

"Look at the surface. There is more structural damage than the last footage suggested. We've got two collapsed towers, and the refinery site is venting."

Spartan shook his head violently and pointed at the smoke rising from the refinery.

"I can promise you the Biomechs won't have damaged anything significant there. Look at the buildings nearby. The place is secure. The enemy will have shattered the defenses and then moved on the site best suited for establishing their compound."

Khan nodded in agreement.

"Yeah, he's right. They'll have their people and our prisoners working on modifying and installing equipment to service their plan very quickly. They are not like us. The minute they secure territory, they begin exploiting it."

Spartan pointed at the refinery and the number of green diamonds that had started to appear on the biometric overlay.

"These are life signs, correct?"

Lieutenant Jenkins nodded, and Spartan traced his hand around where they were positioned. The small icons moved very slowly though. It was hard to tell if it was because the target was static, or just that the technology was slow assimilating new data. The Lieutenant pointed to one of the towers nearby.

"That's one of the damaged relay stations. We modified it to track the biosignatures of anybody still alive on the station. It isn't perfect, but it gives us an idea of what's down there."

Spartan scanned the imagery with a quick eye, taking in the details and adding up the numbers in his head. As he identified each one, the furrow of his brow seemed to widen.

"Apart from what, maybe two dozen, the rest are all in this one area and moving about. This is where they are housing the prisoners while they build their factory system. I can guarantee you that."

Lieutenant Jenkins didn't seem convinced.

"You honestly think they will drop small teams onto Mars just to build a factory? Why Mars? You can see the place. It ain't anything special."

Spartan placed his head in his hands and took a number of slow, careful breaths. Finally, he lifted himself back up and looked directly into Lieutenant Jenkins' eyes.

"You fought in the War, and you must remember what

they did at the Bone Mill?"

The mere mention of that place seemed to drain color from the poor man's face.

"Exactly," continued Spartan, "The Biomechs managed to get some of their technology established down there. Now, we know the Zealots used this equipment to create a massive, and I mean a massive army hidden underground. Hell, it was on one of our own colonies, and we didn't see it."

Spartan paused and then thumbed the screen with his good hand.

"You know why we didn't see it? Because they built it inside a collapsed mine and refinery complex. They had access to technology, machinery, and thousands upon thousands of trapped workers."

Khan nodded at the screen and the shape of the first shuttle as it came down to land.

"Yeah, and what does that place look like?"

Spartan scratched at his cheek, considering the situation.

"They will have this place up and running in months, maybe even just a few weeks. You can expect the first batch of their creatures to be ready. At that point, the only option left will be atomics."

Khan rubbed his forehead and then stood up and walked a few meters away from the screen. He reached a line of seats, all of which were far too small for him. Next to them was a rack fitted out with twenty thermal shotguns, all locked by a triple bar system so that they couldn't be easily removed.

"Look, they're landing," said Lieutenant Jenkins.

He pointed at the bank of ten screens that showed views from the shuttles, as well as the Captain and his six squad commanders. Spartan and Khan moved closer and watched with fascination as the first of the craft moved to the surface surrounded in a cloud of dust.

"It begins," Spartan said quietly.

"Right," agreed Khan, "and it will end just as quickly."

* * *

The landing of the two shuttles was an impressive sight and might have been enough on its own to encourage surrender to most foes. The lightly armed craft swept in like aircraft at an air show. Even before landing, their height had dropped to barely ten meters above the ground. At that height, the landing lights activated and bathed the surface in a dull glow. Contrary to the suggestions of Spartan, the team had elected to land during the night cycle. The rusty iron oxide littering the surface kicked up when they swept in, leaving a trail of what looked like mini cyclones right behind them as they screamed in at high speed.

The signal that the descent had turned to a landing sequence was when the engines reversed thrust and the retro thrusters activated. In an instant, the shuttles lifted their noses and moved in to settle on the ground. The first came in a little hard, and the hydraulic landing skids retracted almost half the way back into the shuttle before it bounced and then settled down on the Red Planet.

Most assumed that Mars would appear red upon a first visit, and as the first Earthsec platoon exited the shuttle, more than a few that were surprised at what they saw. The landing lights and flood lamps fitted to the craft lit up some of the ground around them, but it was the navigation and marker lights fitted all over the refinery that did most of the work. They cast an odd series of hard shadows in all directions, as well as lighting up the ground and highlighting the peculiar array of oxidation and rust on the surface. It was more colorful than the majority had ever expected.

"Move out, people," said Captain Cobb.

He watched the first team leave from the safety of the second shuttle. They moved out as a single large unit toward the surface blast doors. At first glance, it looked nothing more than a crowd of heavily armed men, but as they covered more ground, it became easier to see the three large squads as they pulled apart. Two moved for the array of doors while the third took up positions in cover a short distance away, providing a basic degree of overwatch.

"One more pass," he said.

The second shuttle tilted hard to the left and circled

over the landing zone for the third time. The onboard gunners, as well as the remaining half of the landing party watched in all directions, each looking for signs of the supposed Biomech enemy. Cobb looked at the video image showing on a thick display screen embedded on the wall. It showed the last known positions of the enemy and also confirmed to him that there had been no more than four of the multi-limbed combat drones.

Biomechs, my ass. These could just be private security combat drones.

Like all of the Earthsec operatives in the combat component of the unit, none had experience of the Biomech threat. Only three had ever ventured outside of Sol, and the stories of the Great Uprising still seemed farfetched; even to those who had been to see the sacred sights of some of the larger battles that had since been turned into tourist attractions or memorial gardens.

Captain Cobb had dealt with a dozen minor insurrections and incidents on the colonies of Sol over the last thirteen years. He had even been involved in the Jupiter incident, where a private firm had attempted to take control of the orbital mining facility. It was one of the richest sites in Sol, and his use of forbidden robotics had allowed him to empty large parts of the base into space, making the site uninhabitable for nearly three years.

Tyrant Hawken, he thought bitterly, remembering the odd name the criminal had taken, or perhaps he'd chosen it for himself. In either case the man had escaped, along with his entourage of a dozen combat drones and weapons.

This looks and sounds just like his work.

Cobb watched the first shuttle lift up from the ground to provide a clear landing space for his own craft. Satisfied with the initial dispersal, he gave the order to his pilot to move in. This time the landing was textbook, and no sooner had the skids settled, the doors had opened, and the Earthsec team flooded out.

The atmosphere on Mars was still not completely breathable, but at least the atmosphere itself had begun to stabilize after centuries of development. It was no Earth, but it was a great deal further ahead than the sterile hell of twenty-first century Mars where the first colony had failed in less than a year. With a modest atmosphere, it was able to retain some warmth at night, but it was still a difficult planet to live on. The clothing and armor used by the Earthsec team was more suited to the underground peacekeeping duties that were common beneath the surface of Earth; and lacked a fully enclosed and sealed environment for operating on airless moons or in the direct sunlight. It was another reason Cobb has selected night for the attack.

Captain Cobb was the first out of the second shuttle, and to the horror of his men, he stumbled and dropped to one knee as he moved from the craft. The two following tried to avoid him but only one managed, and the other stumbled and fell down alongside him.

It was at that very moment when the Biomechs struck.

* * *

Lieutenant Jenkins watched with fascination as the four arachnid shaped machines emerged from their hiding places. Even though they were mechanical beasts, they moved with a speed and grace that could easily have been a living creature. The first of them leapt out from inside the shattered wreckage that lay strew about the shuttle landing area. Although he had watched the footage of the initial attack on the refinery, this felt different. Probably because everything he was watching was taking place on the surface of the planet he was currently orbiting, and it was all happening right now.

"Yeah, am I surprised?" complained Khan.

"No...We have to warn them!" muttered Lieutenant Jenkins.

Spartan shook his head.

"They know."

It was true. Even as the machines emerged from cover, the first of the Earthsec operatives opened fire. The initial volley was impressive and showered the attackers with small-caliber bullets. That was the extent of their effectiveness though.

"Now it starts," Khan said in a hushed tone.

Spartan said no more but watched in silence as the four machines split up and did exactly as he would have expected. There were cries of anguish and fear from the small number of crew that had seen some of the footage on the other displays. Only a handful of combat operatives remained, and Spartan spotted one of them running for a plastic bin. The poor man was too late and vomited over the wall and onto another of his comrade's boots.

"This is how it always goes," said Spartan.

He then looked down and checked the details on his own antiquated datapad, a unit he had borrowed from one of the officers' quarters just after the shuttles had left. He lifted his eyes as the four charged into the nearest platoon of Earthsec operatives, with terrifying results. As Spartan had prophesized, their armor proved less than useless. Each machine tore apart two or three men before turning their attention on Cobb's unit.

"We've got to do something!" said Lieutenant Jenkins.

The man lifted himself to his feet, but Khan stopped him and placed his hands on the man's shoulder.

"No, we can't help them right now, but we can learn. It will take hours to get our people down there. Spartan's already on it."

Lieutenant Jenkins' face tightened, and his jaw stiffened, but Spartan also turned to him and nodded at the footage.

"Whether they live or die is down to Cobb, their gear, and their training. I promise you though, we will be there in three hours, and when we get there, we'll fix this. Okay?"

He waited until receiving the nod from Jenkins before continuing.

"I have another shuttle already loaded in the drop bay. We leave in eleven minutes."

It took another few seconds before Jenkins looked back to Spartan and grabbed his shoulder.

"You planned for this?"

The look of disgust was clear, but Spartan was less than amused. He ripped the arm away from his body and sent another batch of commands via the battered looking datapad.

"Are you kidding? We told your boys what they were up against, and they screwed up. So yeah, I made my own plans. Just be thankful I bothered, or we'd be looking at another twenty plus hours before the next shuttle can be fuelled, armed, and rotated in for launch."

Khan raised an eyebrow at the estimated time. He knew that Dauntless was an old ship, but twenty hours seemed excessive to him. He opened his mouth to speak, but unlike the Lieutenant, he knew the facial expressions of Spartan, and this time he let it go. Instead of speaking, he nodded and then looked away; now uncertain as to what expressions he ought to be showing. A long stream of gunfire pulled them back to the terrible scene that was taking place on the surface of Mars.

"The shuttle," said Spartan under his breath.

All three looked back and watched as the machines butchered the men while just a handful returned fire. Out of two platoons, barely a dozen got off any shots, and none succeeded in inflicting anything more than minor damage on the machines. Several video feeds cut off as the men were killed, but also as the machine moved on to crash into the two shuttles, leaving dents and holes through their sides.

"Look, there's Cobb!" said Khan.

They watched him jump back inside the shuttle, and then a moment later he appeared on the other side and rolled down to the ground. One of the machines ripped off the side of the machine and pulled itself inside.

"He's a dead man now," said Jenkins quietly.

To all of their surprise, two more men appeared from the one door and hurled themselves free as the craft tore itself apart in a spectacular explosion. The machine failed to emerge, but the other three then turned their attention on Cobb. Many more of the operatives were now scattered and managed to put down fire onto the machines but to little effect.

"I told them, those guns are just going to spitball out there. They need heavy weapons, the bigger the better," said Spartan.

More feeds cut, including one long-range camera from the communication tower. The last one on the first shuttle twisted and then partially fell off so that it was now showing a view of a crippled tower, and one of the machines stabbing its blades through an unfortunate operative. A bright blue light flashed by, and then the feed flickered blue before fading out to white. Spartan sat up in surprise.

"Uh, what the hell was that?"

Lieutenant Jenkins was already on it and moved the imagery back several frames until they spotted a large bipedal form holding some kind of large gun system. All three sat there in stunned silence. Spartan finally spoke.

"Is it me, or is that a Biomech?"

Khan nodded and said nothing.

"Look, to the left."

They all looked at the target of the dreaded Biomech's weapon where the blue energy has shredded it four frames before the feed cut.

"No, that can't be right," said Spartan.

Even Khan found himself unable to say anything of use. Jenkins enlarged the image to show the thermal blast around the eight-legged mechanical warriors that had been attacking the operatives.

"Why is the Biomech attacking its own robotic soldiers?"

For the first time in a very long time, neither had anything to say.

CHAPTER EIGHT

It would be a mistake to assume that all members of the many worlds, colonies, and empires of the known universe might be alike. On Earth, in the early twenty-first century there were over seven billion people, inhabiting nearly two hundred unique countries. Of these countries, there were scores of ethnic groups, languages, and traditions, even between individual cities. The two largest religions of the times, Islam and Christianity, both comprised of many variants, all competing and often violently. We must therefore approach the new alien domains with a degree of sophistication and consideration. After just a few months, the four social groups of the Helions gave a good example of what would happen if all Helions were considered the same. The picture of alien societies completely transformed upon the first diplomatic meetings with the Anicinàbe, a fragmented nomadic people that occupied over twenty stars, yet inhabited no worlds.

The Races of the Known Universe

Admiral Churchill had moved from his quarters to the command center in readiness for the battle that lay ahead. Reports were still coming in from other Alliance outposts that confirmed unknown ships were on the move. That, combined with the ever-approaching deadline for the arrival of Comet C34 at Helios, told him just one thing; war was coming, and it would be coming very soon. No sooner had he arrived than Director Johnson intercepted him.

"Admiral, I have news from one of my agents on Mars."

He looked to Johnson, a surprised expression his face.

"Mars? I though the Rift had been deactivated on the other side?"

"Yes, it is. My agent sent a distress transponder directly into the Rift. It only started to transmit in the last hour."

"Why?"

Johnson walked to one of the many screens and lifted his secpad to contact the unit wirelessly. It completely bypassed the main computer system and so slaved the screen. The series of thirty-one images showed an explosion and a number of objects falling toward the camera.

"My agent says this is the wreckage from a ship, one that matches the exact configuration described by Khan and Spartan during their captivity."

The Admiral looked a little confused, so Johnson continued.

"This matches reports from Hyperion and Terra Nova where there have been sighting of these ships."

He looked almost excited.

"Admiral, I think it's working. These ships are all on the move, and every piece of evidence suggests they are heading for Helios."

He examined the imagery in detail and moved back to the first frame that showed the ship. There were others of a similar design around it, as well as something blurred but much larger right behind it.

"What was it doing near Mars? Is this one of the ships that tried to move into position over Terra Nova?"

Not waiting for an answer, he brought up the threat assessment from the ships in orbit around Terra Nova. As he expected, the report confirmed four ships had appeared around the capital of the Alliance before being pursued to the Sol Rift. The Rift had collapsed before they could follow the Biomech ships through.

"So, all four ships of those got through. Are they all in Sol?"

Johnson breathed out almost in a sigh.

"Not just the four ships, the big one went through too. Although the distortion analysis suggests at least one was caught in the middle of the Rift collapse. I'd say somebody warned them."

Admiral Churchill shook his head in disappointment.

"So, they stopped one of them coming through, but

the rest made it."

He turned about and sighed, shaking his head.

"Those ships are something else. Bringing one down is quite a feat, but stopping the rest?"

He wiped his brow; his feelings on the matter clear to them all.

"If those ships made it to Mars, then they're lost. The defenses around Mars are ancient and not helped by those fools from Earthsec. Do you know how tough it was persuading them to accept Alliance monitoring stations and a patrol ship?"

Of course, Director Johnson was all too familiar with the difficulty in operating so far on the fringes of Alliance territory. Even as he listened to the Admiral, he was busy tagging and checking more data from his analysts on Prometheus. He opened his mouth to speak but found himself immediately cut off.

"ANS Louisiana is the only warship in the system, and she's nothing more than an old Achilles class frigate. I doubt they would last much more than five minutes against one of those ships, not least the rest of the fleet."

He thought of the crew and small complement of marines that would be present on the ship and felt a pang of guilt. He had access to ships and could send help on to Terra Nova through the local Rift and then on to Sol.

But how would they get through the Rift? It has been closed from the other side. Only a Rift station like ANS Beagle has the energy and equipment to open a temporary Rift long enough for ships to get through.

His attention moved back to the images.

"Wait a second. What the hell is that thing?"

His hand pointed at the dark shape behind the other four ships.

"Yes, that's what I wanted to tell you about. According to the limited data that came through from Mars, well, it would appear several distress signals were being sent from the Mars orbit Rift control station as they came through."

"So?"

Director Johnson tried to smile.

"They were stating that something had taken control of the station and was deactivating the Rift...as the ships were coming through."

"What?" Admiral Churchill answered.

"You're telling me somebody managed to gain control of the station, outside of Alliance control, and shut it down?"

Johnson nodded.

"Yes, Admiral. The only question remaining is whether it was Earthsec, or somebody else that managed to gain access."

Admiral Churchill wasn't sure he liked the sound of either of those options. He had little to go on, and right now the indicators on his heavily fortified base reminded him he had his own problems. A trio of officers marched past and saluted as they made their way to one of the many computer centers buried deep inside the hard rock. The structure had been enlarged and fitted out with the best management and communications equipment available in the Alliance. The facility itself was located on one side of the central hub of the base, but an additional two floors up. There were multiple airlock seals that doubled up as security points, and internal weapons mounts were slaved directly to the base's defense grid. He looked at his tactical officer and wondered what it had been like when the Zealots had run the place.

Something tells me, it would have been pretty similar.

"Admiral, I'll see what else my analysts have uncovered," said Director Johnson as he moved off to the side where had had set up a small station with a group of his senior officers. They had access to a dozen displays, as well as privileged access to the entire base's data banks and communications systems.

"Let me know the minute you have data I can use."

The place was much bigger than its equivalent on a ship and housed officers from the Navy, Marine Corps, and civilian side of the Alliance. There were almost twenty officers and banks of computer screens for monitoring events above and below the surface. Admiral Churchill felt confident in his base, his facilities, and his defenses. Even the supply situation was good, and he had access to large quantities of drinking water, limitless power produced by capping the thermal vents, and several years' worth of preprocessed and stored foods. Like all Naval installations, this one was crewed exclusively by official Alliance personnel and was one of the most efficient, self-sustaining bases in service.

Now we'll see if this plan is worth the paper it was written on.

The massive underground base was not the only resource he had at his control. As well as a small number of warships, he also had access to the Prometheus Seven Station. In the past, it had once been a beacon of private enterprise and later one of corruption and criminal activity. Now it was being used as a major orbital platform to control the region of space around Prometheus, and more important to act as a power station for the Prometheus-Orion Rift system.

Thousands of personnel now called the gigantic structure home. A small garrison protected it as well as several squadrons of fighters. With a circumference of over six kilometers, it was one of mankind's greatest ever construction projects, ranking in importance to other famous bases such as the Titan Naval Station in orbit around Prime.

"Admiral, a message from P7, they have long-range imagery of the ships. Their database matches are already on the displays," said the communications officer.

Admiral Churchill looked to the bank of screens on the wall and did his utmost to remain calm. The generic images of space quickly changed as each screen focused on a separate stream coming directly from the station. They showed the groups of dark shapes as ship after ship emerged from their hiding places inside the storm.

"Get me a full tactical assessment."

He watched carefully, his eyes taking in every detail of the odd assortment of ships. As more arrived, he found his pulse quicken at the realization the planet was now surrounded by enemy ships. He looked to the large tactical display that showed him all of his available assets, and for a moment it improved his confidence. Even though his only ship-based protection was ANS Dreadnought, two small T'Kari vessels, and seven of the new Liberty class ships, he felt sure the additional defenses would be enough.

"Admiral, Colonel Morato requests an update."

He looked at the screens and then spun about, quicker than he intended.

"In a moment. Before we get to that, I need information, and fast, dammit!"

Prometheus was more than just the planet, and to defend it, he would need access to every piece of information and every weapons system to hand. The base itself was equipped with an array of ground-based weapons that would make a direct assault deadly to an attacker. The smaller orbiting transit and defense platforms provided additional firepower. Last but not least, the P7 station was equipped with enough fighters and weapons to take on an entire Battlecruiser.

It's enough to look realistic. Hell, if might be a little too much. We don't want to start a six-month operation just as the entire Helios thing kicks off. No. We need this fleet destroyed and as quickly as possible.

He looked back to his crew of the best men and women in the Alliance.

We have much bigger fish to fry than just some Biomech locals.

The first ships to appear in orbit around Prometheus were seven civilian transports. Each of them was of a vintage older than any other ship in the system. Right behind them came fifteen cruiser-sized vessels, each multi-colored, and protected by thick plating and covered in thick studs that ran along the underside and flanks.

"Get me schematics on those ships, what do we have?" he demanded.

Confidence had started to return, but the sight of these new vessels sent a shudder through his body. Transports and cruisers he could deal with, but unknowns were an ever-present worry with the Biomechs. He tried to forget what had happened to his own ships back in the War, but no matter how hard he tried, the betrayal of the machines that had turned his own ships against him was still a fresh wound.

A quick check on the system by the science and tactical officers came up with nothing. It came down to a chance examination of internal files by Intelligence Director

Johnson, who had been silent until now as he'd been cross-examining the data from Terra Nova with what had been transmitted from Mars.

"I've got something," he said, much to the Admiral's surprise.

"What? How?"

Director Johnson approached him and motioned with his hands to send a stream of imagery to his screen from his secpad. The details of a ship structure and approximate design by the tactical computers had come up with something surprisingly similar to what they were looking at.

"It's the same configuration as the ships reported by Spartan, during their captivity by the T'Kari Raiders."

The Admiral sucked in a long breath as he skimmed through the text.

"This is all we have to go on?"

"His reports are fragmentary at best. Don't forget, the man was away for months while being tortured and trying to escape. He was a prisoner aboard a T'Kari Raider and then a Biomech heavy warship. You know his quality as an observer though."

Admiral Churchill stepped in front of the tactical display. He had already moved in his small force of ships to act as a skirmish screen, with his single Battlecruiser operating as the flagship. It was a modest force at best, and everybody in that room, and probably throughout

Prometheus, knew that as well.

Let's hope they know that too.

"What about these transports?"

Horner, the stations tactical officer brought up three detailed images of the ships, all of them from many years earlier. As tactical officer for the entire base, he was responsible for monitoring everything within range of the base's own sensors and weapon systems, as well as providing tactical assistance via the automated internal defenses.

"Admiral, the computer matches for those ships is accurate. All seven were flagged as lost during the battle over Terra Nova. They attempted to break the Alliance blockade of the Rift to Proxima Centauri, along with two missile cruisers and a single battleship."

"And?"

"Well, Sir, all of the ships were reported as lost."

"Lost my ass," the Admiral muttered, shaking his head in annoyance. "Those ships were part of the Echidna Union, and if I remember rightly, they were used to transport thousands of Biomech creatures directly into battle."

He looked at the ships and nodded grimly to himself.

"Yeah, I've seen those before, and there's no way in hell I'm letting them land a single soldier on Prometheus."

It had taken a few seconds, but now he remembered where he'd seen them last. It has been during the fighting on Euryale in the last part of the War. The fighting had shifted from insurgency and retreat to a full-scale conventional war against the enemy. Those transports had been the backbone of the enemy forces in providing logical support to the battle.

"Captain, I want all weapons in this sector trained on those ships first. We know their weaknesses, unlike the other ships."

"What about the others, Admiral?"

"We'll deal with them next. Our resources are finite. Let's hope theirs are too."

He then turned his attention toward the communications officer.

"Get me Colonel Morato, ASAP!"

* * *

Teresa had only just made it back into the central plaza when the Admiral managed to get back to her. It had taken so long she'd begun to wonder if he'd forgotten about her and her marines as they waited for the inevitable fight. Now that she was encased in her PDS Alpha armor, she had been forced to put the secpad away and rely upon the more comprehensive internal communications system. Rather than an excessive additional display, the Alpha visor featured a detailed overlay that could present all manner of details, including full bandwidth visual communications traffic. An icon appeared and she selected it with her retina.

"Colonel, you've seen the feeds. There's more…"

Teresa didn't like what she was hearing from the Admiral. As he continued, her expression changed to one that became grimmer by the second. Even as he spoke, she was able to sift through additional reports coming to her from the sensors on the Prometheus base. Every single one confirmed exactly what she had expected; that they could expect a major offensive in the Prometheus sector, and more importantly that they were underequipped to deal with substantial space-based threat. Eventually, he finished his hurried summary and waited for her thoughts.

"Colonel, we've got a lot to do, and very little time to do it. Tell me, can you hold this place against those kinds of numbers?"

Teresa nodded in agreement and moved behind one of the defensive lines built in the center of the plaza. She noted with satisfaction that her orders had been adhered to, and more heavy weapons had been brought in. The low wall looked like a porcupine bristling with spikes.

"Admiral, that is a lot of ships. I mean a lot. Seven transports, with anything up to a thousand creatures on board if I remember correctly. As for those other fifteen ships, we don't even know what they're carrying. Do they match the specifications of the craft Admiral Lewis fought near Gaxos?"

He said nothing and merely shook his head briefly.

"Okay, well, do we have any idea of their capability?"

Admiral Churchill called to somebody off camera and then looked back.

"The unknown craft look like assault ships. Director Johnson says their configuration matches our files as having been spotted alongside T'Kari Raider vessels. We suspect these are some of the ships that hit the T'Kari hard in the past."

Teresa considered his words carefully. The Raider ships were something the Alliance had only encountered once reaching T'Karan. Small groups of ships performed hit and run attacks, often to destroy equipment or to take prisoners. The very idea that she was now on the most infamous of the entire enemy's prison worlds sent a chill through her body.

Are we here to be taken prisoner again?

"You think they are here to take prisoners?"

Admiral Churchill considered that, but only for a moment and quickly discounted it.

"I very much doubt it. Our combined fleet is already through the Helios Rift. They will be in range in a matter of hours to intercept Biomech forces on the way to Helios."

He gave her a grim look and continued.

"These ships are here for their commander, and we'll make them pay in blood for him."

That's it. There's no way General Rivers would send away our entire strength when this Biomech threat remained, and Churchill; just look at him. He's almost pleading with me to tell him the plan.

It wasn't much to go on, but Teresa felt a little less panicked having heard the fake details she assumed she was being fed.

Well, I'd better do my part.

"Admiral. The troops you've given me simply aren't up to the job. The weapons grid in bays three and four are offline, and half the marines are still preparing their defenses."

He looked at her, and Teresa was convinced she could see the tiniest of smiles on his face.

"How long do you need?"

Teresa considered that for a moment.

Less than an hour to perform a combat drop, and at least three hours to reach a drop orbit over Prometheus, to push them into action it needs to be soon.

"Six hours, Admiral. Give me that long, and I'll have this base locked down for weeks, maybe even months. I can hold this facility, but not indefinitely. What's your plan?"

He looked back at her as if he wanted to say something. There was the shortest pause, and then he rubbed his nose while speaking.

"As I said, the fleet is en route to Helios, so we're it right now. Our job is to act defiantly, as though we are expecting reinforcements at any moment. We cannot let them know how thinly protected we are."

Teresa looked carefully at him, but apart from the rubbing of the nose, there was nothing she could see to give him away.

Then why explain our most significant military assessment over the comms channel, and minutes before the start of the fight?

She began to smile and did her best to hide it. It was all clear to her now.

"The Biomech Commander, Krani, I have him locked down inside the secure hangar, as instructed. They will not get him. I promise you."

* * *

Admiral Churchill moved his attention back to the scores of feeds coming in from all kinds of sources. Even though Prometheus had become a major Alliance base of operations, there were still plenty of private enterprises in operation. Medium sized commercial space stations orbited the planet, and there were many ongoing mining projects, both on the surface and along the perimeter of the storm region. Almost every one of these had begun sending detailed video streams of the approaching ships, and it was all beginning to worry him. He identified the shapes of the small Alliance fleet and tapped the largest of the icons for the Battlecruiser ANS Dreadnought. An image appeared almost instantly, showing her commander.

"Captain Nikova. Your forces are ready?"

"Yes, Admiral. All fighters have been launched, and our targets are preset. All we need is the word to go."

"Good...good work. Standby."

He looked back at the screens and waited. As well as the feeds from space, there were also internal feeds showing the key tactical areas of the massive underground facility. The nearest screen showed him the plan for the base, as well as live video streams from each of his senior commanders. Movement caught his eye on one of the screens, and then the main screen turned black.

"What's going on?"

A dozen pairs of eyes turned to the black display that flickered between colors and then as quickly as it had been black, it changed to a whirlpool pattern.

"Rift has just opened up on the border of the storm region," said Captain Horner.

Admiral Churchill moved his hand to press a button, but Director Johnson placed his hand over his.

"No, we thought this might happen."

The Admiral raised an eyebrow but left his hand in position.

"You expected another Rift?"

Johnson smiled.

"Not exactly, but if they truly believe we are weakened and that we have their commander. Well, what would you do?"

"Strike at our heart, and fast. They will secure Prometheus, take control of the P7 station, and then split us away from helping in T'Karan and beyond."

He looked back at the disposition of ships.

"The T'Kari can shut that Rift down in seconds."

Johnson shook his head.

"No, let them keep it open. We need all of their forces before we spring our trap."

Admiral Churchill looked at his face, now beginning to realize the man's worth.

"Very well."

He tapped a different icon, and T'Kron, the commander of the T'Kari Exiles appeared.

"T'Kron, it is time."

The T'Kari commander lowered his head and the images vanished. Admiral Churchill then looked back at Captain Nikova of ANS Dreadnought.

"Prepare for your attack."

She saluted quickly and smartly.

"Look at this," said Captain Horner.

Once more, all eyes returned to the view of the new Rift as a large ship entered the system. It was shaped in a similar fashion to that of the other fifteen Biomech ships, except this one was easily three times larger and shaped like a squat trilobite. The short length was very thickly ribbed with bulbous armored sections that gave the impression the ship itself was articulated. Director

Johnson turned away and spoke into an earpiece before approaching Admiral Churchill.

"My agents on P7 have intercepted Biomech transmissions from that ship. They are using the same encoding as those coming from Terra Nova at the end of the War."

That sent a chill down the Admiral's back.

"The AI Core?"

Johnson nodded.

"The commander of the...uh...large ship wishes to speak with us, Admiral," said the communications officer.

He extended his had partially toward the viewscreen, and it changed to show a trio of men. At first Admiral Churchill thought it was an emergency transmission from the Prometheus Seven Station, but it only took a few seconds for him to recognize that the background was black and red, and nothing like any ship he'd ever seen before. The man at the front of the group spoke first.

"Admiral Churchill, I presume."

Before he could respond, he noticed a message had just arrived on his secpad. He looked to his right. Captain Horner was beckoning toward the device. While keeping as calm as possible, he lifted it and briefly scanned the message.

Their fleet is on a course for Prometheus itself. I see.

He looked into the eyes of the man on the alien ship, and only then did he recognize him.

"Typhon," he hissed under his teeth.

The man smiled with unconcealed pleasure.

"In the flesh, as you might say. I have been authorized to grant you sixty seconds to hand over our ally."

"Ally? I don't know what you are talking about? The Alliance doesn't negotiate with terrorists, Biomechs…and especially the dead!"

He'd expected a Biomech or another kind of semi-automated system to communicate with them. The fact they had chosen to reveal these agents from the past confirmed many things to him. First, Typhon was well known as the key figure behind the Biomech creatures in the last war. Second, he also knew the man had been killed, and this transmission now confirmed that this, and possibly the Typhon killed on Terra Nova, were nothing more than fabricated humans designed to do the machines' bidding. There had been much speculation to this point since the end of the War, and he felt almost disappointed at the revelation. He looked to Director Johnson who looked equally fascinated.

So, now we know.

The Admiral turned his attention back to the three men. He examined their faces, gestures, and especially their clothing. It was something he'd seen only in the history books, the garb of the long forgotten and defeated Centauri League that had occurred over seventy years ago. On their chests lay the emblem of Echidna, the mother of beasts, and the hated symbol used by Biomech sympathizers in the Great Uprising. Typhon look unperturbed at what he was saying.

So, the Sons of the League and the Biomechs have been colluding, probably since the cease-fire seventy years ago. That would explain a lot.

"Nonetheless, you now have forty-five seconds to hand over our mutual friend."

The Admiral straightened his back and ran his finger down his neck.

"You're just another one of their pet projects, aren't you? What started all of this? Why are you doing this?"

Typhon looked off camera again and then back at him. It gave the impression he was constantly asking for permission.

"My brothers and I brought the word of Echidna to the League in the last year of the Great War. In exchange for their assistance, we promised technology beyond their dreams. Surrender Krani to us, and we would offer you the same."

Director Johnson looked almost happy as he listened in from the side of the room. Admiral Churchill was less interested in the past right then. He had been given a task, that of the destruction of the Biomech infestation in Alliance territory, and he intended to carry it through, no matter the short-term cost. He looked directly into Typhon's eyes and gave him a withering stare.

"Yes, the last Typhon died like a cheap whore on Terra Nova."

He then turned his attention to the man on his flank.

"And you, Pontus, I believe. Yes, you died in your failed attempt to bring in troops from T'Karan to overrun Hyperion."

His eyes shifted just a little back to Typhon.

"Everything about you stinks of defeat. You had fifty years to plan the Uprising, to make use of the technology gifted to you by the machines, and what did you achieve? Nothing but the death of millions, and still you were defeated."

Director Johnson moved into frame and nodded as though greeting them.

"We've spent much time examining the body of your master over the last months. It would appear they are centuries old, a species in decline, and facing certain extinction."

Typhon's face turned from amusement to what looked almost like fear. He glanced to somebody off camera again and then back, his face now more determined than ever.

"Hand over Krani now, or face the entire destruction of Prometheus."

That was what he wanted to hear, and with just a single gesture, he sent the order to Captain Nikova. The machine lurched to one side as it noticed something happening.

"No, you listen to me. Prometheus is ours. You failed

in your last attempt to screw over our colonies, and you'll fail again. What did you call yourselves…"

He knew exactly what they were called, but he stalled, giving his own ships time to move into position.

"Sons of the League, yes, that was it. You believed you were the harbingers of revenge for the Centauri League. How pathetic. Your forbearers couldn't win the Great War, and then you failed to take control of the Confederacy. And now you're here, looking to cause more trouble again. If you ask me, I'd say your benefactors are not as powerful and all seeing as they believe."

He spat on the ground, a gesture that was as offensive to his own crew as it was for them.

"Now, take your so-called brothers, and get out of our system."

His words seemed to be having the right effect, but he thought just a little more might be needed.

"…And take your robot friends with you."

He watched from the corner of his eye as the T'Kari ships moved in toward the Biomech fleet. The small ships were no match for even a single Biomech warship, but they weren't intended for that. As they moved in closer, they began powering up their weapon systems to collapse the Biomech's Rift and their only chance of escape.

"You fools, so be it," snapped back Typhon. "The Sons of the League have a new master, and they will have their vengeance!"

"Admiral!" yelled Captain Horner.

By the time he'd turned, the first of the T'Kari ships had been vaporized by a massive amount of gunfire. Every single ship in the Biomech fleet concentrated its fire on the vessel. The second almost had time to power up its weapon system before it too was smashed by heavy gunfire.

"Now we will recover our comrade, and your new friends will suffer unimaginable agony."

Typhon's expression changed to laughter, but it was so excessive and odd that it received nothing but a mixture of confusion and amusement. Finally, he stopped and wiped what looked like drool dripping from the corner of his mouth.

"Admiral, I suggest you surrender Prometheus, and fast. If we find even a scratch on the metal work of our friend, we will unleash a terrible horror on this world, a horror the Helions are only too familiar with."

His lip lifted up into a cruel smile, and the Admiral had to turn away to hide his own feelings. If the weapon he was referring to was the nano-weapon used against Helios, then they were in a lot of trouble. There was little, if anything he could do about that right now though. He gave a hand signal to cut the transmission and breathed a long, clear sigh at the conversation. Director Johnson nodded as though impressed at what he'd seen.

"I think they bought it."

He closed his eyes for a second and slowed his breathing to calm his nerves.

Colonel Morato and the cargo are in the correct place, and ready. Yes, now we have to give them a fight, and it has to look good.

He reached for the ancient looking intercom microphone and moved it near his mouth. He started to speak but found his throat dry and empty. It took three attempts to clear his throat before he could finally say what he wanted to.

"Men and women of Prometheus, the enemy from the War has returned, and this time they intend on crushing us, one world at a time. Look to your officers and sergeants, follow the plan and remember...there is no mercy for the Biomechs and their soldiers. Leave none alive."

He lowered the intercom and looked to the video display that still showed Captain Nikova, the commander of ANS Dreadnought.

"Begin your attack. Good hunting, Captain."

She saluted smartly and then moved from the camera, and he was left to watch as the ships of the Alliance moved on the much more powerful Biomech fleet. He was pleased to see the first explosions occur along the two nearest enemy transports. A few seconds after that, the volley fire from many more vessels on both sides began, with ANS Dreadnought providing over half the firepower of the Alliance side.

So, this is the beginning of the end.

CHAPTER NINE

Could the warriors of the future take advantage of the military developments of the conflict around Helios? Some military theorists pointed to the machinery used to create the first generation of Jötnar. Why not combine that with the hardware used to build the supply Rams used by the Marine Corps. The arguments for this level of cybernetically enhanced war machines would only gather pace as the violence and combat losses took their toll.

Robots in Space

Spartan found the trip down from Dauntless to be exciting rather than dull. It had surprised him, and he could only put it down to the mixed feeling of boredom and impotence he'd been feeling while in orbit. He looked to the other side of the shuttle where Khan was wedged alongside a rack mount containing a dozen of the TEK-

40 Bullpup rifles.

"How much longer?" his friend asked.

Spartan looked up at the analogue clock fitted along the top level of the shuttle and almost laughed. He'd not seen such a low-tech piece of equipment on board a spacecraft before, certainly not one designed for actual frontline use as this shuttle was. The circular device was bordered in tarnished brass, and the second hand moved with a gentle stutter. Spartan had never really been much of one for tradition, but seeing something so antiquated on a spacecraft bordered on absurdity to him.

"Well, if that old thing is right, we'll be on the ground in less than three minutes."

Khan nodded.

"You're sure we've got the right landing area? This area is still pretty close to the access doors."

Spartan smiled.

"When am I ever wrong? The back entrance is used for the crawlers and loaders to move inside. We'll have space to move and plenty of cover."

He then looked to the front of the craft and raised an eyebrow.

I just hope the pilot's up to this.

With the landing now out of his hands, he turned back to something he could influence, his equipment. He checked his jacket and ensured the buckles and straps were all correctly adjusted. Spartan was only too familiar with the detailed reports on the surface of Mars. Back in the early days of exploration, it had been a terrible place to have to live. The world was harsh, a cold planet with a barren surface and a thin atmosphere that consisted almost entirely of carbon dioxide. Even now the temperature would be incredibly cold. Like the other operatives that had landed, he had access to a thick balaclava that covered his head, leaving space just for his eyes and mouth, and would in turn be covered by his respirator.

Right, that looks good. Next, weapons!

He unplugged the TEK-40 from its mount to his left and checked that his last-minute modification had worked. The two of them had used what little tooling was available on the ship to link two of the weapons together with two fused plastic modules along the bodies and stocks. Spartan had made one of the engineers on board attach a metal bar to the triggers that joined them together. Khan, on the other hand, had taken two but removed as much as possible and added nothing more than a larger piece of metal on the trigger. The two guns were more like pistols, and he'd decided to carry one in each hand rather than follow the same route as Spartan.

"Spartan, you're moving in on the shuttle bay now," said Lieutenant Jenkins.

The man had been pretty upset at being left behind, but Spartan had finally persuaded him to remain, as he was the only person on the ship he could genuinely trust to monitor the situation from above. Apart from the pilots, the only others in the shuttle were the remaining four operatives, each armored and equipped in the same fashion as those that had already vanished.

"You guys ready?" asked Spartan.

The men nodded at him but none looked as if they particularly recognized his authority to lead the mission, one that consisted of just six men, as opposed to the substantial force that had already landed.

"I don't think he heard you," growled Khan.

The four men might be unsure about Spartan, but their attitude toward Khan was universal. He was treated as a beast, almost a monster, and one they were continually nervous of. As he tensed his muscles, they could see the straps straining to keep him tied down in the craft.

"Yeah, we're ready, for whatever this is," said one of the older men. Spartan looked to the man and watched him carefully. The weapons and equipment will all subpar, but he was surprised at the amount of gray hair showing on the man's head.

Old men and boys, this is going to be fun.

"Remember, this is a recon operation. We land, get inside, and head for the communications tower, picking up any strangers on the way. We get local access to the security net, and from there, Lieutenant Jenkins will direct us to the prisoners."

"We should just go in and get them all, man," muttered

one of the younger men.

Khan could just about reach the man, and he struck his helmet with the back of his hand.

"Wake up, you fool. Cobb landed with all of his men and got his ass handed to him. That's what happens when you initiate a mission with zero intelligence on the ground and no respect for your enemy."

Khan nodded as he spoke.

"Yeah, these machines are tough. If we're going to get out of here alive, we'll need to land smart and fight smart."

"Khan's right," added Spartan, "We can't just waltz in there and be the hero. If we are gonna save your friends, we need to land in one piece and get some solid intel on what the hell is going on down there. Hell, there could be a hundred machines there or just five."

"What difference does it make?" asked the young Earthsec operative.

If Spartan hadn't been strapped in, he would have struck the fool directly in the face. Instead, he was forced to rely upon a less preferable form of communication to him.

"Kid, I've killed hundreds of their creatures, warriors, and machines. Trust me, they are tough, and they'll chew you and your buddies up before spitting them out. Listen to us, and maybe you'll live. If you want to do your own thing, well, just do it, but well away from us."

He lowered his head just a little and frowned.

"You got that?"

The young man bowed his head and said no more.

"Insolent pup!" laughed Khan.

Spartan raised an eyebrow and then looked back at the live overview of their landing area. He had audio communication to Dauntless only, but it was better than nothing.

"Jenkins, any updates?"

"That's a negative. The landing site looks clear. Watch yourselves down there. Oh, there's one more thing."

Spartan almost didn't want to ask.

"What is it?"

There was a pause of nearly three seconds before the familiar sound of Lieutenant Jenkins returned.

"The weather. There's a small dust storm coming in within the hour. After that though, hell, you've got one mother of a dust storm coming in. I estimate you have a little less than seventeen hours before it hits. It's a Martian Category One storm."

"Understood, Dauntless. Spartan out."

"Uh, Spartan. Have you heard about Category One Martian dust storms?" asked the young operative.

Spartan didn't particularly want to speak with him, but they were only a moment away from landing. He needed people on his side, not waiting to do their own thing once their boots were on the ground.

"And you do?"

"Yes, Sir," said the man, finally using a mark of respect for the man leading the mission.

"The storms on Mars are infamous. Once they start, the place goes on shutdown, and nothing lands or leaves till it's over."

"So we wait it out," suggested Khan.

"No way, man," laughed the operative, "Category One storms last weeks, often even months. I know a survey team that came to assess one of the refineries, and they were stuck here for thirteen months."

He looked at Khan with a grim expression on his face.

"If we are down here when it starts, then we're trapped."

Spartan glanced at Khan whose expression had changed from interest to marked surprise. Spartan then moved his attention back to the man.

"What's your name, son?"

"Darwin Moneaux."

"Okay, then, Darwin. We will be out of here in seventeen hours. You got that?"

The man looked less than convinced, but Spartan extended his hand and pointed to the floor of the shuttle.

"Son, I've landed on all kinds of planets and stations. We are not staying here a minute longer than necessary. Even if that means blowing the place sky high. Twenty hours from now, we'll be back on the Dauntless and laughing about this."

The shuttle swung down low and along buildings on

the other side of the landing area. Spartan had specifically requested they avoid the obvious landing site and came down in the dusty road on the other side. Unlike the landing area, this one was devoid of damage but was littered with several abandoned ground crawlers and containers. Spartan pulled the respirator unit down from where it had been resting on top of his head, and the other operatives did the same. They'd been unable to find one for Khan, so he was going to have to manage with just the air supply fitted to a makeshift mask over his mouth.

"All ready?" asked Spartan.

All of them nodded in reply.

"Good, stay close to me and be quiet. This is a recon, not an assault operation."

The landing was fast and a little harder than expected. They hit the ground, and the skids retracted nearly a meter, almost throwing the craft back up into the air. Spartan grimaced as it lurched about, slid to the right, and came to a halt. He didn't even check to see where they were and hit the access button. The side door snapped open and exposed them to the bitter atmosphere of Mars. Even though the world had been subjected to centuries of terraforming, the icy cold chill slammed into them all. Spartan stepped out and felt the peculiar low gravity that made him feel uneasy and stronger at the same time.

"Go, go, go!"

Spartan was out first, and he moved quickly. His fabric

and armor-covered body looked odd against the faded surface of Mars. Spartan looked back at them to check they were moving, but with the respirator and balaclava fitted, there was no way to see his facial expressions any more. Satisfied they were following, he turned back and continued on his path toward the loading doorway. They moved out in a skipping movement, each taking advantage of the reduced gravity to cover ground more quickly than normal. In seconds, the six were out from the open ground and waiting at the massive loading door. A six-wheeled construction crawler lay abandoned to one side and covered in layers of colorless dust.

"Get it open!" snapped Spartan.

Two of the Earthsec operatives moved to the control panel and inserted their override security unit into the system. Almost instantly, the large door shuddered and then hissed as it lifted. The thick metal device lifted up two meters and then squealed loudly before sticking.

"Typical!" grumbled Khan.

He moved closer, bent to one knee, and grabbed the base of the door, pushing it up high with both of his hands. Even Khan strained against the weight of the door, but in a few seconds it moved up another meter before jamming in tight.

"Inside," he muttered.

Spartan was in first, his pair of TEK40 rifles raised to stomach height across his body. The other four operatives followed close behind, and Khan brought up the rear. There was no light, and all of them were forced to activate their lamps that were fitted onto the weapons. The hard yellow light cast long, hard shadows inside the loading area, but so far they had picked up nothing suspicious.

"Dauntless, Spartan here. We're inside," he said over his mouthpiece.

"Affirmative. Looks like you got in quietly for a change."

Spartan nodded, completely forgetting the only communication remaining was audio. The Earthsec teams were less than advanced when it came to the use of technology, and although his armor came equipped with a camera, it was only for the benefit of those orbiting Mars.

Typical Earthers, it's all about top down monitoring and control.

He recalled the plan of the refinery he'd been looking at on the screens inside the shuttle. The structure of the site was relatively straightforward, with a massive shaft buried deep underground and then a series of habitation zones, transport tunnels, storages tanks, and pipelines. The water towers were actually buried deep inside the rock with a small section no more than twenty meters extending out to the surface.

"Spartan, you know the way?" asked Khan.

"It's okay," said Darwin Moneaux, "I studied the plans on the way over. We need to take the secondary passageway past the pumping house. It will bypass the main habitation area and give us a view of the shuttle landing area. From there, it's about a ten minute trip to the base of the water towers."

Spartan bared his teeth in amusement.

"And that's where the life signs are?"

Spartan nodded.

"Until a few minutes ago, yeah. Let's go."

Operative Moneaux led the way, with nothing but their lamps providing light in the darkness of the refinery installation. As they made their way through the substantial loading and storage area, he looked about, ever vigilant and expecting an attack. Incredibly, they made it the entire way across and to the first set of internal doors. These were barely large enough for Khan to climb through, but once inside and sealed shut, they found a little respite from the bitter cold outside.

"Great, now what?" asked one of the older men.

Spartan noticed it was the same one that had been grumbling on the way down from Dauntless. He walked toward the man and twisted him about. Spartan pull up his respirator and instantly felt cooler air on his mouth. It was cold but bearable, nothing like outside.

"You know what is next. We find out what happened and assess the strengths of the enemy. If we find any survivors on the way, so be it. For now the plan is recon. Understood?"

"Yeah, but what about Cobb? We ain't coming down here and leaving without him. Earthsec looks after its own."

Spartan pulled back his new arm and brought the fist in against the man's stomach. The impact was hard, perhaps a little harder than he'd expected. The man jerked back, slamming into the inner wall and slumped down coughing. Spartan almost regretted his outburst but then saw something move further down the passageway. If he hadn't struck the operative, he'd never have been in the right position to see it.

His weapon was up in a flash, and his eyes watching carefully in the direction of the shape. Khan spotted his movement. As one, the group spun about and took aim with their weapons. Spartan aimed from the hip while Khan didn't even bother to look for cover. He extended both arms toward the target like a gunslinger of old. The choking man remained on the ground, providing the only sound until Spartan spoke.

"Who's there?"

A shadow moved out from behind a container and stepped out into the corridor. It was a man, but his form was obscured in thick cloth. He carried in his hands a short but thick muzzled thermal shotgun of some obscure design.

"Spartan, I see you're making friends again," said the man from deep inside the passageway.

Spartan kept his weapon trained on the shape, but as he watched was sure there was something familiar about him. The shadow moved closer until the hard light from the operatives' lamps bathed him in light. The man was covered in layers of loose clothing and a pair of round goggles that made him look like some desert dwelling wanderer. He stopped in front of Spartan, lowered his weapon, and pulled up his goggles to reveal his ebony black face and piercing brown eyes.

"Marcus?"

"So, you haven't forgotten everyone, then?"

The man's voice had always been hidden behind a thick accent, and over time it sounded like it had become even harder to understand. Spartan lowered his crude weapons and approached his old friend. He lifted his artificial arm, but Marcus stood his ground.

"Why are you here, Spartan?"

He lifted his hands and twisted about to look at the dark passageway.

"Isn't this a little out of your usual place of operation? I heard about APS Corps. Tough times, huh?"

Spartan let the air rush out through his teeth.

"Right, I see."

He looked over his shoulder and nodded to Khan who then moved in closer to his flank. He'd not met Marcus before. In fact, he'd never even heard of him.

"This is Marcus, my old friend from back in the day. Last time we spoke was during the..."

"Fighting for Terra Nova," added Marcus. "Yeah, that's

the last time we spoke."

Spartan looked past Marcus, checking for signs of any more people. He had a hundred questions for the man, but now was definitely not the time. For now, he would have to manage with the bare minimum.

"We don't have long. There's a storm coming."

"You don't say," said his old friend, "I take it you're here to deal with our new friends?"

Spartan nodded, and Marcus looked at the small group before shaking his head.

"Whatever you're planning on doing, you won't be doing it with six guys."

"What do you know?"

Marcus pointed to the way he'd come from.

"I assume the loudmouthed guys that came in earlier were yours?"

Khan nodded.

"Well, they ran right in to the hunting parties those things sent out. It's been days since they landed, and I can tell you now, Spartan, they plan on doing a Prometheus, right here."

"How many have they taken?" asked the older of the Earthsec operatives.

Marcus looked at the man and back to Spartan.

"He's kidding right? The machines have every single person that works here. That's hundreds of men and women, and in a few more days, the butchering is going to start."

He wiped his brow, clearly distressed.

"All that's left here are a handful of your men that came in and the work crew in the lower level security station. The whole lot of them tried to escape two days ago, but the machines found them. The survivors have dug in, and nothing short of thermite charges will dig them out now."

He pointed in front and behind them.

"Every access road and tunnel leading from here to the rest of the bases here on Mars is barricaded by them. Once they start making their fighters, they'll open them up and send them out to the rest of Mars. You remember what those things are like, don't you, Spartan?"

Khan grumbled something, and Spartan had to strike him in the chest.

"Speak up, Khan. What did you say?"

Khan bent down and leaned in close to Marcus.

"I said we either help those that made it to the security station, or we get out of here and destroy the site. There ain't no recon left to do here."

"Destroy the refinery, with what?" asked Spartan. "You know the arsenal on board Dauntless. It's got nothing that could make an impact on this place, not with most of it being so far underground."

Marcus reached out and placed his hand on Spartan's new artificial arm. It was covered in fabric and an armored gloved covered his hand so that it looked like any other arm. As soon as he made contact, his face altered slightly. Spartan couldn't tell if it was surprise or sympathy, or perhaps a little of both.

"I see you've hit hard times as well, old friend?"

He then tilted his head and looked back inside the passageway.

"I can take you to the security station. There's another access shaft running ten meters below the entire base."

"How do you know that?" asked one of the other operatives.

The man stepped up to Marcus and walked around him, examining his clothing and weapon.

"So who exactly are you, Marcus? And how the hell do you know the layout of this place?"

The man tried to grab Marcus' shoulder, but as he reached the clothing, he found Marcus had twisted about, grabbed his arm, and spun him about. In a fraction of a second, their man was on the floor, and Marcus had his foot pushed down into his back.

"I've been on Mars for six years now. That's all you need to know."

He then looked back to Spartan.

"Johnson said you would be coming. Now, are we going to get the survivors, or what?"

Spartan was confused with the information heading his way. One thing he did know was that the clock was ticking, and if they weren't fast, they'd end up trapped inside the refinery and possibly unable to leave for a long, long time.

The machines have timed this damned well. They hit just as the storm arrives. While we muddle about, they will use the cover of the dust storms to take every colony structure, base, and facility on Mars. By the time the storm leaves, Mars will be a Biomech fortress.

He shuffled on his feet as numbness had begun to spread through his left leg.

"We get our people, and then we're finding a way to shut these machines down."

Marcus shook his head.

"You know how many of them are here, right?"

"Yeah, three or four of those arachnid warriors," said Darwin Moneaux.

Marcus almost choked with laughter. He looked at the man.

"You're serious? Okay, if you say so."

Spartan nodded in his direction.

"We don't have much time. Take us to them, and fast."

Marcus turned to the way he'd come from, and the rest followed. They moved in silence for almost a minute. Spartan finally asked the question the others were desperate to hear an answer to.

"So, what exactly landed down here?"

Marcus chuckled.

"A Biomech commander, at least a dozen arachnoids, and more than a hundred foot soldiers. They took control of this place in less than an hour. It was brutally efficient."

"Foot soldiers?" asked Khan.

"Yeah, they match the data from those warriors they landed on Eos."

They kept moving down the passageway, all of them keeping their weapons ready and their torches on. Spartan caught a glimpse of Khan's expression, and it was one of clear surprise. Spartan could only assume his friend wanted to know how Marcus knew what was going on at Eos, something he barely knew about.

"Marcus, what do you mean about Eos?"

He looked to Spartan and could see he had no real idea what he was talking about.

"Eos, the moon of Gaxos out in the Helion system. Our marines fought a major battle there and got their asses kicked. Gun and two entire battalions were stationed there. The Biomechs landed these foot soldiers, and they are tough."

He smiled.

"Don't worry, I know you like a fight. If we're going to make it to the security station, I'm sure you'll get a chance to see a few of them."

They moved further inside the refinery, finally taking several turns into darker, cooler parts of the base. There was no sound this far inside the structure, yet Spartan felt no safer. He watched Marcus carefully as he moved, wondering how the man had found his way to Mars, and more importantly, how did he know so much of what was going on?

"Marcus," he called out, "tell me more about Eos."

* * *

The eight legs of the Prometheus underground facility all met at the central plaza. Based on the last minute orders from her, a series of barricades had been put together that were now garrisoned by a mixture of troops, the majority coming from the stern looking Red Watch. The open ground from this thin curtain wall had been left deliberately open to provide deadly killing areas in case any of the enemy broke through. In the center, directly in the base of the sunken plaza, was Teresa's central redoubt with dozens of warriors and almost as many heavy weapons. A pair of Bulldog vehicles waited in the open space with their doors open and their crew waiting outside for their orders. Every single one of them found themselves in awe of what was happening on the massive video projections.

Teresa and the rest of the defenders watched the space battle unfold right before their eyes. It seemed detached to her as spacecraft filled with hundreds, and sometimes thousands of crew fought and died in the vacuum of space. What made it worse for her though, was that Teresa knew the entire operation was a trick. Nothing more than a way of forcing the machines to unleash their war machines on a planet that was expecting it.

Most watched the video streams directly from inside their armor, but many more watched the unfolding battle on large projections that were positioned throughout the underground base. The wall directly opposite, where Teresa and her comrades were dug in, showed an image of the fight nearly ten meters tall.

"They are putting up a good fight," said Osk, who had only just arrived with her small retinue of guards.

"Indeed they are. It hasn't stopped the assault ships though, has it?" asked Teresa.

Both were fully armored, yet they could see each other's faces through the slightly smoked visors. Osk turned from the live feed and toward Teresa.

"True. The transports took most of the fire from Dreadnought, but she's been chased away. I've never seen a single ship put up such a fight before. It looks like the design did its job. Not that it will matter in the end though. They'll be here soon."

Teresa nodded bitterly.

"I know. It's not just the ship. The crew is one of the best I've ever met. If they are leaving, it's because they have absolutely no choice in the matter."

Teresa knew the fleet had little chance against such numbers. Even so, she'd though ANS Dreadnought and her Liberty ships would have lasted more than the thirty minutes it had taken the enemy. One of the Liberty ships had been rammed, and its shattered hulk continued to spin as it moved ever closer to the fiery planet. The remaining Alliance ships were already moving away from the planet and back toward the safety and shelter of the storms.

"Why not head through the Rift to T'Karan?"

Teresa looked at the images of Biomech fighters pursuing the massive Alliance ship and couldn't help but smile as a cloud of turret fire destroyed all five pursuers in a single powerful volley.

Something tells me they are staying close for a reason.

An alert sounded on her secpad, and the imagery transferred directly to her visor overlay. It was Captain Horner.

"Colonel, the external sensor field shows the enemy formation of ships has released their landing parties."

Teresa closed her eyes and breathed slowly. She knew this was coming, but the imagery of the enemy's assault ships had proven more worrying that even she had thought.

"How many?"

The man's forehead tightened as he explained.

"Ten of the fifteen capital ships made it through our lines. The P7 station took out two, and another went down from the combined missile and gun battery fire coming from us. Dreadnought took out two herself."

Teresa was far from impressed though, she knew that ten more had broken through, and they were all the size of a Crusader class warship.

"And the transports?"

"Two were downed, five more got through, but two are burning."

Teresa quickly totted them up in her head.

"So, three of the old civilian transports and ten Biomech ships got through to the orbit of Prometheus? Is that right?"

"Affirmative, Colonel. All but two are the recently identified Biomech assault ships, codenamed Sawfish. They match the designs of the ships that landed troops on Eos. The others are Biomanta class cruisers."

The names might have been amusing on any other day but not now. Unlike most temporary names, these were based on form and function.

"Also, the large single ship, provisionally codenamed a Cephalon class is with them. We suspect it is controlling the operation."

"I need numbers, Captain. How many landing craft can I expect?"

"Expect?" answered the man, "No, they are already en route. We counted at least twenty of the Bioray landing craft heading for the surface, with half as many making directly for the entrances to the docking areas and shipyards. According to the reports from Eos, these things can land up to a hundred warriors directly into battle. Some can even carry their heavy walkers."

Again Teresa closed her eyes, but the images of the fighting on Eos haunted her almost instantly. It wasn't just the massive mechanical machines that the Biomechs had made use of; it was the variety of biological warriors that really worried her. They were fast, violent, and never ever backed down.

"How long do we have?"

He stopped whatever it was and looked directly at her.

"Colonel, the first Biorays are heading your way. I have the surface guns on them but half have already been knocked out."

A loud banging sound came from far in the distance, and it sent Teresa's heartbeat up substantially. She found herself gulping involuntarily.

"Okay, Captain. We'll take it from here. Is the internal grid online?"

"Yes, Colonel."

"Good, do your job, and we'll do ours."

As the signal cut, a group of two dozen marines surged past her position and off into one of the long open spaces that took them to one of the legs of the base. A trio of Jötnar ran right behind them, all of them holding their modified L56 Mark III weapons low and at the ready. The base began to shake again as if it struck by an earthquake, and chunks of rock began to fall from the ceiling.

"What the hell!" Teresa snapped.

She'd planned for many contingencies, but the possibility that the machine would be able to smash through over a hundred meters of solid rock and two plated sections of metal hadn't even occurred to her.

"No, they can't. Surely not?"

As she finished speaking, a massive section of stonework ripped off the ceiling and came down on top of a pair of workers. They vanished in a mist of blood, and she twisted about to avoid looking at the grisly mess. Teresa turned her attention to the ceiling so far above her, but apart from a small number of cracks, nothing else gave away the position of the enemy.

"Colonel, they are past the turrets. They're inside!" said Captain Rivers over the communications network.

"This is it. Now the real fight begins."

That was when a hole the size of a Bulldog appeared in the ceiling, and the first of the large walkers dropped down to crash to the ground. A dozen heavy guns opened fire from her fortified redoubt in the central plaza. At the same time, the barricades installed at the entrance to each of the long legs of the plaza turned their guns on the center. The machine didn't even have time to steady itself before it was shot to pieces. More holes opened up, and this time and as quickly as it had started, the real gunfire began.

"Here goes nothing."

CHAPTER TEN

Commander Olik was one of the old heroes of the Great Uprising. As part of that glorious generation of synthetics, he fought alongside such legends as Commander Gun and Khan in the greatest battles of the War. His reputation for calm-headed bravado stemmed from the deadly fighting on Euryale. The terrible carnage on that world was more than enough to eliminate the entire population, but the Jötnar held firm, and although they sustained heavy casualties, they helped win that most vicious of battles in the War. In the years after the Fall of Terra Nova, he faded into obscurity outside of the Jötnar until called upon once more to do his duty. Prometheus would be the proving ground not just for him, but also for an entire new generation of his kin.

Heroes of the Great Uprising

Spartan found his heart rate had doubled, but not because of the predicament he was in. No, it had increased so greatly simply due to the information he'd heard from Marcus. Although both of them had avoided bringing up the painful past, Marcus had been quite happy filling in Spartan with the major events of the last months; the exploration of Helios, meeting other races, and the beginning of the project to understand the great enemy of their time, the Biomechs. The part of the story that affected him the most was the news of this comet heading for Helios. He knew when he heard it that the attack was part of a greater plan, one that meant much more than just an invasion.

"What is it?" asked Marcus.

He'd noticed Spartan had stopped speaking. They were still working through the never-ending line of passageways, but he knew that wasn't it. Spartan glanced at him and narrowly avoided striking his head on an array of overhead pipes. Khan grumbled and dropped down to his knees to crawl under them.

"When we were prisoners on the Biomech ship, I saw part of their plan. At least, I think I did."

Marcus seemed intrigued at this new information.

"What did you find out?"

"Well, for starters, they wanted us to give up Helios, to persuade our leaders to pull the Alliance away from Helios. They said they had a score to settle with their enemies out there."

"Where?"

Spartan shrugged.

"Well, I assumed the other side of the Prometheus Rift, so all these enemies in the Orion Nebula. Back then I thought they were talking about the Helions. From what you've told me, they are not too happy with these other races either."

Marcus stopped and waited for the others to catch up.

"Thirty more meters and we'll be directly underneath the cooling pipes. We follow those to the pumping station, and next to that we'll find the security station. Now, it is..."

A clanking noise made him stop immediately. They all dropped down low, and almost as one flicked off their lamps. The sound was dull but repeated at equal intervals. It may have been a set of pistons or heavy machinery as might be expected in a refinery, but this was different, if nothing else because it was increasing in volume.

"You know what that is, don't you?" Khan asked as quietly as he could.

None of them could see each other, but Marcus did whisper back.

"It's one of those arachnid warriors. Since they took control of the place, they've been running patrols of the refinery. Why do you think I brought you down here? You stay up top, you die."

The skittering sound of the thing above them grew louder and louder, finally stopping a few meters from where they were hiding. Not one of the tiny group made a sound until it moved away as quickly as it had arrived. The almost indiscernible clatter of metal feet faded, to be replaced by the gentle thumping of distant machinery inside the heart of the complex.

* * *

Olik ran as fast as he could while making sure he didn't hit any of the Alliance personnel on the way. His large size and armored suit would cause vicious injuries to anybody he might strike as he moved. Less than a minute earlier he'd been at the central plaza, but the news from the second leg of the base had demanded his attention.

"Almost there," he said to himself, rounding the next corner in the massively wide passageway.

As he ran, he continued to monitor the video feeds from the other side of the blast doors. They showed the wreckage of the outer doors that had been torn apart by the suicidal ramming of a damaged Bioray landing craft. A myriad of enemy warriors had emerged through that breach, many of which had then been cut down by the quadruple turret mounts fitted ten meters away from the inner blast doors. Only one camera was still transmitting, and what it showed had shocked even him. He reached the inner layer of blast doors on the third access arm and almost ran directly into the entire platoon of the Red Watch that waited for him. The double width line were as

240

still as statues, every single one of them armed with the new heavy weapons that had been hastily fitted just hours before.

"Ready?"

"Ready!" replied the unit in perfect unison.

He'd never commanded a unit of such young and inexperienced warriors from another region before, and these Jötnar were some of the best-qualified and trained Jötnar outside of those fighting on Helios. He almost felt guilty at being given command of them, when he'd barely said a word to even one. Yet unlike most of them, he was one of the first generation of Jötnar. Like Khan and Gun, the enemy had created him specifically for war. He'd fought hard on Euryale back in the Great Uprising and had taken a painful injury to his face that he bore with pride today.

Those that followed had been a mixture of artificially inseminated Jötnar. More recently they had been assisted by the Alliance to reproduce naturally, much to the concern of the citizens of Alliance colonies. The video feed flickered for a moment, and it drew his attention immediately back to what was happening on the other side of the doors.

"Just look at them," he said quietly.

It was like looking into a nest of insects, but almost all of them were different. Those nearest the camera were bipedal, tall, and covered in a dull iron hide. Some were armed with arm-mounted blades, others with firearms of an alien design. Intermixed with them moved the arachnid robotic warriors, as well as a smattering of the six-limbed robotic tanks. One of these had reached the blast door and was using two of its front legs to smash its way through the metal and masonry.

This is going to be interesting.

Olik looked back at his kin and did his best to hide a smile. Whereas his armor was new, unpainted, and unblemished, theirs was dark red and scratched from months of training. To the uninitiated he looked like the rookie, a warrior with little experience in war. It couldn't be farther from the truth, however. Olik had more combat experience than any other Jötnar on Prometheus, and he intended on using that to make his people's most hated of enemies pay.

"There are seven other legs in this base, each one leading to hangars, shipyards, and to the surface. Once they breach one, they will have partial access to this entire facility."

He looked back to the blast door and then to his warriors.

"I've fought these creatures in more than a dozen battles, and I've never lost one. They are emotionless things, and they have no right to existence."

A couple of the other Jötnar growled their agreement.

"They will not get past us, not on my watch. As long as

one of us is still standing, they will be stuck outside. Do you understand me?"

"Yes, Commander!"

The rank was an honorific one, given by the Jötnar to the one they recognized as their leader in combat. Gun, the first of the freed Jötnar, had taken the name. Ever since it had been used to signify anything from a lieutenant up to a general amongst their kind.

A great rumble came from the other side of the blast door, and Olik took it as an opportunity to shut down the visor on his PDS Alpha armor. All of them lifted their weapons to their shoulders and lowered their stances for balance and stability. It was a heady mixture of weaponry, with most having opted for the Bulldog's assault cannon. A few had decided to make use of the 60mm railgun weapon that looked more like a tank cannon when held by one of them. Olik had opted for the Bulldog L56 Mark III weapon, based on nothing more than Gun's recommendation.

"Olik, what's your status?" asked Teresa.

The image of the Colonel appeared inside his visor, and he noticed the gunfire in the background.

"I'm at the blast door. Sensors indicate two of the Biorays have made it to the outer doors and are sending in troops."

"You're ready for them?"

"Affirmative, Colonel. We will hold them until you say

otherwise."

"Good work, Olik. Listen for my order. When it's given, I will need you and your platoon to join me. You know where. Just listen for the code."

"Understood, Colonel. What's happening in the plaza?"

Teresa grimaced, and the video feed blurred a little as she opened fire. It took a few seconds before the feed leveled off, yet the gunfire continued in the background. A shape moved behind her, and he saw a massive blast engulf it.

"Olik, something managed to burrow through the ceiling. They must have found a way through the upper hangars and are trying to get through. We can hold them. You just stop them coming in from the flanks."

"Yes, Colonel."

A bright white light flickered along the blast door and then began to increase in size. Olik glanced down at the video feed from the other side of the door and noticed the large six-legged walker had moved back. In its place had moved a number of the smaller man-sized figures. One placed something in the damaged blast door, and then they moved back.

"Here they come. Hold your fire!" he called out.

The white light expanded, and with a dull crump, the entire passageway filled with dust and debris. A hole appeared the size of an armored vehicle, and through it emerged five of the bipedal warriors. Olik watched them enter with grim fascination, especially the odd way they moved, as though their joints were incorrectly fitted. They looked about as if admiring the passageway, but then one turned its attention directly at him. Its red eyes glowed behind a mask of dull iron.

I don't think so.

Olik tilted his weapon just a fraction and pulled the trigger. The chain-fed ammunition feed rumbled and pumped rounds directly into the base of the gun. The creatures made it less than a meter before being hit by his gunfire. Olik cried out in pleasure at seeing the immense level of firepower coming from the Bulldog weapon. He looked to his comrades, none of whom had squeezed their triggers. Smoke filled the space between them and the breach, while the bodies of the enemy warriors shuddered and twitched on the ground. He lifted the weapon and grinned the widest smile he'd shown in months.

"That is one hell of a weapon."

More noise continued through the breach, and the suit's internal speakers amplified the sound so that he could hear what was coming for them. He turned back to the blast door and took aim once again. Another chunk of the blast door ripped off until a full third of it had been exposed. Now they came on, like a great wave of machines and the living dead. A good half of them fired their weapons as they came, and sparks flashed about the Jötnar as they were struck by scores of rounds.

"Now!"

The Bulldog weapons carried by the Jötnar would have done enough to wipe out the first wave. The L56 Mark III weapon was more than just a bigger version of the L52. They fired larger shells from their five short barrels, and the motorized loader sent in rounds via reinforced feeds running from the ammunition rack fitted to their backs. Previously, the marines of the Alliance had suffered badly in this kind of fight, and neither the L48, nor its successor the L52, had proven enough to hold back a tide of Biomech warriors. This time it was different, and the barrage of large caliber shells tor the enemy apart.

"To the left," shouted one of the Red Watch.

Olik spotted the shapes he was pointing to. It was a pair of the six-legged walkers moving through the massive breach. They used their front legs to increase the size of the breach while continuing forward. Weapon mounts hung on their flanks, like panniers on a beast of burden, and bristling with small and medium caliber guns.

"Gunners, bring down those beasts!"

Until now the four Jötnar carrying the 60mm railguns had been waiting. Two were positioned on each flank, and all held the massive cannon sized weapons at waist height. Olik put down some fire onto the first of the machines but simply drew its attention. A machinegun weapon blasted him and put a series of dents and small holes into the shoulder plating of his armor. He felt pain in his arm but just shook his body and growled.

"Bring them down, now!"

One opened fire, and in less than a second, all four were firing single shots at the machines. Their rate of fire was slow, no more than one shot per second, yet every single round tore a hole the size of a man's head. The roar from the weapons was deafening, and the muzzle flashes from the hypersonic projectiles were like nothing Olik had ever seen. His smile widened with every single shot, even as two rounds struck his helm and visor. A large crack appeared and then spread, obscuring his vision. He was tempted to raise the shattered piece, but he knew the crashed Bioray had breached the air seals of the station. He would see, but not for long.

I can fight, even if I can only see their shapes.

It might have been as well he couldn't see because a pair of Biorays now swept into the cavernous tunnel. They landed and deposited nearly two hundred more warriors. This time most of them consisted of the bipedal warriors with blades and forearms. One of the Biorays then took off to give space for a third that dropped a trio of the walkers. The massive armored monsters set up station at the rear and brought their guns to bear on the Jötnar line. Olik spotted their movement, but there was precious little time to do anything different. He glanced back into the massive passage leading back to the heart of the base and the central plaza defended by Colonel Morato.

We need that second line!

Olik activated the video communication, and the face of Osk appeared.

"Commander, our line is getting hit hard, and we're down to less than twenty percent of our ammunition."

"I know," she replied calmly.

The camera only showed her face, but he could see the flashes of gunfire highlighting the details of her cheeks as she spoke.

"Colonel Morato is holding the plaza. I have marine reserves already in post a hundred meters behind your position. Give me three more minutes, and then fall back in good order."

"The ammunition?"

"It's on the way. Six Rams will be with you in less than a minute."

"Understood."

Olik needed nothing more from her and certainly no explanation. Osk had earned the respect of her comrades in over a dozen battles. Only a fool would consider arguing with the first of her kind, a female Jötnar that was treated almost as a divine being amongst their race.

"We hold!" he growled to the rest of the Red Watch.

They barely moved, each standing like an armored statue, but all of them pouring gunfire into the passageway. If it had been men in the assault, the fight would have already been over. The foot soldiers of the Biomechs knew no fear, and they were mindless synthetic beasts, controlled either by instinct or directly from the Biomech AI Cores.

If only we could control them, or make them stop like in the War.

If was a vain wish though, as it had never again been repeated. The last days of the Uprising had seen the AI Core on Terra Nova turn on the Great Enemy. Only the direct wishes of the Core would prove able to control the warriors on the ground, and even the most advanced technology and decryption hardware had proven incapable of intercepting and modifying the data from these command centers.

The wall of dead now reached almost a meter in height. Large numbers of the creatures were in shattered heaps around the legs of the Alliance soldiers. Yet from the darkness they came, and the attack seemed to increase in ferocity, not less. Olik brought down three more when his weapon ran dry.

Damn it!

More clambered over the bodies, and he saw one of his brothers dragged to the ground. The enemy warriors hacked and stabbed at him and managed to tear off several pieces of the Alpha Armor. Even as they embedded their blades into his torso, the Jötnar lifted himself to one knee and picked up one of them as a club. He swung the howling creature and slammed it into the face of the second. The third lifted its arm to stab again, but Olik was now there. With a quick twist, he threw his right shoulder into the attack and smashed his plated fist through its face. Gore splattered his comrade, but instead of complaining, he spat out the blood and roared with laughter.

"Can you fight?" he asked.

The Jötnar strained and lifted his battered and badly damaged frame back to his feet. Blood ran freely from a deep gash in his upper torso, but he simply shook his head and stretched his shoulders.

"Yeah, where's my gun?"

Olik looked down and found the weapon, or what remained of it. There were four dead Jötnar on the ground, and Olik unceremoniously tore off one of the Bulldog weapons and dropped it into the hands of the warrior.

"Better?"

He smiled in reply.

"Much."

Movement caught Olik's eye, and he twisted his head about to spot some four-legged robotic mules running down the passageway like a small group of horses. They were the pack version, and each had been fitted out with the large box units containing addition ammunition. He indicated to the nearest, and it turned slightly to run up and stop next to Olik. Its legs folded in, and it lowered to the ground as a stationary ammunition store.

Good timing, my little friend.

The other Rams, as they were known, moved into a position behind the rest of the fighters. Olik turned to his left and deactivated the second feed unit on his armor. It disconnected the current ammunition bin with a clunk. The feed rail dropped down, and he grabbed and then pushed it into the hopper section on the Ram. He had no time to remove an ammunition box and so left it fitted to the Ram. He turned back around just in time to see the next wave of machines and inhuman warriors surging over the bodies.

"I've got something for you!" he yelled, much to the amusement of his kin.

The massive shapes of the six-legged walkers moved to give away their intentions to close the distance. Even more worrying for Olik was the Jötnar sized shapes moving alongside them. At first he couldn't believe what he was seeing, but two of them came out of the shadows, and it looked as though he was looking at his own reflection. The creatures were the same massive height and shape as him, yet these were clad from head to toe in dull black iron, or something at least that resembled it. Each carried a different kind of weapon, with some holding large guns, others a bizarre shoulder mounted rocket unit, and the majority with cruel curved blades.

"Monsters!" he hissed.

There was nothing that the Jötnar hated more than their kin that had been forced to serve the Biomechs. Olik and the others were free of the control of the Cores used by the Biomechs, yet their sympathy and hatred of their enthralled brothers was like no other feeling to them. Either they could be turned or they would die. For those that had been manufactured for war, it was almost always the latter of the two.

"No mercy!"

The sound of his gun was barely audible over the rest of the gunfire. It was the six-legged walkers that did the real damage in the end though. Unlike the weapons carried by the other warriors, the Biomechs had learned to fit larger systems to these machines. The great thump of large caliber automatic cannons filled the passageway. The first volley of their guns hit two of the Jötnar in the front rank and cut both of them down where that had been standing.

"Bastards!" Olik snapped.

He could only just make out their shapes far away, but he could see the streaks of gunfire and the status indicators that said two of his brothers were dead. He moved ahead as a score of the warriors ran in. Without giving them a moment's thought, he grabbed one of the shattered arachnid machines and lifted it up in his armored left hand. The eight legs hung down lifelessly, but the shape itself covered over half of his body. Two of the creatures cut at his left, and he slammed his foot into the head of the nearest.

"Die, you filth!"

Another Jötnar hacked the second down. He did the

same as Olik and picked up a turret section that had been blown off one of the walkers. In seconds, over half of the Jötnar had grabbed the fallen enemies' remains and held them as a grisly shield to protect against incoming fire. One of them laughed, hurling a shattered warrior over his shoulder like a cloak and then grabbed another to push in front. More gunfire hammered into them, tearing holes deep into the flesh of the dead. Olik allowed himself a moment to smile as more blood splashed and splattered over him.

Yeah, that's how we do it.

One of the other Jötnar nodded in his direction before turning back to the fight.

"Commander Olik, you're one of us now."

He cut down two more enemies and looked down. Blood ran down his armor in such quantities the color of his armor had changed to a dull red. Even more blood ran down the cracked visor and thickened along the damaged section.

Red Watch indeed.

The smile on his face began to fade as watched the third of the massive walkers drop down over the bodies and landed just ten meters away. The multiple turrets fitted to its flanks swiveled about and pointed at his comrades. One in particular twisted back and forth before coming to a halt with the barrel pointing right at him. He pulled the trigger on his weapon, and to his bitter disappointment, the weapon jammed on a double feed.

"Typical!"

* * *

Teresa rolled to her side and immediately felt one of the articulated sections of her armor push against her flesh. Two hardened metal spikes slammed down a meter from her head, and a third made directly for her.

"Get down!" cried Captain Rivers.

The officer hurled himself at her, and they hit the ground in a mess on the floor. The metal spike struck the ground and embedded itself half a meter into the stone. The digging machine that had begun pushing its way through the ceiling had become stuck, and for whatever reason, the attack from that direction had floundered. Either because of their defensive fire, or some other fluke, the thing was immobile. The enemy had not stayed idle, however, and they had redoubled their efforts on three of the main arms. A second large group worked down from the upper levels over the base and tried to force their way through the winding passageways leading down to the plaza.

"How are we doing?" asked the Captain.

Teresa lifted herself up and opened up her visor to let in some air.

"We're holding. One second, I need to speak with the

Major."

Captain Rivers nodded and moved off to the right to help those defending the barricades. With the attack above them rendered useless, only a trickle of the enemy warriors managed to find their way to the plaza. Even so, he would be damned if he'd let even one get too close. Teresa waited impatiently until the video of the Major appeared on her visor.

"Colonel," he said smoothly.

"Major Terson. What is the status of the ship?"

"She's ready, Colonel. All we need is the order."

Teresa gulped in another mouthful of air and then reclosed her visor.

"Good, that's what I wanted to hear. Standby and wait for the word."

"Understood, good hunting, Colonel."

Teresa didn't really know the Major particularly well, but his reputation was outstanding in the Corps. More than that, of all her officers, he was the only one with a background in the Navy, having changed service halfway through his career to join the Marines. That knowledge and background was exactly what she thought she would need if the plan worked out as intended. Major Terson had come with the personal recommendation of General Rivers himself. He'd been working discreetly in the shadows with the other commanders to prepare her more secretive part of the operation ever since her talk with the Admiral. She'd also left Captain Tycho and Thompson with him to assist, and they had made rapid progress.

Good work, Major, damned good work.

If it hadn't been for the violence in the plaza, she might have been able to calm down. The Biomechs had so far concentrated the bulk of their efforts on one of the legs of the base but still the odd straggler made it in from other parts. An emergency override kicked in from Admiral Churchill.

"Colonel Morato. Our surface guns forced back the next wave of landers. All we have to deal with it those that are already here."

That was surprising news to her. At the last count, almost all of the surface guns had been eliminated. It hadn't occurred to her that the commander of the outer defenses would have kept so many hidden. Her gut instinct would have been to use all of the defenses to stop the first wave. This was a cold, calculated plan, but it put a smile on her face.

That cunning devil!

"Colonel, the enemy fleet will be overhead again in less than an hour."

Teresa hadn't expected to hear that. As far as she understood, the entire assault had already been unleashed.

"What do you mean? You think another wave is coming in?"

He nodded in reply.

"Our recon birds show they are preparing another wave of Biorays. Those we've beaten off are moving to join them. I suspect they will launch a second final assault as soon as they're in position."

Teresa's thoughts shifted to the waiting ship with its precious cargo aboard. The value of a Biomech commander was understandable, but she was surprised they were quite so adamant in their plans to recover it.

Why this one? Why is it so important?"

The only answer she had to hand was what she'd seen in the reports. This one was certainly a regional commander, and it had been trying to make a run for the Black Rift when it had been stopped and captured in battle. Either it was a big risk on their part, or it had been a plan to get captured in the first place. The only option was the most obvious to her; that the Biomech had been as arrogant as the actions it had carried out. If the machine had truly believed it would succeed, then perhaps its own hubris had allowed its defeat.

"Colonel, you know the plan. You have to ensure they cannot get their hands on Krani?"

That's it!

Of all the options, there was only one that really made sense. The machines were on the move, and that was common knowledge. It was also known that their primary objective was Helios, and after that, presumably the chance to open the Black Rift to their homeworld, and whatever mysteries their domain included.

It has to be the machine's knowledge. Their plan is reaching its conclusion, and they are scared we will learn the Biomech's secret.

The more she thought about it, the more convinced she became. Until now, the Biomechs had never put so much effort into recovering one of their own. If this machine had critical information, then there was also another worry. They might be just as keen to destroy it, as they were to capture it.

That could be a problem!

It was all happening much more quickly than she thought it would, and her heart felt like it would explode out of her chest. She checked her overhead tactical display and noted that all of the eight legs were still under Alliance control. Three were under heavy attack, and it would not take much for one of them to break. The only good news was that all the Biorays had deposited their troops, and there was no reserve for them to make use of.

We just need to hold for ten or fifteen minutes, and we'll have time to rebuild the defenses.

"I'm ready, Admiral. I think we should hold on a little longer though. The longer we can hold Prometheus, the harder it will be for them to get Krani."

There was a short pause on the other end. Teresa looked slightly to her right to see on the indicator that their channel was wide-band and using the security coding from over a week earlier. Against any other foe, it would be almost impossible to access, but it was well known that the machines were the masters of ciphers and decryption.

Let's just hope they heard that and take the bait.

CHAPTER ELEVEN

How did the Biomechs travel between T'Karan in the Orion Nebula, and Mars in Sol? It was one of the greatest questions asked by military commanders, scientists, and politicians throughout the Helion Crisis. It had only happened once in recorded history, yet the disappearance of a T'Kari Raider, and the reappearance of Alliance captives near Earth, left a great question unanswered. The only logical answer was that there must be a third place, a missing Nexus between T'Karan and Sol. As more was learned about the Biomechs, it became clear that unraveling this mystery would prove the key to defeating them.

Evolution of the Biomechs

The route inside the refinery seemed to be taking much longer than expected. They had already been making their way inside for nearly fifteen minutes when the first attack came. It started without any warning when a trio of human sized figures emerged from the dark end of the passageway. Spartan immediately lifted his modified TEK40s.

"Hey, get your hands up!"

None of the shapes stopped and actually increased speed. They moved in an odd way, and they were clearly finding the low gravity an issue as they tried to reach the group. One used its arms to pull itself along the walls. Spartan lifted the barrels and took aim.

"Last warning. Stop!"

His finger squeezed ever so slowly over the trigger, and one of the Earthsec operatives stepped out and lifted a hand to stop him.

"No, they might be..."

Khan grabbed the man and yanked him out of the way. Spartan pulled the trigger completely back. It was perfect timing. Another half a second would have resulted in a dead man, rather than one that was speechless from shock.

"Stay back!" he growled.

The pair of TEK40 rifles drowned out his last words and filled the passageway with bright light. The small caliber rounds hit those approaching with a metallic twang and the occasional meaty thud as some penetrated their thick, armor-like hide. Even so, it took a long burst of nearly two seconds in length for them to be stopped.

"That is one piece of junk," muttered Spartan.

He looked back to Khan and then to the Earthsec man. "Don't even think about doing that again, understood?"

The man tried to speak, and Spartan simply shook his head angrily. As the reverberating sound of the gunfire finally cleared, the Earthsec fighters moved up to Spartan. One of them pointed back into the passageway. Spartan could feel his rage starting to build, and he knew from experience it was always best to find an outlet as quickly as possible.

"Watch your fire, Spartan. There are civvies down here."

He made to move, but Spartan grabbed him about the throat with his left hand. The grip would have been strong, even with his real hand, but with his new improved appendage, he found he could snap the man's neck if he so wished; and right then he was very tempted.

"Listen to me, asshole. I know a man when I see one, and I know when it's alien and heading for me with nothing but a bad attitude and cruel intentions on its mind. Next time you want to find out which one it is, just walk toward it and ask nicely, understood?"

He released the man who then proceeded to cough and choke.

"Now, go and check the bodies out. You might be surprised by what you find."

All of them did, and even Spartan was shaken by what they saw. They were quite clearly not friendly, but they were also unlike anything he had seen before. Previously, the warriors sent by the Biomechs had been a mixture of biological monstrosities and synthetic warriors like Khan. Even the machines had a certain form and structure that these new warriors lacked completely.

"What the hell are these?" he said and bent down to examine the nearest.

Marcus walked up alongside him and placed his fist on one of them, checking if it were still alive.

"I've seen these before."

He then looked at Spartan.

"These are the same assault troops the Biomechs used on Eos. It looks like their battlefield assets are as varied as their ships."

Spartan said no more but examined them in detail. Based upon their armor and weapons, they were definitely not friendly and about the same size and build as Spartan. There was a subtle variation in shade and size that betrayed their construction as something more natural than the mass-produced synthetics he'd seen before. Their skin was hard like metal and colored as dulled iron, with almost no reflection given off. The heads were protected inside a thick helm where a pair of dead eyes stared out. Only one was still alive, and unlike the others, its eyes glowed red.

Either they are bred, or they make them from butchered captives.

He wasn't sure which of the two options turned his stomach the most.

"This one still breathes," growled Khan.

Marcus was there first and dropped in front of the machine. The speed he moved to the alien surprised all of them, and at first it looked as though he was genuinely interested in its safety.

"Are you with the Twelve?" he asked desperately.

Twelve? Spartan wondered.

The creature's eyes moved a little to stare at Marcus, and then with a low sigh it breathed its last breath. Its eyes faded to black, just like the other one. After checking for weapons, they pulled the bodies to one side and continued on their way. The small group didn't make it far before Spartan finally stopped and moved back to Marcus.

"Is there something you're not telling us?"

The others stopped and waited impassively, with just Khan standing with his large arms crossed in front of his chest.

"What do you mean?"

Spartan hissed through his teeth.

"Don't play games, Marcus. I checked the plans on the way here. We've moved around the habitation area, and this is skirting around the mining shafts, isn't it? The Twelve? What in the name of all that's holy is the Twelve?"

Marcus looked to Khan and then to Spartan.

"Yes. You're right. There's a lot you don't know."

Spartan lowered the muzzle of his weapons to the floor and took his time.

"So I'll ask you again, what are you not telling us? What is this 'Twelve' you asked the creature about?"

"Why bother asking?" added Khan, "They don't speak the same languages as us, and they never respond."

Marcus considered his response almost too long, and Spartan had begun to take a step closer when he finally spoke.

"Director Johnson sent me information just before the Rift collapsed. He told me the prisoner on the Admiral Jarvis Naval Station had managed to send out a wide area pulse with information on our dig sites as well as images of what we found."

Spartan looked confused. It wasn't just the fact that Marcus was talking to him about dig sites; it was more than this old warrior was speaking of the Director as if he'd known him for years. The history of Marcus was clearly a complex one, and his knowledge of internal affairs suggested he was a deeply embedded operative of some kind in the Alliance organization. It was that part that intrigued him the most.

"Digs? Like the one on Hyperion?"

Marcus smiled.

"You really haven't been paying much attention, have you?"

Spartan raised a single eyebrow.

"Come on, then, tell me."

Marcus smiled for the first time in nearly two decades.

"There are sites throughout Alliance territory; the Bone Mill on Prime, the Anomaly, the remains on Hades in T'Karan. There are more though. Research at the ruins on Hyperion gave us details of many more sites, as well as scattered information on this group known as the Twelve.

Spartan quickly worked out what he was getting at.

"This refinery, there's a reason they've been digging down so far, isn't there?"

Marcus nodded.

"We found this symbol, one that shows twelve mechanical legs in a circle, like a twelve-pointed star with the feet all pointing in the same direction. Once the signal was sent, the Director sent me a message telling me these machines might try and break into the dig site and recover their comrades. My team was given orders to collapse the entire site before they could get here."

"Dig site?" asked Moneaux.

But Spartan was more interested in Marcus' connection with Johnson.

"Johnson? What team are you talking about?"

It was clear they would move no further until some explanation was forthcoming. Marcus appeared frustrated and eventually relented, but only in front of Spartan and Khan. He demanded the Earthsec operatives watched for signs of the enemy while he spoke.

"Look, I've been here as a freelancer for, well, let's just say a long time."

"How long?"

"Long. Now, Johnson sent over coordinates for the archaeological excavations over a year ago. Earthsec thought it was to do with the first failed colony, from way back. They made it to the bottom when they made contact. Alliance moved in and took over. That was two weeks ago. As soon as we cleared the artifacts, the machines came through the Rift."

He leaned against the wall, a look of tired desperation on his face.

"There were a number of blasts down there, and when I made it to the shaft, everything had gone. I mean everything. Whatever was down there, either it left or they took it."

Spartan wanted to know more, but the sound of shouting from far into the distance cut short the conversation.

"Come on, that sounds like our people. We'll come back to this later."

His interest in the mysteries of Mars paled in to significance when compared to the lives of around three hundred innocents, as well as however many of the assault team still remained. There was also the issue of over three hundred thousand citizens that were scattered throughout Mars, and all of them would be at the mercy of these machines.

"Where does this go?" he asked Marcus.

"Fifty meters and then up the access ladder to the

security station. We can reach the water towers from there. That entire area is triple layered in case of quakes or drilling ruptures. It's the strongest and most secure part of the entire facility."

"And right next to the shaft you had them digging. Didn't any of you have the guts to tell them what they might find?"

It was a weak argument, and even Spartan knew this kind of information was best kept private. Worse than that, he knew deep down that if the information had been made public, the Biomechs would have arrived earlier, and the losses could have been even greater. It didn't make him feel any better though.

"Give me a hand up."

Khan held out his hands and hurled Spartan out through the hatch in the ceiling. Spartan could have climbed it, but his new limb was still causing him a little trouble. Spartan was the first of the small party to make his way into the large compartment immediately below the security station. He had to lift his hand to ensure he didn't strike the ceiling while reaching for the nearest grab rail. He staggered but quickly regained his balance and looked back to Khan.

"I said a hand up, not a throw me up!"

Containers and crates had been piled high near the doors, but the burn marks and bullet holes showed there had been some major fighting in the last few hours. It was large enough to park two or three land cars inside, and the tracks on the floor suggested a tracked vehicle had been parked there at some time recently. Spartan looked down to the others but stopped to look at Marcus.

"I thought you said this place was secure. There's damage up here."

"Any blood?" asked Marcus.

Spartan look back around and noted with interest that although there were marks on the walls and floor, there was nothing to indicate any of the survivors had been hurt or killed in the fighting.

Strange, he thought.

It wasn't so much that there was no blood to be found. It was that Marcus had asked that as his first question.

It's like he never expected there to be blood.

Khan was next, and the ladder groaned under his weight as he squeezed his way up. To all of their surprise he made it through after much groaning and complaining. This particular section of the refinery was at least tall enough for him to stand without stooping. He moved to the damaged sections of the wall and looked at the burn marks.

"These aren't ours. They're Biomech weapons."

Marcus was next but before another could follow a massive boom shook the structure. Dust and dirt filled the air and drifted about in a dirty cloud. Each of them waited for the sound to fade, but instead of becoming quiet, it increased in volume and was then joined by loud banging sounds.

"Sounds like machines."

Then came a sound none of them expected to hear. It was a booming voice, machine like, and completely artificial. The words were alien and meant nothing to any of them, yet there was something that astounded them all. They were angry words and being shouted out. Another powerful shockwave struck the walls, and something howled out in pain.

"They must have reached the survivors. Come on, we have to stop this!" said Khan without thinking.

Spartan tried to hold his friend back, but either from lack of action or perhaps just boredom, Khan had no interest in staying back any longer. He moved in front of the doorway and smashed his shoulder against it. The door burst open and revealed a cavernous structure with a tall ceiling supported by thick columns, each one spaced apart at very wide intervals. Large water towers extended up from the floor up into the ceiling, and gantries ran along the upper levels. He looked left then right, and stopped in his tracks.

"What is it?" called out Spartan.

The sound of a major fight in the distance made keeping quiet almost irrelevant, and the entire group moved out and took up cover behind one of the massive water towers. All of them watched on in awe at the sight before them. To the right were a large number of people, most of whom wore the overalls and helmets of the refinery workers. Some hid behind the towers while others had climbed the gantries and were firing their few weapons at the fight below.

"What the hell!" cried Operative Darwin Moneaux.

A dozen shattered metal arachnids lay smashed about the floor, but that wasn't what had drawn their attention. It was the sight of two Biomech warriors, each nearly twice the size of Khan. They were great robotic monsters, heavily armored, beautifully constructed, and covered in marks, cuts, and scratches. The one machine was faded red and instantly brought Spartan back to his time as a prisoner.

"Biomechs!" hissed Khan.

Spartan grabbed his friend and pointed to the other machine. Its armor was devoid of paint and instead just a rusted steel color. On the legs and shoulders were the markings of the twelve machine arms.

"The Twelve," said Marcus, as though it was some great revelation.

The two massive machines fought like a pair of medieval wrestlers, but they were not the only part of the battle. At the end of the open space, a hole had been torn through the wall. It was easily large enough to squeeze one of the Biomechs through. Dozens of the bipedal warriors came from the gap, and almost half were armed with firearms. The largest group moved in on the humans while the rest ran at the faded and battered looking Biomech.

"Drop them!" snapped Khan.

Spartan, Khan, and the small group of Earthsec operatives took careful aim and then sent down a volley of gunfire. It cut down five of the creatures in as many seconds. The shooting continued, but now a few had turned and began to shoot back.

"Use the cover. Your armor is useless!" said Spartan.

Marcus was already staying well back behind the base of one of the towers, so was Operative Moneaux, who seemed to have finally accepted the authority and knowledge of Spartan and Khan. The others still stayed out and blasted away, taking two more of the enemy apart with automatic fire.

"We can end this if we stay together!" said the oldest of the group.

Spartan did his best to cover them, but the creatures quickly isolated the small group of operatives and put down considerable gunfire in their direction. Worse was the fact that the red machine had hurtled the other machine to the ground and turned its attention on the operatives.

"Run!" screamed the nearest, but it was too little, too late.

The machine laughed something in its own tongue and then sent a ball of energy toward them, vaporizing the little group and sending their fused remains in all directions.

"Bastard!" roared Spartan, and he lurched around the

corner and blasted away. Khan did exactly the same, but apart from adding a series of dents and marks in the metal, they achieved little. The smaller warriors scattered with only a few making their way toward Spartan. Two made it close enough to attack with their edged weapons but were torn apart by gunfire from the battered looking Biomech. It shouted something and then threw itself back at the red machine.

"Finish them off!" cried Khan, and this time he ran from cover and into the small remaining group of the enemy. He crashed into the first and sent it to the floor, and then chased after the rest who turned and made for the breached wall. Even the civilians shouted and cheered; a small number even joining in with whatever weapons they'd salvaged.

"Get the machine!" said Spartan.

He moved out along with Marcus and Operative Moneaux. The three of them put down ineffective fire on the machine, but it did achieve one thing, it caught the attention of the thing. At one point it paused and look back, only for its opponent to deliver a final massive strike. The rusted looking machine slammed its right arm up in a savage uppercut that sent the other robotic monster flying through the air to crash into a lifeless heap on the ground. It turned about to face Spartan and Khan, lowering its arms as if to say it meant them no harm. A few gunshots from the gantries bounced from its armor, but it chose to ignore them.

"Cease fire!" Spartan shouted.

He looked back to the cover he'd so recently vacated and then again to the machine. Khan and Marcus followed him out, and they moved in a widely space line toward the huge machine. Operative Moneaux was close behind them. Those in the gantries finally stopped their fire upon seeing the machine begin to walk toward the newcomers, but without threatening them. Then it stopped and lifted one arm to point at them.

"Uh, Spartan?" said Khan.

The three stopped, but no one wanted to lift a weapon for fear of drawing the ire of the massive machine. A multi-barreled weapon with a short set of barrels began to glow, and then a blast of blue energy tore past the group and vaporized a metal shape just a few meters behind Khan. Two more shapes moved out, and this time they could see what they were.

"Take cover!" cried Spartan.

Both he and Marcus rushed to the first piece of cover, but Khan refused. He aimed at them both with his arms and blasted away, even as they moved in to within a meter. The closest leapt up, its front legs extended like spears. Khan beat aside the first and then threw himself at its body. In one moment, they turned to a brutal melee on the ground; Khan punching and kicking while the robotic warrior did its best to embed its bladed legs into his flesh.

"Drop it!" said Spartan, firing single shots with his weapon for fear of hitting Khan.

"Get back!" said the Biomech that had moved closer to Spartan.

Spartan looked at the thing, speechless as it grabbed the leg of the machine and tore it from Khan. With a single flick, it cast the machine to the wall and aimed its left arm at the robot. Once more the blue glow engulfed it, and half of the machine vanished in a spray of molten metal. Marcus moved from the safety of the column and approached the Biomech, stopping three meters from its feet.

"I'm Agent Marcus Keller, Alliance Special Intelligence Division."

Spartan and Khan looked equally surprised as Marcus explained his rank and position. Even stranger was that he was announcing it to the machine. It seemed to look at him, but then turned its attention to Khan and Spartan. Spartan was still on his feet, but he helped his comrade stand before they all moved to face off against the battered and rusted looking metal monster. Spartan opened his mouth to speak, but the machine beat him to it.

"Spartan and Khan, warriors of Hyperion. I am Z'Kanthu, warlord of the Twelve and one of the Steersmen."

The small group of humans said nothing. Every one of them waited in shock as it continued to speak in crystal clear English.

"The long sleep is over. It is time for us to direct the end of this war, once and for all."

Spartan looked to Marcus, noticing even he looked surprised at the words coming from his mouth.

"Us?" was about all he could muster.

"Yes," answered the machine, "The Twelve will finish what we started. We are the Steersmen, and we direct the flow of life."

Spartan stepped a little closer, lowered his weapon, and stared directly at the head of the machine. He shook his head slowly.

"Prove it."

* * *

The last few arachnid warriors had long vanished into the gloom, and the area of the refinery occupied by the small band of humans was safe, at least for now. The odd sound of movement and very occasional gunfire continued far into the distance, as some of the refinery workers shot at anything that seemed to come closer to this part of the refinery.

"Shall we follow them? Spartan asked, "Those machines are falling back into the refinery. When they are deep enough inside, they will regroup and then reassess their plan. These machines never, ever back down."

"Spartan is correct," said the machine in a perfect, slightly clipped accent.

"The enemy, the ones you call the Biomechs, is already deploying their forces from their crashed vessels. They will be back within the hour."

Marcus looked to Spartan and could already see the question forming on his face. He looked back to the machine and pointed into the darkness of the refinery.

"The enemy?"

"Yes," answered the machine, "we are known as Kybernetes in your languages. Steersmen, I believe, the people that would steer a ship through water. We are the last of our great people that once ruled the stars. All of us are now entombed inside these machine bodies or inside our Cores."

Khan wasn't in the least bit interested in a background tale of woe and pushed past Spartan to speak.

"Who cares? So, your people are dying. If you ask me, that can only be a good thing. Now tell us, how many of them are there on Mars?"

The machine either already knew or simply performed a quick calculation.

"There is just one other Steersman, and she is now gone."

He looked back at the machine.

"No. That's a stupid name. We haven't been fighting for years against an enemy called the Steersmen or Kyber whatever you said." replied Khan, "We call you Biomechs, and that's the way it will stay."

The machine concentrated its attention on Khan.

"As you will. In answer to your query, six landing vessels made it to the surface, as well as a command lander carrying one of my…Biomech brothers."

The machine lowered its head solemnly, nodding toward the shattered machine that was already oozing some unrecognizable fluid on the ground.

"That was Dersna, one of the few that was trapped in this part of space before our exile. We have been sworn enemies since the War. She led a force of seven ships in the past, but your sensor log shows only three made it through into this system before the Rift collapsed and destroyed the other four."

"So?"

"I estimate approximately six bandon, assuming they are using the old way."

Khan raised his shoulder in confusion.

"Bandon?"

The machine looked at him for a moment and pointed its arm at him. An image flickered and then settled that showed a schematic of a Bioray landing ship.

"Bandon is the word we use for a force of warriors. One steersman, no, one Biomech normally commands a force of five or more bandon."

Spartan looked to Khan and shrugged. The machine

already had access to an impressive level of vocabulary and had no problem in understanding this particular gesture.

"It is true. For over a thousand years our people, what you call Biomechs, have made use of these ground forces made up of our machines. The standard complement is three Eques heavy walkers, ten Decurion assault machines, and a cohort of eighty Milites foot soldiers."

Spartan walked to one of the shattered foot soldiers and pulled its iron colored form up the height of his waist. The eyes had already faded from the red glow they had seen earlier.

"So this is one of your Milites?"

"Yes."

Spartan shook the warrior, but it did nothing. With a mutter of disgust, he cast it back to the ground.

"I don't like any of this. What happened to their ships? There's no way in hell the one frigate and the war barge stopped them."

"That is correct. My security protocols were activated the moment you accessed my burial chamber. It was I that connected to your security grid. I am also responsible for collapsing the Rift as the enemy entered the system. The timing was…ah…beneficial."

Spartan paced about the machine as though entering a debate with an equal.

"So you're saying that you wiped out their fleet by collapsing the Rift."

"No, I destroyed three ships and crippled all but the command ship. It was heavily damaged before your two ships finished the job. The landers on your world are all that remain of the Bandon of Dersna."

Cobb and three more of the operatives form the original landing moved out from cover. Three of the civilians joined them and all carried a mixture of thermal shotguns, each one of a different age and manufacture. The weapons were puny in comparison to the gear being used by the operatives and even less impressive than anything carried by the Biomech. The majority of the civilians was much less confident and kept themselves well hidden.

"Spartan, I owe you an apology...and my thanks," said Cobb, extending a hand.

Spartan took it and nodded grimly.

"Yeah, it usually works out this way. Ever the easy ones."

All of them looked back to the machine that waited in silence. Even as it had been explaining itself, the survivors had been checking the area, patching up the wounded, and ensuring every door and access point was secured. All while this was going on, the machine just waited, as though it had never even moved. The preparations finally stopped, and Spartan, Khan, and Marcus moved in front of it and joined the Earthsec operatives who'd kept their weapons trained on it all this time.

"You might as well lower those things," Spartan said.

Khan nodded in complete agreement.

"True. A TEK 40 is about as much use as indigestion against that thing."

It was hardly the most sophisticated joke in history, but Spartan laughed to himself, partially because of the unusual situation they were in, but also because he could remember Khan and Gun from back in the beginning. It was at that time when saying just a few words was a big deal. These days Khan was cracking barbs and jokes just like the rest of them.

Times definitely change, he thought and lifted his gaze to the machine.

Indeed they do.

The machine lowered itself down to one knee and tilted forward upon seeing Spartan's interest. An odd assortment of whistles and grinding sounds emerged from the thing, as panels and sections moved aside from the central torso until the remnants of its ancient host was on display. Unlike others that they had seen, this one was encased inside a transparent metal cylinder that had been fused inside the body of the machine itself.

"It will not be easy for you to trust me. You have my word, and that of the remaining Twelve, that I will not stop until my brothers are made to pay for what they have done to all of us. The last of their kind must be banished to their domain, and they must be stopped from ever returning."

Khan looked at the inside of the machine with great

interest. On the outside the robotic structure look impregnable, but from inside it reminded him of images of the human womb, so soft and vulnerable. He even felt a moment of weakness and was tempted to reach in and cause damage, but a look from Spartan stayed his hand.

"No, not this time," he said quietly.

Spartan looked at Marcus, and the man didn't seem surprised.

"You knew?"

He grabbed his shoulder, but as his hand reached the man, he twisted aside to avoid it and look back at him. He shook his head angrily.

"While you've been busy fighting and killing, some of us have been trying to understand what's been happening for the last few decades. You think it's a coincidence that we found the Anomaly at the heart of the Confederacy right when we were losing the War?"

Spartan looked up to the machine and then took a step forward.

"How long have you been here?"

The machine closed up its body, and it looked like it might be offended at the way it had been spoken to. Instead, it stretched its limbs as if they were weary from use.

"The last of the Twelve and our enemies have been scattered through your domain since our exile half a thousand of your years ago. We continued our war among your worlds, built our warrior factories, and sent ships through the Rifts."

"You built the Anomaly?" asked Khan.

The machine looked at him for much longer than Spartan. It was hard to detect any emotion from a machine equipped with none of the bodily features required to do so. It was the time it took, and the way it moved its upper body and head to look at him that betrayed an unusual degree of interest in the warrior.

"One of our factory soldiers," he said in an odd way.

Spartan looked at Khan and then spoke to the machine. "What do you mean?"

The machine turned its attention back to Spartan, and at the same time large numbers of the prisoners moved down from the gantries. Each of them was curious to see what was going on. A number retained their weapons, and all that were armed kept them trained on the machine.

"We created your kind in our factory stations and ships. My people are few, and you were constructed to protect us from those that would threaten us. Before the War, our domain was weak, our numbers small. Our bandon are limited by the resources of our own world, and the Biomechs to command them. We crafted your kind to respond to preprogrammed Cores to create a safe buffer area around us while remaining fully autonomous and self-serving; and always remaining loyal to us."

Khan spat on the ground.

"You mean you declared war on your friends and occupied their worlds, to keep the last ancient Biomechs safe?"

The machine didn't seem offended at the question.

"Yes and no. Most of the fighting was done by the biologicals. We merely direct them. They do the fighting. Our bandon are used only when direct action is necessary, or where we do not have access to factories and supplies for our biologicals."

The machine sounded remorseful, and that was unexpected to Spartan and Khan.

"Not all of us agreed. We joined with the Twelve and refused to take part. For this betrayal, our kin turned on us and committed a great genocide. We tried to warn the Helions and the rest, but they refused our overtures and instead declared the Twelve the servants of the enemy. We were hunted and killed by both sides, and so the last of the Twelve escaped across the stars to what you call the Anomaly. We built a new home there for the living and for machines while our enemies were banished to their own Black Rift. This lasted almost five of your years until the others found us."

Marcus looked to Spartan.

"The Biomechs from the Black Rift?"

Spartan shook his head.

"You don't say."

He then looked back at the machine.

"So they found you, killed most, smashed your tech, and then just vanished?"

The machine shook its head.

"No, when they arrived their numbers were also few. With no access to Helios, there is no chance of reinforcement. In less than two years, our Biomech numbers fell to less than twenty. Life is more important to us than anything else, even for the enemy. The last battle took place at the place you call the Anomaly. It was a terrible fight and ended with the destruction of the Rift and the scattering of our ships throughout the stars."

"That's how you came to be on Mars?" asked Spartan.

The machine twisted a little to look at him.

"It is how I came to your star, before your people had conquered your own nearby stars. My ship crashed here, and I was lost to history."

Spartan shrugged.

"Well, while you've been sleeping down here, your kin have been manipulating my people through icons, prophecy, and technology to make us turn on each other. Why would that be? If they want us dead, why don't they come out and fight us?"

The machine paused but did not move.

"In the minutes I have been freed, I have already accessed your data device."

The machine pointed to Spartan's antiquated datapad.

"I have absorbed the information on your wars and of

my brothers. It is true, they have worked against you, but you misunderstand their strategy. It is not to destroy you. It is to use you as an asset."

Marcus seemed to be nodding in agreement as it spoke.

"The enemy wants you strong. They never intended on your destruction, just your obedience. They have planted agents and artifacts for many years to prepare you for their leadership. They will remove your authority and take control in their name. I have seen the evidence from the factories you found on Prometheus to the ruins on Hyperion. Your people have improved themselves and honed your soldiers and ships into powerful weapons. They will be their weapons to subdue the other races."

Khan laughed at its explanation.

"Yeah, the trouble is, they already tried that. We fought a war against our own people who had been controlled and supplied by the Biomechs. We beat them. So what can you do now? We don't need your help."

It took a step closer to Khan and pointed at him.

"The comet marks their return to Helios. Those not banished through the Black Rift at Helios escaped the exile and have spent the centuries rebuilding their bandon for their return. That is why we have remained hidden, until this day came. The enemy wanted to use you as a weapon, but we, the last of the Twelve can help your people and stop my kin seizing Helios."

"The Twelve? Who exactly are they, and how many of

you are there?"

Marcus interrupted.

"Spartan, the Twelve were one of the old races, named after their twelve worlds. They were the friends and allies of the Biomechs. They intermingled and interbred with them for centuries until the War. The Biomechs turned on them first and exterminated the entire race before moving on to the others. Some of the rebel Biomechs took the sign of the Twelve and fought back. Our research over the last year has confirmed part of this story anyway, as well as the suggestion that some of these rebels escaped into our territory."

Spartan smiled.

"So, that's what you've been doing all this time. You've been helping Alliance Intelligence to locate and dig up surviving Biomech rebels. Why?"

Marcus looked to the machine.

"Because it was their inscriptions on Hyperion that got us to Orion in the first place."

For the first time in many years, Spartan found himself at a loss for words.

CHAPTER TWELVE

Ships of the Alliance have a long and proud history, but few could argue that the glory days of humanity could be traced back to the dark days of the Great War. Before the Confederacy, and a long time before the rise of the Alliance, was a period of time where colonies were responsible for their own vessels. Colony sponsored vessels and competition resulted in some of the largest and most elaborate vessels ever constructed. ANS Invincible, as she is now known, was the most famous battleship of the Great War, but far fewer recall the infamous incident concerning TNS Endeavour, the flagship of the Terra Novan fleet. It was the destruction of this ship and the loss of nearly twenty thousand men and women that brought about demands for a ceasefire and the end of the War.

Ships of the Interstellar Navy

Teresa watched the tactical overlay of the base and

then the movement of the enemy fleet. The two were intrinsically linked together, and she knew too well that if she timed her part in the operation badly, the entire plan would fall apart. The three legs of the base had been hit much harder than she could ever have expected. Captain Rivers approached her, moving quickly from behind the emplacement he'd been using just a few minutes before.

"Colonel, Commander Osk wishes to redeploy our reserve to form a secondary line for Olik to fall back through."

"How hard are they being hit?"

The Captain's face was hard to see through his visor, but she could tell from his voice that he was worried.

"Twenty-five percent casualties, and another Bioray has landed a final assault wave."

"I see."

Teresa indicated for Osk to approach, and they retired to the safety of the second wall that was only partially completed.

"Commander, we can't hold them back at the entrance. We need to pull back to the base of the leg, right over there."

Teresa pointed off to her right where the passageway Olik was defending could be seen. Passageway was something of a misnomer though, as it must have been at least thirty meters wide at its vast entrance. A number of Bulldogs had parked in a short line to create a temporary barricade while marines assembled additional defenses right behind them.

"Olik, Morato here."

"Colonel," he replied over the communications channel.

Teresa could hear the sound of violence in the background, but none of it stopped Olik from answering her questions.

"We need another four minutes to ready the defenses. Can you hold?"

Then came the hesitation, something unusual from Olik and his people.

"We can hold, but only until they overrun us. There are more coming this way. Sixty seconds at the most."

His voice tailed off as more gunfire drowned him out. Teresa spun about to face Captain Rivers and Commander Osk. She knew they needed a few more minutes, but it was already beginning to fall apart.

Now we have to move to the next stage.

Teresa connected on the open channel to every officer on Prometheus. Osk watched her, waiting for the word. Finally it came.

"This is Colonel Morato. Code Hypos Alpha. I repeat, Code Hypos Alpha."

She looked at Osk, and the warrior did nothing more than nod in her direction.

"Understood, Commander, good luck."

Osk waited in the central plaza along with Captain

Rivers while Teresa ran to the long line of Bulldogs. The side doors of the nearest were already open, and she ran inside to find the crew waiting.

"To Olik," was all she needed to say.

The large wheeled armored personnel carrier squealed as it moved away, and the others followed in a wide line that fill the passageway.

"Olik, we are almost there. Give the order to your troops. It is time."

The journey to Olik took less than twenty seconds, and when they moved to close range, Teresa almost gagged at the sight. Those Red Watch still standing protruded out of the dead like small islands, each surrounded by the dead of the enemy as well as their own dead and wounded. Olik had already pulled back some of his people, and four were dragging wounded warriors from the firing line.

"Protect them!" Teresa shouted.

Her Bulldog skidded to a halt and presented its armored flank to the smashed entrance to the base. Gunfire already struck its armor, and the automated turret mount swung about, adding its own heavy gunfire to the battle. Teresa headed to the doorway and ducked back as a cannon round put a hole through the plating.

"Watch your head!" said the Bulldog's gunner.

Teresa nodded and then moved out toward the Jötnar. It was like a scene from hell, with blood, gore, bodies, and smashed armor as far as she could see. If it had been regular marines in this place, the tunnel would have fallen a long time before, but to the Jötnar it was just another fight. Even as they were cut down or wounded, they kept on; and it was working. Only a scattering of the enemy remained, and the bodies littering the place slowed them down further.

They're insane, all of them, Teresa thought, watching with an odd mixture of horror and fascination.

One of the robotic arachnids reach Olik, but he smashed it aside with his armored limbs and then blasted it from less than a meter away as he roared in anger. Another small group of the bipedal warriors climbed over a fallen Jötnar, only to run right into the path to two injured Jötnar. The gunfire tore the enemy soldiers apart, and they then dragged their wounded comrade back to safety.

We need them out, fast!

Teresa took aim and fired a burst with her L52, noting with satisfaction as one of the creatures stumbled and fell. It tried to get back up, but another Bulldog tracked its movement and decapitated the thing with a short burst. The other Bulldogs soon arrived and joined in. From within each vehicle came a small fire team of marines, each moving out and keeping low. They went to the fallen Jötnar and helped remove their heavy weights to the waiting vehicles. The entire process took almost a minute, but with the heavy gunfire from the vehicles and the last few Jötnar, they were able to get the last of them on board until only Olik remained. The lone Jötnar waited just three meters from Teresa's vehicle and continued firing; the muzzle of his gun already glowing red hot from the massive quantity of ammunition he'd fired.

"Olik, now!" Teresa shouted.

He looked at her, then back to the Biomech horde continuing to come. A few more bullets bounced off his armor and struck the Bulldog before he dropped the unit and threw himself into the back.

"Go, go, go!"

With the screaming of engines and burning rubber, the Bulldogs turned and rushed back as fast as their drivers could safely do so. As quickly as that, the leg that Olik had defended so capably fell, the Biomechs redirecting their efforts into that single location. Teresa watched them climbing through the shattered entrance as they pulled away and turned her attention back to Olik.

"That was a mighty fine piece of soldiering, Olik."

He pulled up his cracked visor and opened his mouth to speak. Thick blood dripped from his lip, yet the smile was impossible to ignore.

"Is it working?"

Teresa nodded, as much for her as it was for him.

"Yes, so far. Now comes the interesting part. Are you ready for it?"

Olik seemed a little out of breath but managed to answer before leaning back inside the vehicle. It was cramped enough for Teresa, and she was surprised he'd managed to find a way to fit. They passed the new line of defenses and hurtled onward to the barricade that guarded the entrance to the hangar containing the Biomech prisoner. The gunner jumped in surprise.

"Holy crap! We've got two up top!"

He spun the turret about, but Teresa grabbed his hand. "No, not yet."

He didn't look convinced, but the stern expression of Teresa, combined with the blood splattered and angry looking Olik, quickly deterred him. They carried on with two of the Bulldogs following. The rest pulled to the right and formed up behind the defensive line, waiting for the assault. Those inside watched the two creatures holding on to the top of the Bulldog with fascination. This was the closest any of them had been to the beasts without them trying to kill them. Even as they rushed past the barricade and into the hangar, they stayed on the surface of the vehicle.

"Now?" asked the gunner, his nerves beginning to fray. Teresa shook her head.

"No, just keep your eye on them."

As quickly as they had passed the outer barricades, they were inside. The thickened steel barriers dropped down behind them. For a moment they were safe. The vehicle continued forward and moved alongside the massive ship that sat waiting. The powerplant was online, and of the crew and marines she'd stationed there, only a handful remained on guard along the base of the landing ramp.

As soon as the Bulldog stopped, Teresa hit the door button and lifted her weapon. In perfect synchronization, the two Biomech warriors dropped down, their red eyes glowing with evil intent.

"Drop 'em!" she cried.

Those inside opened fire, as well as the gunner that had been monitoring via the top-mounted turret. The two didn't stand a chance and were quickly cut to pieces. Olik laughed at seeing the destruction and forced himself from the vehicle and onto the ground. He groaned when he put weight back on his legs.

"Are you okay?" asked Teresa.

"No problem, let's do this."

She nodded and walked back to the ramp. As soon as her feet hit the metal, the sound of the engines began to build. Major Terson met her at the top and beckoned her inside.

"Colonel, we're all ready for the next phase."

Teresa stopped but only long enough to make sure the rest of them climbed inside. The massive, spacious hangar was now completely empty, even though it was still being guarded from the outside. The door slid shut with a slow groan behind her, giving her just enough time to contact Admiral Churchill. Before that, however, she connected to directly to Osk.

"Commander."

"Colonel Morato, I see you've made your move. Good luck, we'll do our part here."

"Thank you, Gun would be proud."

Teresa then connected to the Admiral. The door now closed firmly, and a loud hiss spread through the vessel as the seals pressurized.

"Colonel. Are you on board?"

"Yes, Admiral. Tamarisk II is ready to leave Prometheus."

"Good. You know the plan. Next time we meet, we'll raise a glass to this little adventure."

"Indeed we will, Admiral."

"God speed, Colonel Morato."

* * *

Admiral Churchill could hear the sounds of battle from his post and from the myriad of camera feeds leading directly to this one place on Prometheus. The bulk of the attention had taken place at the base of the section that Olik had been defending. He tapped the icon near the heaviest fighting, and an image of Osk appeared.

"Commander Osk, what is your status?"

"Admiral, the enemy has launched a final assault with their remaining forces. The main tunnel is full of their foot soldiers."

He looked over his shoulder and watched the external

feeds as Tamarisk II lifted slowly from the mighty hangar and ignited her engines. It looked like she might crash into the sheer wall, but the huge section of metal and stone slid apart allowing them access. The ship was out of the base in seconds, moving faster and faster through the shaft as it headed for the surface. He waited until the vessel was clear of the ground before speaking again.

"It is time to end this. Are all your people clear?"

"Affirmative, Admiral, we have fallen back to the plaza."

"Good work, Commander. Enjoy the show."

The signal dropped, and he gave the signal to Captain Horner.

"That's it then. Activate the charges."

The station's tactical officer turned to his display and ran his hand over a series of detonation icons. They required a specific order and timing, but after four seconds of tapping, the system was ready. He held his breath and then tapped the display. All of them watched with satisfaction as a number of charges fitted along the flanks of the vast tunnel were triggered. Each one sent a great gout of flame, sharp metal, and broken rock into the center where the Biomech horde stormed ahead. When the dust finally began to clear, only a handful of the enemy remained standing, and all of them were badly injured. Admiral Churchill couldn't have been happier at the result.

"Great work. Send in the marines to finish to job."

* * *

Teresa pulled on the thick safety straps and locked the buckled. It clamped shut with a reassuring firm clunk sound. From where she sat inside the armored cockpit, she had the perfect view of the escape from the Prometheus facility.

"Come on, pilot, get us out of here, and fast!"

Teresa hadn't even noticed until now that the man at the controls was none other than Intelligence Director Johnson. The side of his face was unmistakable though, and when he spoke to Captain Tycho, she knew immediately who it was. There were only four of them in the cockpit, and they sat in two pairs, Johnson and Captain Tycho at the front, she and Captain Thompson in the next two. Olik and the other members of his team had moved to the cargo area and joined the platoon of marines already stationed on board.

"Hold on to your hats!" said Director Johnson.

He dumped more power to the engines, so much so that the internal gravity system struggled to match the acceleration, and Teresa could feel herself pinned to the seat. It calmed down a little after a few seconds, but only because the system had caught up with the ship's escape.

"What in the name of all that is holy are you doing here?" she asked.

Teresa's voice was hoarse and almost out of breath.

Johnson twisted in his seat and glanced at her, smiled, and then looked back.

"Teresa. Good to have you back there, just like old times!"

He wasn't wrong either. Teresa found it hard to not think back to their time aboard the original Tamarisk. It was the insertion craft for the original Prometheus rescue mission. It made her feel old thinking about that event, especially as it had been so early in the last war. Right when Kerberos had fallen to revolt.

A lot has changed.

She looked at her two captains, both of whom were busy checking the monitors for signs of trouble. It wasn't really necessary though. She spotted the ships through the mainscreen in front of them and lifted her arm to point.

And a lot has stayed the same.

"Yeah, I see them," said Johnson.

The ship shared much in common with the basic philosophy of the original Tamarisk. The vessel was relatively small but equipped with armor, powerful engines, and was surprisingly nimble. As they burst out from the low orbit of Prometheus, the engines rumbled even harder.

"Look!"

Johnson pointed slightly to their right where a whirling maelstrom had appeared.

"The Rift," Teresa said quietly.

"Twenty-three minutes to get there at this speed, assuming there are no problems. Those ships are out of range right now."

He was referring to the craft Teresa had pointed out to him. The large formation of ships was moving around the planet, but it was hard to tell exactly what was happening from the visual feed alone.

"They might be out of range, but they know something's up," said Captain Tycho.

He focused his attention on the largest of the ships, the one that matched the shape of a massive trilobite type vessel. On closer examination, he could see an increase in the glowing around the engines. The numbers alongside the ship confirmed his assessment. The computer performed a very quick series of calculations before giving him a simple figure. It left him feeling numb.

"Director, that ship has changed course. It's not on a pursuit vector anymore."

They all knew what he was saying, but it took Teresa to ask the question.

"They're heading for the Rift?"

He nodded slowly.

"Not just their command ship, their entire fleet. And at that speed, they will arrive at the Rift within two minutes of us."

Johnson nodded.

"In that case, we'd better make sure we get there with

time to spare."

With almost perfect timing, as he finished speaking, the ship shuddered as though it had just broken the sound barrier. The view from the cockpit shifted slightly and then adjusted to level them off.

"Problem?" asked Captain Tycho.

Director Johnson tried to look at the status screens, but more heavy impacts shook the ship, and he was forced to concentrate on keeping Tamarisk II on a level course. Captain Thompson accessed the gunnery controls and camera units so that he could scan the surface of the ship.

"Nothing yet. I don't see any ships out there."

Teresa remembered the images of the battle around the moon of Eos in orbit of Gaxos in the Helios system. There had been many different types of ships, but also a large number of Biomech fighters, something that was new and hadn't been seen in numbers before.

"Check for fighters. Remember, they are fully automated, no biological signatures, and difficult to spot on the heat trackers."

Both captains altered their settings and began a detailed scan of the area around the ship. On one screen in front of Captain Tycho was a schematic of the ship, and around it a chessboard type design that showed space in three dimensions. One red dot appeared, and then another, and then a total of seven small shapes filled the unit.

"Oh, crap, we've got trouble," Teresa said, "Get on the

guns and bring them down."

Director Johnson shook his head.

"Sorry, Teresa. That's one thing we didn't quite have time to finish."

"What? You're telling me we have no guns?"

He turned to her and grinned, an expression that almost matched something she would have expected from Spartan.

"No, the guns and turrets are fine, but there's no automated computer control of them yet. They need to be controlled and tracked manually via the monitoring station back there."

He pointed at the small computer room behind the cockpit. It was narrow, and banks of computers filled both sides. Teresa ripped off her straps and immediately bashed her head on the ceiling. Luckily, she'd lifted her hands, but the bewildering array of forces from the gravity generator and the accelerating ship made it almost impossible to move.

"Shut off the damned gravity generator. We'll do this the old way."

She then looked to her captains.

"Tycho, you stay here and help Johnson. Thompson, you're with me."

The gravity shut off as he unbuckled himself. The two of them carefully entered the next section of the ship, while keeping a firm grip on the multitude of grab handles fitted throughout. Teresa bashed her PDS Alpha armor several times before making it to the seating and dropping in. Captain Thompson went past, but as another strike hit the ship, he lost his grip.

"I've got you!" Teresa called out.

She swung him down with one hand. He grabbed another handle and dropped down into the position behind her and facing away.

"Thanks, that could have been…painful."

Teresa said nothing and turned her attention to the targeting matrix. It was modern, state-of-the-art even. It showed a view from the turret mount on the side of the ship, as well as a radar system for identifying and tracking the movements of the Biomech fighters.

"I'll take the dorsal mount."

Captain Thompson nodded in agreement.

"Sure. I'll take the flank guns."

Teresa put her hands on the unit and moved it to control the target selection of the weapons. As soon as she tapped it, there was a clump like something had just broken off the ship.

"It's the turret covers. Don't forget, we're supposed to be an unarmed transport."

The Captain nodded and returned to his own screens and controls.

"Colonel, whatever you're doing, it isn't working. We're taking gunfire to the starboard engine mount. A few more hits like that, and we'll get to the Rift too late."

"I know," she shouted back, "Just give it everything you've got!"

Each of the dorsal turrets adjusted to track exactly where she was pointing, and they moved quickly and precisely. Although there was no way for sound to travel outside the vessel, she could certainly feel the grinding of the massive motors as they rotated above and behind the crew module.

There you are.

The shape of a tiny Biomech fighter came into view right behind the ship. For a second, it vanished too low for her to hit, but as it popped up, she flagged it and then hit the burst button. The transport vibrated a little as the row of four turrets opened fire, each of them emptying their cargo of 20mm flak rounds right at the craft. The guns were primitive in design and far less advanced than the railgun or particle beam technology used on almost all warships.

"Come on, they're hitting the engines again!" shouted Director Johnson.

Teresa ground her teeth and swung the turrets a few degrees to the right. Most of the rounds missed, but at least one struck the lead fighter. The initial impact was less than inspiring. It began to spin. After a few more seconds, it lost control and then spun out of view.

"One down!" she said.

Captain Thompson monitored the flanks from the multiple cameras fitted all over the outside of the ship. While one group of fighters hit the rear, the second larger group zigzagged slightly above and below so that one moment they were on the left, and the next they were on the right.

"Stay still, damn you," he muttered.

The transport thundered on, its engines continually dumping more fuel into space as they accelerated faster and faster. The Biomech fighters had no problem in keeping up and even after three of the seven were downed, the remaining four split up to harass the aft of the ship.

"How's she doing?" Teresa asked when one of the fighters vanished once again.

"Not good, one of the fuel feeds is severed. Any second now, and we're going to lose power to that unit."

"What about that?"

Although she was seated in the next section, she could still see inside the cockpit and the view out through the main screen. Right in front of them was the unmistakable shape of a Biomech warship. Director Johnson nodded in agreement.

"I know. It's one of their Ravager class ships. I assumed they would stay in low orbit and continue dropping off troops. It looks like your plan is working after all."

The clatter of auto cannons persisted as the turrets continued their work against the fighters. From outside, it looked as though a small cloud of flies were buzzing around a sugary treat. Gray streaks shot out from all directions about the ship, as gun after gun picked out at them, and one more fighter exploded in an orange flash.

"Yes!" cried out Captain Thompson, forgetting himself for a moment.

"Great work, now all…" she said before she spotted what the last three fighters were doing.

"Brace, brace, brace!" was all she had time for.

The three remaining fighters must have received a signal because as one they accelerated at high speed toward the rear of the ship. The two Alliance officers pumped round after round at them, and even though they managed to cripple one, it wasn't enough to stop the combined wreckage of three Biomech fighters from hitting the rear. They struck with a sickening crunch that echoed throughout the ship. The hum of the engines stopped immediately and was then followed by the sound of alarms.

"We're in trouble," said Captain Tycho.

"He's right," confirmed Johnson, "Engines are offline, guns too."

He turned back in his seat to look at Teresa.

"We're a sitting duck."

Teresa didn't say a word. She was busy looking at the image of the large Biomech ship coming at them. She lifted her hand to point at its biological design.

"Now we're done," Captain Tycho whispered.

The bitterness and disappointment in his voice was hard to hear. Teresa, on the other hand, looked positively angry, but far from beaten.

"That's not an attack ship. It's a Bioray."

All of them looked as the colorful vessel moved ever closer. Johnson considered it and then turned to the others.

"You're right. They mean to board us. That means we have a chance. I need anybody with technical knowledge to come with me. We need to get the generators back online. Then we'll have minimal engine power and guns."

"What do you want me to do?" Teresa asked.

Johnson had already pulled himself past her before stopping for a brief moment.

"Get down to Olik and the others and prepare to repel boarders. Something tells me we'll have company very soon."

* * *

Admiral Churchill watched the shape of Tamarisk II as the explosion enveloped the rear of the ship. He felt his heart almost stop for a moment. It looked like the ship had been destroyed. Unlike other regions of space, this particular point was surrounded by thick energy storms. The deadly unchartered parts of the storms were a block to direct travel, and for the last few weeks the storm area had drifted ever closer to the Rift entrance. The crippled Tamarisk II drifted out of control only a short distance from the deadly tendrils of the storms. Even as he watched, a series of small flashes marked secondary explosions along her aft.

"No, it can't go, not yet," he said quietly.

He didn't want to, but something forced him to look up. He was astonished to see the ship was intact but venting substantial amounts of propellant into space. It had started to roll but very slowly.

"She's dead in the water, and the enemy has ships moving to blockade the Rift. We also have a single Bioray on an intercept course."

The Admiral rubbed his hand on his chin.

"What about the rest of their forces? Tell me they are falling back."

Captain Horner checked the status indicators on his display for all the combat units in the base. Most of the action was still taking place near the plaza, and it took only seconds to get the full picture.

"Commander Osk has full control of the plaza. Biomech forces have been routed from all areas other than the hangar for Tamarisk II."

"So, more made it in, how?"

Captain Horner pointed at one of the screens. It showed the tunnel the ship had used to escape to the surface. All of the defensive turrets had either been destroyed in their crash or during the short and bloody battle.

"Two Biorays made it down the tunnel and crashed inside the hangar. Osk has sent two platoons to deal with them. Other than that, the base is safe and secure."

Admiral Churchill looked unconvinced.

"Two Biorays, that's about two hundred enemy troops. Am I right?"

"Yes, Admiral, but Osk sent in the Red Watch. They are more than capable of dealing with them. After the fight with Olik, I think the rest are looking for some payback."

He looked back at the images of the ship.

I bet they are. Still, rather have them with us than against us.

"So, the primary assault here has failed, and their fleet has redirected to deal with Tamarisk II."

He pointed at the Biomech ships on the screen.

"All of their ships?"

Captain Horner nodded.

"Yes, Admiral. The entire Biomech fleet is redeploying around the Rift to block their escape and to take control of Tamarisk II. Unless she gets her engines operational soon, they will not make it."

"I see."

He tapped the icon to the ship and reached Director Johnson almost immediately.

"Director, what's happened?"

The video connection was down, but the partially jammed audio remained intact.

"Admiral, we have engine damage and breached

compartments. I have teams moving back to restart the generators, but it's going to take time."

"You don't have long. They are sending a Bioray right for you."

"Understood, Admiral. The engines should be back in a few minutes, but we're not gonna be fast."

"What about your guns?"

"Computer targeting is down until the generators are back. I have the Colonel getting marines in position to repel boarders. The guns can be worked manually if necessary, why?"

"I see. Forget defending against a boarding action. I need your troops to keep them busy until..."

"Until what, Admiral?"

"Just hold them for twelve more minutes, and you'll be clear to make a run for the Rift. Just make sure you use any power you have left for the run. Have you got that?"

The audio cut, and the Admiral looked to the Captain who'd been listening to the entire conversation.

"Is it time?" he asked.

Admiral Churchill nodded.

"Send the signal to ANS Dreadnought. It's time for them to come out of hiding."

All eyes inside the Prometheus base turned to the vast storm clouds that surrounded the world of Prometheus. Arcs of lighting flashed back and forth, and the clouds themselves seemed to glow with pure energy. One crashed down only a short distance from Tamarisk II and faded away into the blackness.

"There she is!" said the Captain in a much too excited tone.

At first it was just the bow, but then the entire bulk of the heavy warship emerged from the clouds of energy. She had been lashed from bow to stern, and there were scorch marks and superficial damage to almost every external part of the hull.

So, the displacements fields worked, to a point.

He made a mental note to thank the engineer teams for those modifications, especially the work of the renowned scientist, Sanlav.

CHAPTER THIRTEEN

Hyperion had proven itself many times to be a valued training ground for Alliance marines. Through an agreement forged with the Jötnar leadership, a number of training bases were established so that new recruits could hone their skills on such a dangerous world. It was the only place where the offspring of the Biomechs' hideous beasts were allowed to live and roam in relative peace. The large numbers of dangerous creatures gave the marines a new way to test their survival skills, and more importantly to the Jötnar, it gave them another reason to hold their infamous hunts. These events were known throughout the Alliance as an almost guaranteed way to get a nasty injury or possible even lose your life. For most, that was a risk too far, but to the Jötnar, it made the adventure all that more entertaining.

The New Colonies

Spartan paced forward and backward and then stopped

in front of Marcus. Khan and the Biomech Z'Kanthu were also there but said nothing. He looked at his old friend and though he wanted to trust the man, he was still finding it difficult to shake of their last encounter. There was little love lost between them now, and under other circumstances, he might have simply struck him with his fist. He seemed to have firsthand knowledge of the Mars installation and access to Alliance Intelligence.

I still don't trust him, he realized.

"Marcus, are you certain this will take us to the top-level landing platform? Is it even intact?"

Marcus nodded quickly.

"Trust me, Spartan. I know my way around this place. This access shaft is for tracked vehicle to take parts and supplies from the platform to the lower levels."

He then indicated toward Z'Kanthu with his thumb.

"Plus, it's the only way up that is big enough for him to get through."

Captain Cobb moved closer with his small group of operatives and an equal number of the civilians that they'd rounded up so far. He had said relatively little up until this point.

"Spartan. Isn't it time we made contact with Dauntless? We need help down here."

Z'Kanthu moved his torso slightly.

"That would be unwise. The enemy could intercept communications other than direct line-of-sight. We can hold them here, but not indefinitely."

"How tall is this tower?"

Marcus looked up. The tunnel was a wide, winding affair that had been cut directly into the rock of Mars.

"It doesn't so much extend out of the surface. It's more a deep tunnel that runs to a landing system about three stories above the surface. The bulk of the tower is under the ground. For safety, it is completely isolated from the rest of the base. The only way in is either from the bottom or from above and through the landing platforms themselves.

Captain Cobb seemed satisfied with the explanation.

"Makes sense. My plans for the site show three similar structures. What about the rest of my civilians back there?"

Spartan shook his head.

"Not today, Captain. We get this group to safety, and then we can start thinking about what to do with the rest."

"Spartan, I have my own resources. We can..."

Khan moved between them and raised his hand to point, but Cobb assumed he was about to strike him. He lifted his weapon, and Khan merely batted it aside, knocking the rifle to the ground.

"No, not with these people. You saw what happened when you went up against the Biomechs. You fought and they kicked your ass, plain and simple."

Khan was correct, but the pained look on the Captain's face betrayed a helplessness Khan would never truly understand. He lowered his head just a little and moved to the fallen weapon. He bent down, grabbed the rifle, and then looked back to Spartan.

"We might not have the weapons, the armor or the training, but I'll be damned if we're going to leave our people to be butchered down there. I've seen the stories from Prometheus and the Bone Mill. Those things...it can't be allowed to happen."

Spartan placed his hand on the man's shoulder.

"I promise you, once we have these people away, we'll work out a way to help the rest. Better some saved today than none saved tomorrow. Understood?"

Captain Cobb nodded reluctantly and walked back in the direction they'd been heading for some time. The rest kept on moving with him until just Spartan and Z'Kanthu remained. As Spartan followed them, the machine spoke.

"I am detecting the presence of the enemy. They are coming."

Spartan closed his eyes a little, and they looked back down the tunnel. It was a long way back inside.

"How long?"

The machine paused, and it seemed Z'Kanthu might not have heard him. Spartan started to speak again, but it interrupted him.

"There are few at the moment."

Again it paused, looking back in the same direction as Spartan.

""'They are Thegn scouts. It will take them nearly fifty minutes to make this climb. We must keep moving. As soon as they find us, they will call upon the rest of the bandon, and then the main attack will begin."

Spartan needed no further encouragement.

"Then let's get to the top of this place and get a signal out to Dauntless."

He was about to move but looked back.

"You said you deactivated the Rift back to Terra Nova, didn't you?"

The machine nodded it archaic armored head.

"That is correct."

"Can you reopen it?"

The machine extended its arm, and a panel opened to reveal some kind of computer communication system. At least that was what he thought he was looking at.

"Of course, why?"

Spartan grinned so widely his crooked teeth showed.

"Because we're going to make a telephone call."

The machine's grasp of Spartan's language had been impeccable up until this point. As the Alliance warrior moved away, it watched him and tried to understand exactly what he had just said.

Telephone call?

* * *

The journey to the outer hull of ANS Tamarisk II had been a truly worrying experience for Teresa. She'd only made it halfway to Olik when Director Johnson had contacted her and given her the change of plans. Her APS suit had been designed to operate in all environments, including deep space, but it was something she'd never been fond of. With the artificial gravity system offline, it reminded her of the old days when the fleet had been based around large ships packed with rotating sections.

Here we go.

Teresa pulled open the final airlock door and instinctively held her breath. It slid open smoothly and with no noise of any kind. Moving from the ship required a sharp tug on the grab handles, and then she was out in space. Captain Thompson followed behind, along with four more marines; each armored and armed in the same fashion as her. Teresa moved aside so each of them could move from the airlock. She then ensured it was closed and sealed behind her.

"You know the deal, and the plan has changed. Johnson needs the guns online while the engineers get the generators back. Each of you to the turrets, and keep your heads down."

A chorus of acknowledgements came from them, and then they were off. ANS Tamarisk II shared a basic design philosophy with the original ship, but the actual layout was completely different. It was a much more streamlined and far more elegant vessel that demonstrated the sweeping technological changes that had torn through the Alliance following the Uprising. That had been partially to advances made during the military build-up in the War, but mainly down to the reverse engineering of captured Echidna technology.

Keep your eyes on the job.

Teresa traveled along the side of the ship and pulled herself over the top and onto the dorsal section. Large container sections were dotted along the hull, giving the impression they were designed to carry all manner of supplies. In reality, these containers were armored sections that hid the guns systems from view.

Almost there.

It took Teresa a little longer than she'd expected to reach the already open section. The route she'd taken required climbing around a large number of communication arrays and escape systems. It was a little confusing because from a distance the upper hull looked much smoother and clearer than it actually was.

"Colonel, are you there?" asked the Director.

"Johnson, have some patience. Half of my unit is in position. I'm almost at my station."

"Okay, good. Can you see the Bioray?"

Teresa stopped for a moment and looked slightly to the left off the bow to look for the ship. It wasn't easy to spot the shape even at this close range, and it took a few seconds her eyes to adjust until she found it.

"Yeah, I see it. How long do we have?"

"Well, she's holding position at one eighty kilometers."

"Holding, why?"

"Because they've launched small assault craft. I estimate they are about the size of a Cobra, maybe up to the size of a Hammerhead."

Teresa shook her head and sighed.

"How much time?"

Again there was a short pause, and then he returned. Teresa could tell from the tone in his voice that it wasn't good.

"Forty seconds! Teresa, you have to stop them coming aboard. My guys need five more minutes at the very least."

"I'm on it!" she replied and pulled herself inside the shallow container where a pair of quad mounted auto cannons sat motionless. The sides of the container had folded back so that they now only extended about a meter from the hull. It left the turrets exposed and vulnerable but also provided them with a full degree of movement from the front to the back of the ship; as well as an almost completely clear three-hundred and sixty degree view of the upper side of the vessel.

"Fifteen seconds!" said Johnson again.

"Got it."

Teresa activated the channel to the marines on the ship.

"Incoming boarding parties at ten o'clock high. Don't

let them get here."

Teresa moved to the armored mount between the pair of turrets and pulled herself behind to where a small display and set of manual controls was fitted. Compared to the system inside the ship, it was positively archaic. She looked closely and quickly recognized the unit as one of the shielded emplacement controls used for base turrets by the Corps.

These aren't even naval weapon systems.

In some ways it was better this way though. Teresa was very familiar with the technology, even if she hadn't had much access to it for well over a decade.

"Five seconds!"

The panel flipped open with just a tap on the spring mechanism. It was nothing but a rudimentary and unpowered iron sight, without even an optical stabilizer or level of magnification. The gunnery controls based round a torsion bar connected directly to the turret mechanics. The powered system was offline, but in the weightlessness of space it was not an issue. Teresa moved the sight so that it pointed directly at the dot that was the Bioray. She put her fingers on the angled bar that functioned as the override trigger. The first of the assault craft almost flew overhead before she spotted it. The multicolored shape flashed by so fast she had no time to track it.

"Damn it!"

She swung the turrets back and looked for signs of the

rest. Then she spotted a third and fourth craft circling around the damaged rear of the ship. Without a computer or any tracking guidance, she quickly estimated how much lead would be required and then depressed the lever. The turret shook violently, and the case flew from the breaches as the quad weapons blasted away. The violence of the weapons fire seemed odd compared to the complete silence in space. Even so, the first six rounds flew in front of the craft and missed. Teresa held down the trigger long enough for the craft to move directly into her fire. It was moving so fast that only three of the flank rounds struck it.

"Got you," she muttered, swinging the mount back to track another target that had appeared to her right. As the other marines spotted the targets, they flagged them via their own sensors and shared the information with the rest controlling the guns. It was a far cry from the tracking systems used on the ship, but it was the next best thing. In less than five seconds, the six marines had established a digital dome around the ship that extended over two hundred meters.

"Good work, people," she said as one of the craft was hit by the concentrated fire of three turrets.

The remaining craft moved back to the rear of Tamarisk II and opened fire on the already damaged engine section.

"Teresa, you have to keep them from the stern," said Johnson over the intercom.

Teresa was already on it and had swung the guns back but was unable to depress them further without striking Tamarisk II herself. She didn't even notice the group of fighters coming in from the left flank. Streams of gunfire peppered the dorsal turrets, and she was forced to pull herself behind the first gun mount as cannon rounds smashed the weapon systems apart.

"Colonel, we have fighters all around. Port and stern guns are down," said Captain Thompson.

Teresa shook her head angrily as she looked at the ruins of the two turret mounts. The guns appeared to be working fine, but the mounts were smashed and locked so that the guns were pointing exactly where there was no enemy. More shots hit the ship, and reports from the other marines announced the same problem.

So, our guns are all gone. Now they will board us, and this will all have been in vain.

"Colonel, what the hell is going on out there?" demanded Johnson.

Teresa looked at the formation of assault craft behind her and noted the icons on her visor showing the growing number of fighters. She tried to stay calm, but the prospect of being surrounded and boarded by the Biomechs was something she would never allow. She closed her eyes for the briefest of moments and then opened them to the horror of the Bioray. It must have been moving closer during the battle because when she looked back to the bow of ANS Tamarisk II, it filled her entire view. An image appeared on her visor. It was Johnson.

"I've got power back online, and half of our engines are operational. Get your people back inside."

"Johnson, have you looked outside?"

"I know. They won't risk any more damage against us with the Biomech on board."

Teresa looked back at the Bioray and noted the large number of ports opening up and the shapes of more assault craft moving into a launch position. To her horror, there was something even more disconcerting to look at, the shapes of gun systems tracking in the direction of ANS Tamarisk II.

"Johnson, I think you might be wrong on that one."

Two of the assault craft jumped out from the ship and made directly for the flank of her own ship. At this range, she could see the groups of the horrific bipedal warriors holding onto the sides of the craft. She reached to her thigh, pulled out her service pistol, and flipped off the safety.

You're not taking me alive.

The craft moved ever closer, and even as the engines on Tamarisk II powered up, she knew there was absolutely no chance of escape. With the engines damaged, they might still make it to the Rift just as the rest of the Biomechs arrived, but not while a squadron of fighters plus a Bioray and its complement of assault shuttles were moving in on them.

Teresa hadn't expected them to shoot first, and the bright white light blinded her so quickly she didn't even have time to grab for her pistol. Something hit her hard, and she crashed into the back of the container section and was almost knocked out. Her fear of being taken by the machines overruled any mental or physical damage though, and she fought off the blackness.

My gun, I need my gun.

She opened her eyes to see nothing but flames and wrecked metal all around her. The pistol was long gone, and everywhere she looked was the sight of terrifying destruction. She looked out into space, but again there was nothing identifiable, just the wreckage and mutilated ship sections.

How did I survive that?

"Teresa, are you there?" asked a familiar voice.

She tried to speak, but no sound came out. She swallowed, coughed, and then tried again. Her voice croaked, but at least it worked.

"I'm here, what's our status?"

It was a pointless question, but she was intrigued to know how the two of them were still alive. It was only then she noticed the wreckage was moving out of her view. With great physical effort, Teresa pulled herself to the edge of the shattered container and shook her head in astonishment.

"Tamarisk lives?" she said.

"You bet your ass she lives. Now get inside and fast. We have a date with a Rift!"

Teresa pulled herself from where she'd been sheltering, noting that of the six of them that had moved to the outer side of the ship, only she and two others were still showing on the status list.

"Marines, get inside and fast!"

She paused and looked up to the wreckage. It hadn't even occurred to her that the chunks of shattered metal had been from another vessel. Light from behind the remains of the Biomech craft turned the sections black, and then Tamarisk II broke out into open space and gave her the perfect view.

"Dreadnought," she said happily.

It was more to herself than to anybody that might be listening on the audio channel that she'd still left open. The massive warship had positioned itself along their flank, and even now continued to bombard the wreckage of the Bioray while using its turrets to cut down the remaining assault craft and fighters. Her hull was heavily scored and that could only mean the vessel had been waiting within the storm clouds.

Captain Vetlaya, you crazy woman!

Teresa grinned happily and watched as a squadron of Alliance Avenger drones chased after a pair of Biomech fighters. They seemed equally matched in size, speed, and firepower. Both Biomech fighters were blazing wrecks in seconds, and one of the Avenger drones had been eliminated. Teresa took a long, clear breath and turned her attention back to Tamarisk II.

We might just make it out of here, after all.

She inched along the flank of the ship and eventually made it to the access hatch that led inside. The outer airlock was already open, and Captain Thompson was waiting there for her. She felt relieved that he was one of the survivors, but also guilty that she would place his life above the others she barely knew.

"Colonel," he said smartly.

"Captain Thompson, it would appear the rumors of our demise were somewhat exaggerated."

"Quite," he answered quickly.

She moved inside and to her surprise found herself being pulled to the floor. The hatch closed shut behind her, and with just a few more steps, she was through the layered airlock and into the lower compartment. Waiting inside was Major Terson and a handful of marines.

"Colonel, glad to see you're safe."

Teresa noticed the marines had opened their visors, and she did the same. The slightly cool air of the ship was a welcome relief to the warmer air she'd been breathing inside her suit. Olik appeared at the end of the compartment, and he was pointing back to where he'd come from.

"Colonel, there's something not right here."

"What is it?"

"The cargo hold. We checked to make sure the machine was still operative."

"And?"

Olik looked a little confused before he answered.

"Well, it's not there. Just a load of computer equipment and some kind of reactor."

Teresa nodded and placed her finger to her mouth.

"Let's keep it that way then, shall we?"

Teresa walked through the ship while the other marines returned to their posts. Olik followed rather than head back to the storage part of the hull, scratching his head as he walked. He didn't ask again until they were moving through the gunnery control room that also doubled as a war room. He could get no further, but at least he could see the cockpit, and Director Johnson and Captain Tycho.

"Good work, Colonel. That was pretty close."

Teresa nodded in agreement and moved closer to look through the main screen. The Rift to T'Karan was active and swirled around like a whirlpool in front of them. They were already being buffeted by the odd combination of the outer tendrils of the Promethean storms, and the vast energies being used at the P7 station to keep the Rift open.

"Look!" said Olik.

He pointed at a shape as a Biomech Ravager ship went through the Rift.

"How many more have gone through?"

Johnson shook his head.

"That's the first. I think they're trying to persuade us not to go through."

"Why don't they collapse it?"

"Because they're arrogant. And they want it open so they can capture both parts of it."

Teresa looked at the radar scans of the area around them.

"The entire Biomech fleet is going to be here in less than two minutes. What will they do?"

A video appeared on the mainscreen. It was a direct transmission from the Biomech flagship, the massive vessel dwarfing every ship near the Rift. Teresa instantly knew who it was she was looking at.

"Typhon, what do you want?"

The man looked much less confident than normal. His face twisted as he looked back at her until he finally spoke.

"Enter the Rift, and we will destroy everything that you hold dear. We have access to over..."

Teresa cut the audio feed and shouted back at him.

"Typhon, Pontus, and the rest. You're just emissaries, nothing more. We're done with you, all of you."

She didn't even bother to listen to his reply and simply cut the feed. Teresa then looked to Johnson who did his best to hide his smile.

"I take it negotiations are over?"

Teresa didn't even need to answer that question. Director Johnson hit the engine override on his console, and the ship shuddered as more fuel was pumped into the remaining engines. The effect was nothing as great as before, but it did push them along almost an additional twenty percent.

"We go through!"

* * *

Admiral Anderson watched the mainscreen with growing impatience. This was his first voyage aboard ANS Terra Nova, and although he remained completely confident in her capabilities and her crew, he was still finding the mission to be one of the most stressful he'd ever undertaken.

I've stripped the AJ Naval Station of her ships. If they get wind of this, there'll be hell to pay.

Again he looked at the screen, but there was still no change.

Nothing.

The officers continued their work scanning the Rift, but in the three hours they had been stationed not a single ship had come through. For the umpteenth time, he looked to his science officer.

"The signal jammers and disruptors are all ready?"

"Yes, Admiral," answered the officer just as quickly.

He turned his attention back to the mainscreen and ran

his eyes along the list of ships he'd brought to bear. As well as his flagship, there were eight brand new Crusader class ships and thirty of the newest Liberty Class. It was a formidable fleet and probably overkill, but he was taking no chances with the Biomechs.

Will they work? he wondered.

The scientists on the Admiral Jarvis Naval Station had promised him the jamming hardware fitted to ANS Beagle would do the job. He'd seen the data and in that they were right, but he'd seen plenty of theories smashed when it came to battle. He tapped the button on his screen and brought up the video report from Admiral Lewis for what must have been the tenth time that day.

"Admiral. We are in position and are assisting the Helions in assembling a blocking force. We have no idea of the enemy's strength, just that they are on a direct collision course with the planet, and their arrival is imminent. I have sent additional scouts to the other races to plead for help."

He skipped ahead to the section that dealt with Eos.

"Initial scans of Eos show the majority of the Biomech ground forces have been eliminated. Small groups of survivors have made contact. I have arranged for New Helion Army units to assist them until we can provide additional forces."

He looked at the ground scans for the last message and noted the irritation in Admiral Lewis' tone when he mentioned the lack of additional forces.

I know you need them, but there's a war to fight, and Eos is at the bottom of the list, old friend. We'll go back for them. For now they'll have to rely on their own skills.

"Admiral, something's coming though," called out the tactical officer.

This is it.

He took three quick breaths and then sent the signal to the fleet to open their gunports and take aim. Everything had been prepared, and there was no need to say or do anything, just to give the signal. The green indicators for the banks of jammers on the ANS Beagle station flickered on, indicating the systems were active. That was when the Ravager came through. It took just a few seconds for it to fully clear the entrance, and its scanners and radar system immediately activated. A grim smile appeared on his face as he looked at the shape of the enemy's vessel.

"Fire!"

* * *

Tamarisk II entered the Rift with ANS Dreadnought running right beside her. At a distance of less than a hundred meters, the transport was well protected from the barrage of fire coming in from the first wave of Biomech ships. Gunfire from the first group of three Biomantas smashed into the layered armor of the Battlecruiser, but apart from external damage, she managed to reach the

Rift without sustaining any major damage. Both vessels vanished through the Rift, just as the first Biomanta skimmed past overhead and vanished into the Rift as well. Teresa watched the camera feed that showed the pursuing ships as they entered.

"They are close. I mean really close!"

The scene that greeted them in T'Karan rendered them speechless. Both Alliance ships crashed through a light cloud of broken metal and then continued forward while a vast tide of gunfire smashed into the ships coming in behind them. The first Biomanta was hit, but the gunfire from over twenty ships at once vaporized it in a bright blue flash just as another came through to meet the same fate. Finally, Director Johnson spoke.

"This is a massacre."

Teresa put her hand on his shoulder and shook her head.

"No, not a massacre. It is payback."

"Damn right it is!" snapped Olik from the compartment behind them.

ANS Tamarisk II moved off to take a safe position near the Beagle station, while ANS Dreadnought moved into position alongside her almost identical sister ship, ANS Terra Nova. As each Biomech ship exited the Rift, it was hit by wave after wave of railguns, particle beams, and missiles. In less than three minutes, the entire fleet had been reduced to a mass of floating wreckage and shattered hulls. Even the mighty Cephalon, the suspected command ship of the fleet, was unable to withstand such overwhelming fire. It lasted less than ten seconds before the heavy beams tore it into three equal pieces, each of which was then vaporized by the smaller ships.

"Incredible, just incredible," said Teresa.

The others just sat there stunned at what they could see. Olik finally spoke up, now no longer able to contain his questions.

"So this whole thing was a trick, to get the Biomechs through the Rift without securing it first?"

Director Johnson looked to Teresa and back at him.

"Yeah, something like that."

"What about the Biomech prisoner?"

"Oh, he's still on Prometheus."

Olik still looked confused.

"Why did they keep chasing us, then?"

Teresa returned to the same section as Olik and pulled herself into one of the seats. The flashes of the battle had already faded, with the only bright lights coming from those hulks still burning from within.

"This ship isn't just a transport. Tamarisk II has been fitted out to intercept and bounce Biomech transmissions."

She looked back at Johnson who seemed surprised she had known.

"Isn't that right?"

He raised an eyebrow but said no more.

"So everything on Prometheus was bait, nothing more than a trap?"

Johnson's brow creased a little, and it looked as if he was becoming nervous at what the warrior was saying. Major Terson arrived from deep inside the ship and toward Teresa. He'd heard the last part of the conversation and focused his attention on Olik.

"Your warriors put up one hell of a fight. Our estimates were put at over three thousand dead and wounded to give the right impression down there. I've seen the figures coming in already from Admiral Churchill. Less than three hundred casualties on the entire base."

He extended his hand out to Olik.

"Your people have given the Biomechs one hell of a bloody nose."

Anybody might have felt a little offended at having been used in such a way, but all Olik's face betrayed was the sheer joy at having been given the chance to fight in such a significant way. He lifted himself up and immediately struck the armored top of his helmet on the ceiling of the compartment.

"My Jötnar are always ready."

Teresa looked happy, but her expression altered slightly, and she turned her attention to Director Johnson as radio chatter filled the cockpit.

"What did they just say?"

Johnson pressed two buttons, and the volume doubled,

instantly making the sound of an Alliance officer clear to them. Teresa knew immediately who it was, but it was Captain Rivers who spoke first.

"It's my father."

"General Rivers," agreed Director Johnson.

"...assault. The Sol Rift has been reactivated and contact has been made via the Earthsec ship, Dauntless. Biomechs are on Mars. I repeat; Biomechs have landed on Mars."

Teresa didn't know what was worse. The fact that Biomechs had made it to one of the old worlds of the Alliance right under their noses, or that Spartan was somewhere in Sol. She just knew that if there were any fighting to be done, he would be involved.

"Johnson?" she asked.

He was already looking at her as she spoke.

"I know."

"Really?"

"You want to go back, am I wrong?"

They had known each other a long time, but even Teresa didn't realize she was quite that transparent.

"Yes. I'm not waiting a day more to find Spartan."

He turned back to his system and sent a series of coded messages on the secure computer system. All of them waited and listened for a little while longer as the General's voice continued to brief them on what was happening. Finally, Johnson turned back, and even he looked surprised.

"What is it?" asked Teresa.

"Admiral Anderson wants to tell you."

"Do it," was all she could muster.

The face of the familiar Alliance officer appeared right in the center of the main screen. He looked older than the last time they'd met, and she could tell the growing responsibility for the defense of T'Karan was taking its toll on him. Upon seeing Teresa and Johnson together, his face seemed to soften though.

"Director, Colonel. Your forces have performed admirably as part of this complex plan. Again, I apologize for keeping the details to the minimum. I'm sure you understand. Local forces will mop up what's left, and I believe your Promethean troops have already secured the underground facility. Very impressive."

Teresa tried to smile, but it simply wouldn't happen, not on demand.

"Thank you, Admiral."

"This does leave me with a dilemma, however. I will be returning to the border with Helios immediately. My forces are needed there, but I do have a dozen spare Liberty class ships that are available to escort you and Dreadnought back to Prometheus."

Teresa sighed, clearly irritated.

"I take it you've seen the news from Sol, Admiral. General Rivers says Mars has been attacked, and the Rift has been reopened."

Anderson nodded.

"Yes, I know. Admiral Churchill and Commander Osk are already arranging a strike team for you as we speak. Take your ship and get back as quickly as you can. Admiral Churchill will command the operation."

Teresa was confused.

"Operation? Did you know about this Admiral?"

He raised one eyebrow at her question.

"Colonel, you know how these things work. We are at war with these machines, and with their fleet smashed; there is just the force in Sol left to deal with. Admiral Churchill will command the fleet element. You will liaise with him on the ground package."

The image vanished, and she looked dumbfounded as the other officers looked at her. Again it was Olik that spoke first, and unlike the others, he had no problem in speaking his mind.

"Back and forth we go. Does this mean I'll get to kill more Biomechs?"

Teresa thought back to the fighting on Prometheus, the blood and carnage that had littered the place. After all of that, and the first thing Olik wanted to know was if he would be doing more. The thought that Spartan might be there filled her with an odd mixture of joy and desperation.

"Olik, we're going to the Rift right away. Once we're through, we're taking the Terra Nova Rift and then on to Sol. If there are Biomechs there, I promise you, you'll get first go at them."

Olik looked more than happy at this news.

"Good. That's what I wanted to hear."

Major Terson was the only one that didn't seem particularly overjoyed at the prospect of their return.

"I thought the Admiral said we were to meet Churchill at Prometheus first. Then assemble ground forces and move on to Mars?"

Teresa shook her head.

"No, that is all going to take too long. We have Dreadnought and Tamarisk. We'll go there first. Churchill can come after us."

She looked to Director Johnson and expected a fight.

"Agreed?" she asked.

Director Johnson just smiled.

CHAPTER FOURTEEN

After the disaster of Eos, there were many throughout the Alliance that clamored for a complete pullout of the Orion Nebula. The Rift operated from Prometheus was the only link to this new part of space, and it was there that much of the ire was directed. The Alliance plan, known later as the Prometheus Offensive, proved a political masterpiece. Few could deny the effect the destruction of the entire Biomech fleet in Alliance territory had on its citizens. If the Biomechs could be beaten at home, then they could be beaten at Helios. The bold move by General Rivers and his key commanders put the Alliance's attention back on Helios and its new friends and enemies so many light years away.

Orion – The future?

They had been on the landing pad for over two hours now and were still waiting for help. Though a few had complained at falling back, the sight of more than fifty enemy soldiers moving across the open ground toward the more distant landing area had reminded them of quite how precarious their position was. The pad itself was much larger than Spartan had expected. His initial estimate was that something the size of a medium sized Alliance transport or even a military escort minesweeper could probably make it down there. With its raised height, it gave an excellent view of the surface of Mars. A low folding wall ran around the outside of the flat surface, but it did little to protect you if you inadvertently stepped off the edge.

"Any news from Dauntless?" he asked impatiently.

Captain Cobb looked up to the sky as if expecting to see the craft right above them.

"They sent our emergency evacuation signal through the Rift as soon as we broadcast it. There's nothing coming back yet though."

Spartan grumbled, and Khan walked to one for the railings and struck it hard with his left fist.

"Maybe being up here wasn't such a good idea," said one of the operatives.

Z'Kanthu, the Biomech walked around the perimeter of the landing area and looked down into the damaged sections of the base. The distant mountains were already well obscured by the dust storm that was moving ever closer.

"If we are to leave this place, we will need somewhere

a ship can land."

He then pointed down over the edge of the platform to the refinery complex and into the deep depression that looked much like the center of a volcano. Spires, shafts, and towers all pushed upward to give it a half completed look.

"The enemy controls down there. They have cover, darkness, and a storm to help them. The only way to reach us here is through that passageway."

He looked to the direction of the entrance. It was very wide, and as well as space to walk, there were also two separate sets of maglev tracks for the rail system back into the base. Z'Kanthu moved toward the entrance and lowered down onto his haunches.

"They are coming."

Spartan and Khan went to his right, both holding up their weapons to point in the same direction. Cobb and the other operatives stayed further back on the platform, behind the cover offered by the containers and discarded machinery lying about. Marcus moved to the communications gear and continued to send information up to Dauntless.

"How many?" Spartan shouted out.

The machine twisted his head and looked down at the human. Spartan was a big man, but even he looked puny when compared to the monstrous Biomech.

"More than you will be able to stop."

Khan laughed.

"We've killed enough before, and we're going to keep on doing it."

The machine turned his attention to Khan and then looked back down the tunnel.

"They are not interested in you. Now that the enemy knows I am alive, they will stop at nothing to take me prisoner, or to destroy me. The destruction of one of the remaining rebels is worth an entire planet to them."

"So go back down the tunnel and leave us be," suggested Cobb.

The machine swiveled about to stare at the man from Earth.

"If it would protect your species, I would. My life is better spent making a difference in this war. I have knowledge of the old Bridge network, and a deep understanding of their strengths, numbers, and strategies."

"He's right," Marcus agreed.

He had left the equipment and joined Spartan on the firing line at the mouth of the tunnel. There were more than twenty civilian workers on the platform, of which only half carried weapons. They had joined Cobb and his own team behind cover.

"The shuttle is on its way. ETA four minutes."

He looked to Spartan and then tilted his head and indicated toward Z'Kanthu. There was no need to say anything even though it had evidently not occurred to the others. There was absolutely no way that all of them and Z'Kanthu would be able to escape the planet on just one shuttle. Spartan nodded, agreeing without opening his mouth.

"Now," said the machine.

The first to move out from the shadows were the bipedal warriors Z'Kanthu had called Thegn foot soldiers. Seven ran as fast as they could, their red eyes dancing about like glowworms as they moved. Spartan and Khan fired first, and their accurate fire hit the first few directly in the face. Two dropped to the ground, but the rest kept moving. More shapes moved behind as well at the glinting of bare metal machines.

"Spartan, the outside!" Cobb shouted out.

Spartan emptied his clip before turning to look at the Captain.

"What is outside?"

He didn't want to leave the line, but Z'Kanthu turned his main guns on the enemy, and for a few seconds at least, he had cleared a path and given them a moment's breathing space. Cobb waved at them desperately, and Spartan broke ranks, cursing under his breath.

"What the hell is..."

He leaned over the side of the landing platform and look down its steep sides. The first tendrils of the dust storm had already arrived and had washed out the ground to give the effect of a yellowish fog, made worse by the rising sun in the distance.

"There!" Captain Cobb interrupted.

Spartan looked at the actual bedrock the tower had been built on top of. At first he saw nothing, then the movement caught his eye.

"No, it can't be?"

He lifted his weapon and used the optical scope to improve the view and almost dropped the weapon. The eight-legged robotic soldiers had found a way to the base of the tower and were climbing their way up like a group of horrific metal spiders. He lost counted at eleven, and below them he could see more shadows.

"Great, that's just great!"

He turned back to Captain Cobb and grabbed his shoulder.

"Get the civilians along the wall. Use guns or throw machinery. I don't care, just keep them busy."

Another volley of gunfire announced the next major wave through the tunnel.

"I need your operatives with me."

He ran back and almost made it to Khan when two of the machines clambered over the edge near to where his friend waited. It pulled back its legs and then kicked out to jump toward him.

"Khan!" he shouted.

The Jötnar warrior had blocked his line of sight, and even as he ran, he knew Khan was going to be struck. The machine lurched from the ledge and flew through the air. Khan had already turned about but was only half there as it reached him. With a sickening crunch, Z'Kanthu smashed Khan aside and took the impact directly on his chest. His immense size and weight stopped him from falling, but he still staggered back and was unable to shoot for a few seconds. The machine roared something in his own tongue and over speakers installed somewhere inside the armored carapace. With a hard tug, it tore the limbs from the machine and threw the flailing wreckage over the edge.

"Spartan, the tunnel!" Marcus shouted.

The enemy was now out of the tunnel and swarming about the open space on the landing platform. Khan and Spartan moved off to the one side to join the three Earthsec operatives who continued to put down heavy gunfire into the approaching Thegns. More had reached the fight with firearms, and these Thegns were much more cautious and made use of the cover offered by the dead. They stayed low and managed to pick off two of the operatives without them even being seen. Spartan tried to drag the wounded men back, and then they were on them. The first brought down both of its blade toward Spartan who lifted his left arm, blocking them with his new armored forearm. It flashed and sparked but incredibly absorbed the impact.

"My turn!"

He lifted his modified pair of TEK40 rifles and riddled the creature with holes. Even this rifle had no trouble causing damage at a distance of less than a meter. Another two knocked him back, and one stabbed at him. This time Spartan barely managed to avoid the strike and took a painful slash to the leg. He instantly felt the cold air of Mars rushing in around his flesh. The next one moved in to stab at his face, but Cobb emptied a full clip into its torso, almost cutting it in half.

Z'Kanthu roared again and manhandled several of the Thegns out of the way, using his body to shield the two of them.

"Stop them getting up here!" he said, turning back to swing and strike against the never-ending attackers. Spartan began to move and then stopped, only for a second to watch the mighty machine tear the Thegns apart one by one as they swamped him.

Damned crazy machine.

He was impressed with his combat abilities but far from concerned for his fate. That wouldn't happen just because he'd killed a few expendable Thegns.

"Khan, with me!"

They ran over to the edge and joined the rest of the civilians at shooting the machines climbing up the sides. They were now less than thirty meters away and making good progress. Spartan took aim and fired, but the machines were tough, and not easy to hit as they lifted themselves up the vertical surface. Half of them were now obscured by the rising tide of dust.

"Marcus, where is that damned shuttle?" Spartan hollered.

An explosion knocked Marcus to the ground, and he was dragged behind the overturned containers being used by three of the civilians. Thegns had now taken control of the entrance to the tunnel back into the base. They had dragged a large container and a number of bodies to create an improvised barricade from which to launch additional attacks. Dozens more were engaged in a brutal firefight and melee throughout the landing pad, and it had quickly degenerated into a series of small skirmishes.

Z'Kanthu helped where he could, but most of the Biomech creatures seemed to be attacking all of the time anyway. Every time he threw one over the ledge, another three took its place. One of the eight-legged machines managed to tear a chunk from the motorized knee joint on his leg, and Z'Kanthu dropped to one knee. On his own, and in the middle of the landing pad, he was overwhelmed. They piled onto him like bugs devouring a carcass. Khan shook his head angrily and looked down at the bodies of the Thegns. He dragged the nearest one to him and ripped out the blades from its arms.

"Spartan!"

He tossed one to his friend and then broke from cover, ignoring the bullets striking his armor and barged directly into the nearest Thegns around the fallen Z'Kanthu.

"Help him!" Spartan ordered.

Few could respond, but by the time Spartan had reached Z'Kanthu, there were another four civilians with weapons taken from the dead doing their best to help. A Thegn killed one, but the others made their presence felt. A dozen of the enemy was killed in as many seconds, and Z'Kanthu managed to lift himself up slightly, only for the shape of one of the massive six-legged walkers to emerge from the tunnel. A loud voice boomed from inside, and the Thegns quickly scattered to leave the damaged Z'Kanthu, Khan, Spartan, and two of the remaining civilians exposed in the middle of the platform. The gun turrets swiveled to point at Z'Kanthu, and a high-pitched whine built up pace as the barrels began to rotate.

"No!" Khan screamed.

He stepped in front of Z'Kanthu and aimed his shortened TEK40 at the machine's torso. He didn't even consider negotiating and pulled the trigger. Lights flickered about its armor as the bullets scratched and dented the metal plating. Then the machine opened fired and vanished in a bright yellow explosion that sent metal and ammunition flying in all directions.

"Get down!" shouted one of the civilians.

More gunfire struck around them, and scores of Thegns were cut to ribbons by large caliber guns. Dust filled the platform, and the scream of machinery deafened them all.

Spartan was knocked to the ground. He looked up to see a Thegn looking down at him, its weapon lifted high above its head. Then everything above its waist vanished, leaving the lower half of its body standing there like a broken statue.

What the hell is going on?

He rolled over and lifted himself back up to his knees. All around him lay bodies, but he could still see Thegns heading for him. He took aim, but more powerful guns slammed into them. These were no TEK40 rifles though. High rates of fire and powerful cannon tore them apart like the guns of armored vehicle. He twisted back and saw a dark shape on the platform. He'd expected a small shuttle, but instead the craft barely fitted on the platform. It was a small transport about half the size of Dauntless. Its engines sent dust flying all about and directly at his visor. Six shapes moved toward him, and he lifted his weapon.

"Spartan, stay down!" said one of them.

He didn't recognize the voice, but the fact it knew him gave him a moment's hope. He kept his head down but only for a moment. More heavy gunfire followed, and then the dust began to clear a little. The shapes altered to show the forms of six warriors, each in dark red armor. They reminded him of conventional marines but were bigger, and equipped with the additional neck and collar protection fitted on all current issue armor patterns. They were much too big to be normal marines.

Jötnar?

They moved toward him, each carrying the biggest weapons he'd ever seen in the hands of a humanoid before. They carried on past him at a slow walk, each of them blazing away and cutting down every last Thegn. Spartan shook his head in shock, but it wasn't the Jötnar that made his heart almost stop. It was the shape of a woman that had just emerged from the flank of the ship. She reached the bottom of the ramp and then flicked open the outer screen over her visor. He knew the face instantly.

"Teresa?"

Spartan moved toward her, completely forgetting about the fight they were in the middle of. Even though the ship and its Jötnar had cleared an area, there were still Thegns about. One of them leapt out in front of him, its firearm pointing directly at his face. A hole appeared in its forehead, and blood sprayed over him as it slumped forward. Right behind it was Teresa, her carbine raised and pointed straight ahead.

"Spartan, where the hell have you been?"

She rushed to him and grabbed him hard, pulling the battered and exhausted Spartan to her. As they held on to each other, the Jötnar pulled back and formed a defensive curtain around the ship. More conventional marines came out with stretchers and helped carry the wounded back inside. A few of the machines attempted to climb over the sides of the pad, but with numbers now on the marines' side, they were quickly shot down.

"I've been waiting a long time for this," said Teresa, ignoring all that was happening around them.

Marcus saw her and walked over to them both. He reached out to Teresa, and she spotted him at the very last moment. Without letting go of Spartan, she dropped her carbine so that it swung down on its sling, and flipped out her sidearm to point it directly at his face.

"What are you doing here?"

Spartan released his hold just a little so that he could see what was happening. At seeing Marcus, he placed his one good hand on her pistol and pushed it down gently.

"He's okay. It's a long story."

Z'Kanthu was back on his feet again and now looked even more battered and worn out than when they had found him. Four Jötnar waited in front, each with their guns trained on his head.

"I can hear your people. They are being attacked inside the refinery."

Spartan listened and looked back at Teresa.

"The last of them have taken the workers of this place prisoner. They are going to turn this place into another Prometheus."

Teresa raised an eyebrow at that unfortunate reference.

"You're more right than you know."

She then looked up at the Biomech.

"I suppose there is a reason you have a Biomech helping you?"

Spartan shrugged sheepishly. They were interrupted by the sonic booms of something overhead. They all looked up as the long black shape of a large capital ship soared overhead at very low orbit. It wasn't the ship that had made the noises. It was the half dozen landing craft coming down, each leaving long black trails of smoke behind them as they entered the Martian atmosphere.

"You brought friends?" asked Marcus.

Teresa ignored him and looked at Spartan.

"Admiral Churchill gave me access to a few ships and a battalion of marines."

Teresa signaled to Captain Rivers who had just come down the ramp along with Major Terson. He ran over and saluted smartly. Teresa pointed up at the craft on their way down.

"How long until the next wave lands?"

"Twelve minutes, Colonel. Any later and the storm will swallow them up."

Another pair of medics ran past, and one thrust an L52 Mark II carbine into Spartan's hands before moving to one of the badly injured operatives. The second then joined his comrade. Spartan caught the carbine it in his right hand and rested the barrel on his left. It felt like an eternity since he'd held such a well-crafted and useful weapon.

"Here they come!" Captain Cobb shouted out.

Spartan twisted about and aimed the carbine at the first shape that emerged. More marines rushed out and formed a thin line, along with the red armored shapes of the Jötnar, and then the gunfire started. The first few creatures were cut down, but as before more came behind them. Olik looked back at Khan and waved his gun in the air triumphantly.

"Let's finish this!"

The crazed Jötnar charged directly into the fight and blasted apart the new arrivals before vanishing into the entrance of the tunnel. Two had remained on the platform and were helping Khan to his feet. At seeing his kin rushing off, he tensed his shoulders and then called out to one of the Jötnar for a weapon. Only then did he notice Teresa. He staggered forward and grabbed her so hard he almost buckled her armor.

"It's good to see you," he said with a growl.

Teresa couldn't find the words and instead just laughed as he squeezed her. Spartan checked the status of his carbine and then looked back at Khan and Teresa.

"We have a few hundred Biomech warriors down there and thousands of civilians. What do you say?"

A Jötnar handed him a massive gun that looked more like a tank's main gun.

"What the hell is this?"

The Jötnar grinned.

"New standard issue, recommended by General Gun."

"General?" laughed Spartan.

He looked at Teresa.

"Well?"

Teresa slid her pistol back into its holster and raised her carbine to her waist.

"I say we take back Mars."

"Yes!" roared Khan.

One of the medics moved on to Marcus who watched the trio rush off into the tunnel, their weapons raised and their bloodlust up.

"They are in trouble now," he said to himself.

The medic heard him though, and as he applied the emergency dressing to the fragmentation wounds Marcus had suffered, he leaned in.

"Why, what's down there?"

Marcus looked into the medic's face and grimaced as the patch pulled down tightly onto his injured flesh.

"No, not them. I mean the Biomechs."

The medic shook his head.

"Haven't you heard? The attack on Helios is imminent. All forces are rallying at T'Karan for the counterattack. That's where we will be going after mopping up here."

"Perhaps," he replied.

"Even so, the Biomechs should be worried."

The medic tightened the last patch and then looked back to Marcus' face and raised an eyebrow.

"Eos was lost, and they are about to assault Helios. What do they have to be worried about?"

Finally Marcus smiled.

"Because Spartan's back, and his war has only just started."